Finding the Bastion

K. A. Gandy

THIGPEN-
GANDY
PUBLISHING

Thigpen-Gandy Publishing

Contents

One

Reverberate

"Oh my God, we have to go back." My hands gripped the steering wheel so hard, my fingernails hurt. I stared in slack-jawed horror out the back window as a mushroom cloud of orange dust and smoke billowed up from whatever remained of Coyote Springs. Sadness, sharp and pungent, bloomed in my chest.

"Nyx, no. You need to step on it," River urged. "That jet could turn around."

"But everyone I know is back there! I gave some of them coordinates, but I don't know if they've left. They might be dead anyways, but how do we know?" I cranked the wheel hard right, but before I could turn a one-eighty, River reached over and slammed the shifter into park.

"Nyx! Stop! Look at me!" His panicked tone finally caught my attention, and I looked into his eyes. "I know this is terrible, but there is *literally* nothing we can do. We're not medics, we have no supplies, and also, by going back we might get ourselves blown up, too."

I shook my head angrily at him. "River, you can't seriously want me to just walk away from the only people I know in this world when they're injured or dead!"

"If they are dead, they won't miss us; and if they're severely injured, we're not qualified to help. What good are you to them if you get blown to smithereens, too? Some people already left, and you gave everyone you cared about the new coordinates. They weren't going to sit on that information. *Surely* they left already or are at least far enough out that they didn't catch the brunt of the explosion. Right? We're fine, so most of the people back home probably are, too."

I pursed my lips, considering. Much as I hated to admit it, he wasn't wrong. I had no medical training beyond basic stitches and slathering on whatever goop Lesina whipped up and told me was beneficial. I wasn't qualified to handle major injuries or burns. Though, he'd said something that didn't make sense. "They already dropped the bomb. Why do you think they'd come back?"

He ran a frustrated hand through his short blonde locks, but he still answered. "Haven't you studied our history? Things got bad, Nyx. A quarter of the cities no longer on the map weren't only covered by sand, they were bombed out. And the people back then never left it at one, to leave behind survivors who'd hold a grudge. They came back for a second pass, to make sure they did the job right. We need as much distance from Coyote Springs as we can get."

A fresh wave of horror rolled across me as I considered the cruel irony it would be if I finally had a chance to find Chace, and then got blown up before I'd left Coyote Springs. I drummed my fingers on the steering wheel for another second, then dropped my hand to the gear shifter. I cut him an accusing stare. "If you ever touch my gear stick again, I'll open that door and boot you out of it. We clear?"

"Crystal." He held up both hands in a display of surrender, then leaned back into his seat.

I threw the Bronco back into drive and stepped on it.

Thirty minutes later, we heard the aircraft coming towards us again, this time from behind. River leaned forward tensely in his seat as if it would get us out of Dodge faster, and I pressed a bit harder on the gas, eking out another five miles per hour. It was nothing against an aircraft moving that fast, but it was all we had.

"Should we try to find cover?" River's voice was tight with unease, which surprised me after how forceful he'd been about getting as far away from Coyote Springs as possible.

"The only cover around here is a Podunk town half swallowed by sand already. Even if we could get to it, it wouldn't provide any protection against what they just did." Chace and I had visited it more than once over the years, scavenging. It was nothing but a skeleton, the bare ribcage of roofs poking above the orange sand.

"That answers that, then," he said solemnly.

And solemn we were, as we sped across the dunes, bumping and jostling as we ran over uneven patches, and dune crests gave way beneath our lumbering bulk.

The jet quickly overtook us, traveling overhead at only a few knots to our right. The noise rattled the windows in the Bronco, and my knuckles whitened in the moment after they passed. The spot between my shoulder blades itched, as if waiting for a bomb to drop on them, too.

They didn't drop another bomb, though. We watched as they flew past, then angled to the right and disappeared from our line of sight.

It wasn't until then I managed to let go of the tension rolling down my spine.

I was still mentally kicking myself about not going back, when we heard the percussion of another bomb going off ahead of us.

"Oh, God. They're still dropping bombs." My voice came out hollow, visions of helpless street orphans playing on repeat in my head.

"Whoever it is, they want to wipe out this entire area. Was there another occupied city in that direction?"

I shrugged. "They're moving fast. I've never been that far west, so I couldn't say."

He made a low, disgusted sound in his throat, before we fell back into tense silence. We watched in mute horror as the bomber made two more passes—each time further and further north until it disappeared from sight.

Several hours after our last sighting of the bomber, we parked out in the open in the valley between the tallest dunes we could find. While I might typically find a little town to settle into for a windbreak, that felt less safe than taking our chances out in the open.

We didn't get out of the truck, only leaned both of our seats back, and stared up listlessly at the roof of the Bronco.

"Do you think the Bastion's people were flying that jet?" I blurted.

River rubbed his forehead, tiredly thinking it over. "Maybe," he finally said.

"It doesn't make any sense. A few months ago, they're stealing our people. Now, they're bombing our city? What are they *doing*?" I wondered aloud, not really looking for an answer.

"It could have been someone else; we don't know. Or . . . maybe they have all the people they need."

River's dark words echoed in my head as sleep eluded me, nearly drowning out the eerie singing of the dunes.

Two

CAMPING

The next day passed in a silent slog, both of us tense, neither of us wanting to be the first to bring it up. On and on we drove, thankfully with no sign of a doomsday jet overhead. Still, it weighed heavily on me. It had crossed my mind a hundred times that I nearly sent River back to Coyote Springs, and if I had, he'd have been blown up, too. It was a horrifying thought, and I found myself praying on loop that more people had gotten out. Hoss. Marl. Lesina. Maisie.

Good gracious, the street children. I gave them water, whenever I could spare it. Which wasn't often, granted, but I had a soft spot for them since I'd been raised on the streets myself. I closed my eyes for a second, pain lancing my heart at the thought of their small, dirty faces .

. . gone. I caught my breath, trying not to cry as the horror set in deeper by the hour.

Sometime in the afternoon, River finally broke the taut silence.

"Nyx, you don't think they went after unpopulated areas, do you?" His tone was edgy, and it made my anxiety ratchet up a notch.

"It didn't seem like it, no. They passed right over plenty of cities we've scavenged before."

He nodded but didn't speak. From the corner of my eye, I could see him clenching and unclenching his jaw, the muscles popping in and out with the action.

"Why?" I prodded, my patience for our mournful silence at an end. If I spent one more minute alone in my head with the imaginary horrors reel, I was going to turn into a soggy mess of tears. Not my style.

"I was just thinking . . . the people who left for Wolf Well wouldn't have arrived yet. Hopefully, they left the new water source alone. Otherwise . . . we've got nowhere to go back to."

I hadn't even thought of that. I should have thought of it; I mean, we'd seen them fly another pass overhead, until they zig-zagged out of sight.

"They left us alone, so we just have to hope that occupied cities were the only target, for whatever reason."

"Yeah, that's been bugging me, too. Coyote Springs has been there for years, right?" He looked over at me, elbow propped tensely on the windowsill.

"Yeah," I confirmed.

"Okay, why now? Why has so much changed in the last few months? You said it was all weird. The people getting snatched, then water running out, then they send you so far into the wastes—it was *all* different. And then the city gets blown up. I don't know why, but it feels related."

It felt related to me, too, but . . . "I think everything is paranoia, right now. Someone just blew up the city right behind us. It could have been the Bastion, but if there's *one* super city we didn't know about, there could be more. Heck, there could be a whole network of them. We'd never know; most people can't drive more than a week one way before they're bone dry and out of water. You're stuck where you are." Bitterness tinged my tone as I rehashed the truth of my entire life before this. I had been stuck, hopelessly, firmly stuck, when all I wanted was to go north to a better life.

I ground my teeth together and kept my eyes on the sand. I was going to have that better life. Hopefully with Chace—and maybe even River—by my side, even if it took me the next twenty years to figure it out.

A while later, I'd zoned out with the radio playing some retro Queen and sand disappearing
beneath my tires, when River pulled me out of
my reverie.

"What is that?" he asked, and I let my foot off
the gas pedal.

"What is what?" I looked over at him, the sinking sun gilding his viking-esque features like
a statue of old. Blonde hair glinted along his
forearms, and I was nearly overcome with the
urge to run my fingers over his smooth skin.
His pale and gold, with my deep brown . . . I
shook that thought out of my head when he
answered.

"Look, over there. It's some sort of . . . spikes?"
I followed his pointing finger, and finally saw
it, northeast of our path. Sure enough, the
ground was dotted with tall spires. "Huh, I don't
know. They look natural, but the shape is odd."

"I think we should go investigate." He leaned
forward excitedly in his seat, squinting for a
better look.

I chuckled at his eagerness and shook my
head. "Uh-uh, we aren't going to side-trip every
time you see something you think is cool. You're
too easily bored. Read a book. I've got a whole
backpack full of them. Do you know how rare

that is?" I reached behind the seat and shook the backpack by its top handle to make my point.

"Ugh, books are boring."

"*You're* boring."

He cast me an exasperated look, his eyebrows lowering dramatically. "I can't help it, I'm a hands-on person. Sitting still for hours with a dusty stack of paper in my hands doesn't do it for me."

"We're still not going over there. We'll run out of water if we go off course every time you see something."

"Okay, *one*"—he ticked off on his fingers—"there's barely anything to see except sand dunes. We get a close-up tour of those right from the truck. Two, did you forget I have the water finder? Get-out-of-jail-free card." He reached back and jiggled his pack, mocking my earlier suggestion that he, *gasp*, read a book.

"Okay, yes, that is helpful. But what if the ocean throws it off—did you think of that? We can't drink ocean water, even if it is liquid."

He slumped back in his seat. "No, I didn't think of that. Dang it." He stared longingly out the window at the mystery spires and let out a sigh. "See you never, cool mystery rocks."

"Oh, you are pitiful. *Fine.* But just this once, seriously. I didn't plan water for two." I gave him a pointed look, and he had the good grace to look sheepish about originally blowing me off.

"Yes!" He leaned forward again, excitedly eyeing the rocky protrusions.

It didn't take long to cover the distance. The sand flattened within a few minutes, and we cruised across pretty quickly.

I stayed a ways back—wary after my catastrophic run-in with the tent pole, I quickly rubbed my water droplet charm for luck—and he was out of the Bronco before I'd even dropped it into park. I was slower but followed. Up close, the tall rock spires were interesting to look at, even I could admit. There were six of them, all different heights, reaching up like gnarled fingers toward the cloudless sky. River circled and wove between them, while I gently rested a palm on the sunbaked surface.

"What do you think they are?" he asked, coming to a stop next to me.

With a shrug, I answered, "No idea. Never seen anything this tall and skinny before that wasn't man-made."

"Me either." He gazed appreciatively up at the tallest one. "Do you want to camp here tonight?"

The sun was half hidden below the horizon, so I shrugged agreement. "Sure. Truck, or . . . ?"

"Tent, for sure. One night of truck sleep is enough for me." He rubbed his lower back with a grimace.

"You know, I've actually got a big tent now, but I've never put it up. Haven't had the chance," I mused, not at all sure it was worth the work.

"What? Well, we've got to try that out." He gave me a lopsided grin, and, for a moment, I forgot all about the world around us. I was truly glad I wasn't alone, and that he had decided to come along after all. Did that make me pathetic? I hoped not. I'd never been dependent on a man before—and wasn't *dependent*, now; the opposite, actually. But it was so nice to not be alone.

"Sorry, my tent is for book lovers only. All others must stay in their own tent, lest I bore them to death with my reading." I cast him a haughty glance then walked jauntily back towards the Bronco.

"Oh, not cool. So not cool," he called out to my back, and I couldn't help but crack a smile. It faded quickly, though, as I looked past the truck and towards the remnants of Coyote Springs. It was out of sight, now, but in my mind I could still see a faint cloud of smoke from the burning rubble left behind.

Reminders of the trouble we were in were never far. Maybe one day we would actually know who was pulling the strings.

We set up our tents between the Bronco and the rock spires, and it was surprisingly easy. The Bronco provided a decent windbreak, and once I rolled out my fancy new neon purple sleeping mat for the first time and laid down, it was downright cozy.

"How are you doing over there?" River hollered, overloud for the few inches separating our tent walls.

"Fine, and you don't have to yell," I called back.

"Oh yeah?" he answered in a normal tone. "I just figured you might be so absorbed in that book that you couldn't hear me over all the breathy moaning."

I snorted. "You are ridiculous, this isn't *that* kind of book. It's a mystery . . . but for the record, there's nothing wrong with that kind of book, either."

All was silent for so long, I thought he'd given up on talking and fallen asleep, until his next words came softly through the wall. "What kind of mystery?"

"Well . . . don't laugh."

"I wouldn't dare—you're my ride," he said drily.

It was me who laughed, appreciating the fact that he could still keep a sense of humor, after all he'd been through. I needed more of that, myself. "Okay, well, it's about this grandma. She lives in a small town, and her next door neighbor gets murdered."

"I'm feeling less humor here, and more concern that you're going to get ideas." Rather than dignify that with a response, I whacked the tent wall with the palm of my hand, causing a loud *whump* sound. He laughed. "Okay, okay, sorry. Tell me the rest."

"Well, once the neighbor gets murdered, she and her cat go and investigate. They find a magical—"

"Wait!" He interrupted again and I groaned, dropping the book against my forehead.

"What?"

"She solves mysteries with her cat?" His voice held a hint of repressed laughter.

"Yes, that's *literally* what I just said."

"Well, go on—I'm intrigued now."

I could hear the smile in his voice and decided to do him one better. I was only two chapters in, so I flipped back to page one, and began reading aloud. When my voice and arms grew too tired to continue, I tucked a stray piece of paper between the pages and set it aside. River had been silent for so long, I was sure he was asleep.

With a yawn, I reached over and turned off my lamp before getting cozy on my sleeping mat. Moments after my eyes drifted closed, his low voice crossed the distance between us as softly as a caress.

"Sweet dreams, Nyx."

Three

PLOTTING THE COURSE

Time passed as quickly as sand disappeared under the Bronco's tires, with no more sign of bombs or jets as we headed steadily northeast for the next three days. River and I fell into an easy rhythm, our days and nights taking on a comfortable predictability; drive in shifts, stop mid-morning and mid-afternoon to stretch, then a final leg of driving until sunset, when we'd stop to pitch our tents. To my surprise, each night we turned in, River happily listened to the next few chapters of our mystery story and made no more jokes about my taste in books.

When we woke on the fifth morning, I was lying in my tent, staring at the cheery green nylon fabric overhead when a thought struck me. I scrambled off of my sleeping pad so quickly, I tripped over the corner and had to catch myself on a tent pole, nearly bringing the whole thing down on top of my head.

"Nyx? Everything okay over there? You didn't find a scorpion in your—"

"River! We have a comm device!" I yelled through the tent wall.

"Err, what? There's a scorpion in your comm device?"

"No, be serious! The Sidewinders gave us a comm device, remember? I'm going to stick it into my wristband and see if I can get in touch with anyone." I unzipped my tent mid-sentence and jogged the couple of steps around the Bronco to pop open the glove box. "Please, please, ple-ase," I muttered under my breath as I riffled through the junk that lived inside the glove compartment. Finally, I found the tiny stick and oh-so-carefully inserted it into the side of my hydration meter.

My pulse pounded in my ears as I stared at the wristband, waiting for something—anything—to happen. For a few painfully long moments, nothing did. Then, an orange tower symbol popped up on the screen, and flashed three times before fading back to the usual hydration display. I waited, but every two minutes the signal repeated itself, and the device stayed silent.

With a disappointed groan, I trudged back around to find River stretching in front of his tent, which was already half-disassembled.

"Anything?"

"Nothing useful. There's a little tower symbol that flashes every couple of minutes, but nothing else is happening."

"Huh. Let me see." He gestured to my wrist, so I held it aloft until the next flash of the orange tower.

"Oh, that's a radio tower. However this thing works, it's probably out of range."

"Well, that sucks."

"Yeah . . . it's supposed to be for when we make it to the Bastion, right? Maybe they have whatever technology that will make it work. Or, maybe it needs to be closer to something. Hard to say, when the Sidewinders didn't give you details."

I snorted and pointed at his still-healing gang tattoo of a cottonmouth snake. "Don't you mean 'my delightful brothers in arms, the Sidewinders?'"

"Oh, was I unclear? Yep, that's exactly what I meant." He shook his head at my sarcasm, and bumped shoulders with me before turning back to the business of packing his tent away.

I followed suit, and in under five minutes we were ready to roll out.

"You mind driving first today?" I asked as I closed the back door.

He swallowed the date he'd been chewing and shook his head. "'Course not."

"'Kay." I climbed into the passenger seat, then pulled a meal bar and water orb from my top cargo pocket. He turned on the stereo, and then we were back on the move.

At midday, I did a quick assessment of our water supply while River jogged laps around the Bronco to burn off energy. "You know that's freaking weird, right? Literally nobody likes jogging in sand," I called as he passed me by for the eighth—ninth?—time.

"Lots of people love running, Nyx. Just because you would rather stuff your nose in a dusty book and live on crumbly twig bars doesn't mean everyone else wants to," he replied cheerfully. "Running is great. Makes you feel alive." He pumped a fist in the air as he jogged out of talking range.

"Being alive does that also," I said with an eye roll and finished my tally. He eventually wound down and trotted up to where I sat on the back bumper, stretching my legs out and enjoying the shade.

"Hey, good looking, pass a guy a water orb?" He waggled his eyebrows at me, and I snorted.

"Is that supposed to be seductive?" I leaned back and snagged an orb from the overhead net and passed it back to him.

He clutched his chest dramatically, a wounded expression painted on his face. "Words hurt, Nyx. I was *absolutely* trying to seduce you."

"Uh-huh. You maybe should have thought of that before you got all sweaty." I wrinkled my nose as I looked him up and down.

"Aren't women supposed to love sweaty men?" He rubbed the back of his neck, causing an impressive bicep flex.

"Sure, yep, we're all falling over. Dead of exploding ovaries." I rolled my eyes. "My turn to drive, poky."

"Poky, really? I just ran *actual* laps around you."

"Uh-huh. Good luck doing that when I'm in the driver's seat," I called over my shoulder and climbed in, his good natured chuckles following me every step of the way.

That night as I lay in my tent, restlessness wouldn't let me sleep. I'd read three chapters before my arms got tired, and I set the mystery book aside and doused the light. Still, though, I stared up at the nylon overhead, mind churning.

"Are you asleep over there?" River's soft words startled me out of my reverie.

"No," I whispered.

"Can't sleep?"

"Can't stop thinking. You?"

"Same."

We fell into silence briefly, and I toyed with the edge of my thin blanket. "Have you ever wondered what the ocean's like?" I finally asked.

"Of course. Doesn't everyone wonder? Although . . . I mostly wonder what it *used* to look like. You know, when it was full of water, and wouldn't kill you."

"Oh." I frowned, disappointed. Somehow that wasn't the answer I was hoping for.

"What?"

"Well . . ." I trailed off, feeling silly. He didn't interrupt, though, and ultimately I spat the words out. "I was thinking of changing course. Not completely, of course, but . . . going straight to the coast. Seeing the ocean—or what's left of it; I'm not picky—sooner rather than later. Then following the straight line up to the city. It's not the *most* efficient, though, so there's always a risk—"

"I say yes. If you want to see it, then yes." His voice was unwavering, resolute.

"But our water supply—"

"Our water supply is more than most people have at once in an entire lifetime. We have a water finder, and we know now there's wild water out there. Remember our oasis? God, I think about showering all the time now." He sighed, and the wistful feel of it resonated in my soul. Showers *were* magical.

"Me too."

"So, let's do it. It might add, what, a day or two to our trip? It's worth it. Who knows when we'll get to see it again?"

"Yeah, I was just lying here thinking, what if we never make it there? Or that jet comes back." My throat tightened painfully, and my words stopped. Raising my wrist, I stared at my hydration meter until the orange tower signal popped back up before dropping it back to the sleep mat with a thud.

"That jet is long gone, Nyx. It's awful. Really, truly awful. But you will survive, no matter what you find out when we get that comm device working. I promise."

He would know, after losing his entire city to a gang raid. He was still fighting, still surviving. The memory eased the tightness in my throat bit by bit, until I could speak again. "Thanks."

"'Welcome," he murmured, a hint of darkness to his words.

The quiet drew out between us again, but this time I sank into sleep instead of fighting it, visions of the ocean painting the back of my eyelids. Whether it would still be the beautiful cerulean I imagined when we got there, nobody knew.

I was still excited to find out.

Four

Baby Scavenger

After tossing and turning all night thinking about the ocean—and wondering if I was making the wrong decision in deviating from the straightest possible path to Chace—I was happy to let River take the first shift in the driver's seat. I was cranky and antsy, and no amount of pink skies painted overhead or cheery music on the radio—River was a *morning person*, blech—was going to make it better. Laid back in my seat with my eyes closed, I was shutting everything out this morning.

We were heading due west now, over land I'd never traveled before, but it looked like every other stretch of desert I'd seen. While I had no desire to jog laps in the sand, I needed to *do* something. Despite making fun of River's running yesterday, if we didn't come across a city soon, I was going to go mad with boredom.

Long-haul driving was not for me, and I'd been doing way too much of it the past month and a half.

I sighed, and flipped to my other side, staring out the window at the dunes rolling past, each one the same.

"Stewing won't make it better, whatever it is," River chided.

"You don't know that."

He chuckled. "I mean, not officially. But . . . there's a ninety percent chance I'm right. What's wrong? You were so excited about the ocean last night."

"I'm bored. And anxious. And I want to tear something apart with my bare hands and find cool stuff to trade." I flopped to my back and threw an arm over my eyes to block the sun.

"Ahh."

"That's it? Ahh?" I scowled at him from under my arm, but he rudely ignored it.

"If I suggested you run like I do, you might bite me."

A snort turned into a chortle, which was followed by a full body laugh, and I dropped my arm to roll my eyes at him. "Oh, my word, you are ridiculous."

He grinned shamelessly at me and gave me a wink. "Told you stewing wouldn't help."

I lightly smacked his arm and hit the button to raise my seat back upright. "Fine, fine. But

I'm going to find us a city. Maybe we'll find something of value to these people when we get there. Assuming they're into trading," I added under my breath as I fished my atlas from the back of the truck.

"Good plan. Want some dates?" River passed me a handful of the sweet, sticky dried fruits he loved so much.

I accepted them and took a bite, but I was already focused on the ancient, leather-bound atlas in my lap.

It took two more days of driving and three should-have-been towns before we finally came across something on the horizon besides sand. When we spotted it, my heart froze in my chest.

"Is that . . . is that a signal tower?" I blurted, pointing out the driver's side window to the southern horizon.

"It's definitely a tower of some kind." River shaded his eyes and squinted, leaning across the center console for a closer look and invading my personal space in the process. "It's too alone for a skyscraper, and too tall for a normal neighborhood building. Not the right shape for a water tower—though wouldn't that be something?" He turned to me and grinned, but I couldn't return it.

"It looks like a signal tower. The question is, does it use the same frequency as this thing?" I jangled my wrist, my hydration meter glowing a respectable green seventy percent. "I think we should go check it out. If there's a tower, there could be a town there, too."

"Let's go, then." He leaned forward in his seat happily, always excited for something different.

I turned the wheel, arrowing straight towards the tower. "Do me a favor—keep an eye out for anything sticking up out of the sand."

"Okay . . . any particular reason for that?"

I snorted. "Yeah, last time I was on a long trip and got too curious, I almost killed myself by puncturing my water tank."

His pained grimace said it all, and he closely scanned the ground with me as we approached. Thankfully, the way was clear. The tower loomed larger the closer we got and hope warred with bitter apprehension as the shape of a small town came into view, clustered not far from the tower. I rolled through the town cautiously, checking for signs of inhabitants. Like most dry places, it seemed deserted. After several passes with no movement—plus heavy dust caking all the windows, and major sand drifts piled up against the northern sides of the homes—we parked the truck and got out to explore on foot.

I loaded my pants pockets with all the usual culprits; my breaking and entering tools, net bags, a couple of water orbs, and a meal bar for good measure.

"You're definitely the pro at this," River said after watching my preparations. He only grabbed a water orb and a crowbar for himself, which he hoisted to his shoulder like a baseball bat. "Lead the way, boss-lady."

I snorted derisively. "I'm nobody's boss but my own, and I like it like that."

"Whatever you say." He winked before bumping shoulders with me, to which I responded with an eye roll.

At least he didn't call me mama.

"So, are we heading straight for the tower? See if we can get your comms working?" he asked, craning his neck to look up at the top of the rickety-looking tower.

"No, let's save it for last. Hit the houses first—it'll probably be quick; most everything is picked over nowadays—and then we can climb the tower."

He lifted one eyebrow in question but didn't argue. Instead, he shoved his hands into his pockets and whistled as we walked down a sand-laden street lined with homes.

"Stay sharp. Even if there are no people, that doesn't mean no danger," I warned to get his head back in the game.

River's expression sobered quickly, and I knew he was thinking of the wolf who'd almost made himself a tasty River sandwich on our last excursion.

The first place we tried was a squat, ranch-style house with dark, water-stained wood paneling and a moldy odor permeating the air. I decided to pass, since anything inside would likely stink every bit as badly, and I didn't want to haul that around and stink up the truck.

The next house was much better; dusty for sure, but tidy and with full sets of furniture in place inside. River made himself at home on a plush floral couch while I tossed the place. It was nearly untouched, and I found myself being far pickier than usual, given our limited storage space and long drive. I collected hard bars of soap from the bathroom closet, a jumbo-sized container of salt from the pantry, and a dozen vacuum-packed freeze-dried meals. After making rounds of the whole house, I also came back and emptied the silverware drawer, collecting dozens of forks, spoons, and knives with delicate rose patterns on the handles.

River lay happily stretched out, his fingers laced together behind his head, and his ankles crossed on one arm of the ancient couch. My jangling steps as I approached prompted him to crack one eye open.

"Find some stuff?"

"Yeah, I really did. Soap, salt, freeze-dried meals—" He perked up at that, and lunged to an upright position in a single, fluid motion.

"Can I see?"

I nodded and passed him the net bag with the various silver pouches. "Look while we walk to the next one. I've got a good feeling about this neighborhood, I'm going to mark it on the GPS when we get back to the truck," I said with barely concealed enthusiasm. If the first town we ran across had this many tradable goods in *every* house, this would be a major score, and worth coming back to once we found Chace.

Assuming he wants to leave the Bastion. Doubts niggled at the back of my mind—he might not want to leave, if the city was really a technologically advanced mecca—but I shook them off and let myself sink into the joy of my job. We would cross that bridge when we got to it.

House after house, River found a spot to watch while I methodically scavenged the best items from each place. Occasionally I'd need his muscle to move something, and he'd leap up and help before getting back out of my way. The first side of the street yielded more than I could fit into the truck, unless I was ready to load the tailgate rack, too. I wasn't, given how heavily loaded we still were with water. As we moved through the houses, I got pickier. Only selecting the best food items, and those I knew had the highest trade value back home. While I didn't know for sure what the people of Bastion City would need, food and supplies were always scarce.

If they didn't need the stuff, we could use it when we moved on. Eventually, the sun began to lower; we'd drained our water orbs—plus the ones River had retrieved from the truck to replace the first ones; and my bags were full to bursting with my haul.

"Ready to head back and unload, so we can head up the tower while there's still light?" River asked, shouldering both bags.

"Almost," I called from the kitchen. Something was off about this house. I couldn't quite put my finger on it, though. I paced the length of the kitchen, looking high and low for whatever was giving me that feeling, but finding nothing. I rubbed my water meter, and idly looked down to check it. Green, eighty-four percent. I was really staying well hydrated these days, even when I forgot my water for a while.

I still couldn't let go of that niggling thought, and walked to the wall of windows lining the back of the living room. There was nothing but sand outside, and the long shadows cast by the homes along the street. Looking left and right, I finally spotted it. "Hey River, come here, please."

He wandered in, hair mussed from a day of stretching out on every piece of furniture in every house. "What's up?"

"Does this look weird to you?" I stood perpendicular to the hallway and squared my shoulders, lifting both arms and pointing out the window to the back of the house, and down the hallway, which was dotted with bedroom and closet doors.

"Uhm, maybe? How big are the bedrooms?"

"No, not that. Look how far down the bathroom door is. Yet the house comes out there." I moved my hands forward and back, showing what I meant.

"Yeah, that doesn't seem to line up."

"Exactly," I agreed, and jogged across to the bathroom door. "Yet somehow, this bathroom is the size of a broom closet." I stepped inside and he followed, lips pursed as he took in the tight, narrow space. It was poorly lit, the small window built into the shower wall half-covered by sand accumulation, and the top half grimy with dirt. It was enough light to see the blue and green striped wallpaper on the walls was crinkled with age and excess heat, sagging away from the ceiling. We could only both fit in if I stood in front of the toilet, and he squished next to me in front of the pedestal sink.

"What are you thinking?"

"I'm thinking there's something behind this wall." I tapped the wall behind the toilet and got a hollow thump for my efforts.

"How the heck do we access it, though? Do you want to tear down the wall?"

I ran a hand through my hair absently, raking it up off my neck for a moment, the sweaty tendrils still trying to cling to my skin. "No, I don't. If it's worth building a secret space for, I want it to still be here if we have to come back for it. We need to find the entrance."

"Fair point," he agreed, and we both got to work. River lifted the mirrors off the wall, the ancient brackets squeaking in protest while I circled back to the hallway. I felt along the wall paneling for any dips or crevices that might have concealed an opening but came up with nothing.

River popped his head out of the bathroom doorway. "Hey, Nyx, you've gotta see this!" The low hum of excitement in his voice had me hurrying to wedge back into the uncomfortably small space.

"What is it?"

"You see many toilets with *pedals*?"

"Err . . . no? Just the normal flusher handle thing. Why?"

River grinned ear to ear as he crouched down and pointed to the back of the squat, yellowing toilet where a brass pedal poked out, seemingly from the base of the toilet. It only stuck out an inch or two past the base, which was probably why I hadn't noticed it nestled against the plumbing behind the toilet.

"Did you try it?"

"Nah, seemed weird enough I thought I'd wait for you. You know, in case zombies come out of that wall when it opens." He waggled his eyebrows, more excited than he probably should have been about *zombies*.

I rolled my eyes at his antics but couldn't help a small smile in return. His exuberance was contagious at times, even when I didn't have any of my own to spare. "Well, I'm here now, so let's try this thing." I rubbed my hands together in excitement as he stood and rested the toe of his boot on the gleaming pedal, then pushed it down to the floor. He had no trouble with it, but I could hear a faint grinding noise as if corrosion or grit had built up inside whatever mechanism it worked. After a few seconds of nothing, he lifted his foot and stepped back. As soon as the pedal sprang free, a dull click sounded, and a fissure appeared in the wall.

"Yes! A door!" I stepped forward and fitted my fingertips into the floor-to-ceiling crack and pried, wedging my thumbs against the wall for leverage. With a scrubbing sound, the door gave inward, and a burst of stale air wafted out of the concealed room. With a quick grin over my shoulder to River, I fished a small light from my pocket, clicked it on, and stepped through. The room wasn't all that large, but two of the walls had floor-to-ceiling metal racks, shelves stuffed to the edges with survival gear and provisions. "Get in here," I called, gesturing for River to step in.

His chest brushed my left shoulder as he squeezed in behind me, and an overhead light flickered once, twice before solidifying.

"What the— They must have solar!" River's voice grew excited at that, more so than the gleaming shelves of trade goods I was drooling over. He spun and began inspecting the far end, where a complicated web of wiring laced up the wall. Sure enough, he moved a panel and revealed a bank of black and gray batteries, tidily nestled inside a rack which fed the wires. He was immediately sucked into examining the solar system, and I turned my attention back to the racks. Against the short wall, it was floor to ceiling food stuffs. The rack immediately to the right held medical supplies, clothing, and blankets, and the bottom two shelves held giant sacks of dried grains.

"Peas, wheat, barley . . ." I murmured as I read some of the labels. "Why do you think they left all of this behind?" I asked River, continuing to examine the contents. I spotted a rack full of alcohol, and immediately lifted the two largest bottles off the shelf. I didn't drink the stuff, but there were plenty of people who would pay big bucks to drink it, and it was great for medical purposes. Sterilizing wounds, pain numbing . . . it was useful.

"I don't know, maybe where they were heading already had supplies? This stuff could have been more than they could carry. There are empty spots on the shelves, so they took *some* stuff." He pointed to a few block-shaped slots, where something had been stored previously.

"Lucky them, lucky us," I muttered, grabbing up all the things that were hard to have manufactured by a replicator. Batteries, flashlights, and mobile solar charging packs were so complex they cost more water credits to create. I'd never had that kind of credit, so all of my gear was pilfered on scavenging missions.

"This is a really advanced system," River gushed. "It's got a full power bank, a redundancy, encapsulated wiring, and I bet a really nice panel cache somewhere. Maybe the roof? It's not covered, if it can still turn on the lights here." He looked over my shoulder into the bag I was topping off with the best bits from this hidden storage.

"That's cool. Is it something we can take, or would that destroy it?" I asked, finished gathering what I could carry; I even left a few less important things in their place.

He sighed, and I had my answer.

"Well, we'll mark it on the GPS and come back. If we hurry, we can still make it to the top of the tower before dark."

"Okay. Hey, did you check that cabinet?"

"Hmm?" I spun to see where he was pointing, and sure enough, a floor-to-ceiling cabinet was tucked in the corner wedged between the metal shelving units and painted the same color as the wall. Curious what else this hidden cache of wonders held, I swung open the tall, skinny door, and burst out laughing. "We're going to need to run to the truck and empty out these bags. I'm not leaving a single one of these behind!"

"What? What could possibly be so great—" He peered over my shoulder, and his eyebrows flew upward. "Is that an *entire cabinet* of snack cakes? Holy mother."

"It sure is, and we are the luckiest two people on the planet right now." I was already drooling, thinking of the light, sugary filling. It always made my jaw twitch, but I loved the taste more than anything else on the planet. There was nothing like a Twinkie, and there were at least twenty boxes, plus chocolate cupcakes and a few chocolate swirl cakes I'd never tried before.

He grabbed my bag before jogging out of the room, a much more excited spring in his step. "You stay here, I'll be faster!"

I chuckled, and started pulling the boxes of precious cargo out, one by one into tidy stacks. This day just kept getting better.

Five

New Heights

T he sun kissed the horizon as River and I stood shoulder to shoulder, staring up at the giant, creaking metal tower. There was a zig-zagging staircase in the center, which was our way to the top. I had a box of Twinkies under one arm, and River had a small tool pouch slung over his shoulder, in case he needed to tinker with anything at the top.

"Are you ready?" River asked, studying the side of my face.

"I—No. No, I am not ready," I admitted, anxiety churning in my gut as my gaze landed on section after section of worn metal, blasted thin by years of constant pelting by sand.

"Okay, well, we saved it for last, there's nowhere else to go, and the light's going to be gone soon . . . Are you afraid of heights?" he teased.

"No, I'm not afraid of heights," I growled back. "I climbed to the top of Wolf Well with you, remember?"

"True, true. So, what's the problem? Do you want me to go first? You can stay down a few steps in case they give out, so I don't squash you. Or you could just stay down here. Honestly, if I can't fix it, you won't be much help. No offense."

I tilted my head to the side and glared at him. "None taken, but, it's fine. I'm going to go. I just needed a minute, okay? I get that this is big, and I get that we probably won't have this opportunity again. But . . . while we're down *here*, I can tell myself this is purely a technical issue. Once we're up there . . . this might not be working because the system's destroyed—along with all the people who were supposed to be on the other side."

"Ahh."

I groaned. "You and your 'ahh.' I don't need a therapist. Let's go." Shaking my shoulders loose, I started up the spiraling corrugated metal staircase. Each and every step creaked ominously under my weight and groaned a little louder as the heavier River followed behind. I glanced up and did some quick math; it looked like we easily had a hundred plus steps left to go. I blew out a fortifying breath, then moved a little quicker. Twenty steps up, I had to jump over the first hole, where a tread should have been. My breath was starting to come in shorter pants, but I forced myself to keep going.

Make it to the top, and you might get to hear from Coyote Springs. Make it to the top, and you might get to hear if Marl and Hoss are alive. A lump rose in my throat, nearly stopping my already erratic breaths at the thought of the only people who'd ever cared about me back home—besides my brother—dead and burnt to ash. Like Jaen.

I sucked in a strangled breath, and forcibly shoved the thoughts down. Thinking about them now wouldn't help them. Make the comm device work. Call back. See who survived. That was it. That was all I could do. And if no one answered . . . we'd go straight north when we found Chace. There had to be better out there than the life we'd lived so far. There *had* to be.

I pumped one arm as the other hand skated up the railing, and kept my eyes trained on the next stair tread, doing my best to blank out my mind. So blank, in fact, that I didn't notice the thin spot in the railing under my left hand until it gave way. I stumbled, and my shins bashed painfully into the stairs. My breath hissed out in a sharp grunt, but before I had time to process, River's arm snaked around my waist and lifted me upright, off my smarting shins.

"Hey, are you okay?" he asked, scooting past me so he could look at my face. I inspected my palms, a reddened diamond pattern etched into my skin where they'd been bitten by the patterned tread. *Better than my face.*

"Yeah, fine. Just didn't see the weak spot in the railing." I grimace-smiled and brushed my hands off on my pants. My shins, however, throbbed like they'd been seared with a hot poker. Once I'd removed the dust from my palms, I gingerly rolled up my pants to check the state of my abused legs.

"Ooh, that is going to bruise," River said with a wince. He knelt down and inspected more closely, gently brushing his fingertips over the angry red lines indenting my flesh. "It didn't break the skin; your pants protected you from the sharp corners, at least. Can you keep going? If not, I really don't mind going up alone." He looked up, his eyes full of sincerity. It would be easy to get lost in his crystalline gaze that never judged me and only offered help and friendship. Maybe one day . . . more than friendship? Could he accept a free woman, and could I put that level of trust in him—open up to him? I wondered, as we stood there buffeted by the wind, half-way up a decrepit radio tower.

I didn't ask any of that, though. I kept those thoughts locked deep inside, where the answers couldn't break me. "Of course. I'm fine.

Ready when you are." He nodded once, studying my face for a second longer before brushing my fingers away, and rolling the pant legs back down. His fingertips danced gently against the back of my calves as he did it, and the unexpected touch shook me to my core.

"How about I lead the way?" he offered. "We can go a bit slower. This old thing isn't going anywhere."

"Sure. Lead the way." I gestured up the ladder, so he turned and continued up, setting a more sustainable pace.

My breathing slowed as we crisscrossed back and forth. As we gained altitude with each turn of the stairs and each landing we passed, the view became more and more impressive, but I doggedly pressed on without stopping. One foot, one stair. Other foot, next stair. Ignore the creaks, don't get distracted by the pained sounds each stair makes when River steps on it, or the visions of him falling to his death because you want to climb the next generation's Radio Tower of Pisa.

Finally, we made it to the top. The wind up here was vicious, cutting through the holes in the top of the tower like knives, and our flimsy linen clothing just the same. The space inside the tower was larger than it looked from the ground, and I kept close to the center, away from the open windows that showcased a very steep drop to the ground below.

"Nothing like a good climb to get your heart pumping, right?" River grinned at me, already digging in his tool bag for a pair of pliers. Apparently he wasn't as freaked out at the idea of plunging to a sudden death as I was for him.

"Uh-huh. We've been over this before. You're weird. Exercise is not fun."

"Hey, you think it's fun enough when trade goods are involved. I get to mechanic at the end of this one, so it should count."

"Fine, go mechanic. I'll be here, staring at the toes of my boots and not thinking about anything besides how many Twinkies I can eat without puking."

He chuckled but didn't wait around to argue. In a flash, he was across the floor, sliding onto an old metal stool and tinkering with an impressive control panel with a full bay of blank screens. A few were cracked, but most seemed to be in good repair. It was a good sign, and I tried to stay positive as he pulled out a pair of needle-nosed pliers and another hand tool I couldn't remember the name of.

River was going to fix it, and we were going to hear from the Sidewinders that everyone we knew—and hopefully many of the townspeople of Coyote Springs—were all safe and well. I stared off into the distance. The sun sank slowly behind the horizon, painting the sky, as I noshed on hyper-sweet cakey goodness.

I finished two of them, one slow, luxurious bite at a time, before I allowed myself to get up and check River's progress. After wiping the excess oil off on my black pants, I stood and crossed to stand beside him.

He was muttering under his breath and twisting something inside a computer panel with a screwdriver the size of my thumb. "How's it going?" I asked, interrupting his stream of thought.

"Fine. Hey, hold this for me, please?" He reached under the screwdriver arm and passed me a handful of tiny screws. I cupped my hands to receive them and watched in silence as he continued to fiddle with the electronics.

After about ten minutes, River sat back and scanned the surface. "I think that's it, now we just need to find how it turns on—Ahh! Red button. I love a good red button. Hopefully it's power, not missile. Do you think this town had missile support?"

"After Coyote Springs, I'd be okay if no one had missiles anymore."

"True, sorry. Just trying to lighten the moment. I have no idea if this is going to work." He gave me a thin smile, then pressed the red button, stood, and stepped back to stand at my side. He seemed to hold his breath as he leaned his shoulder into mine.

The screens in front of us responded instantaneously. The broken screens flickered, before going back to black. The rest all flashed green, and then black text began scrolling across the screen at a rapid clip.

"Should we be reading that?"

"No, I think it's a startup sequence."

"You're smart for a grease monkey," I teased, and he turned to squint his eyes at me in play-accusation.

"I didn't hear any complaints when I grease-monkeyed your electrical system on the Bronco."

"And you never will. You've got real talent." I gave him a genuine smile, and he lifted a finger to trace along my cheek and down to the curve of my jaw.

"You've got a dimple, but you're stingy with it. It almost never shows."

"Mm," I responded vaguely, but the panel in front of us emitted a series of beeps, and he turned to see what was going on. I blinked rapidly a few times, trying to get my head back in the game.

"Okay, we have liftoff." He turned and gave me a boyish grin. "It's booted up."

I watched in expectant silence as the screens flashed and text whirred across, while River rapid-fire typed on the keyboard. In less than a minute a dashboard appeared, the large display taking up six monitors.

"Hey, that looks like something," I said, stepping closer.

"Yeah, I think so. As far as I can tell, this is tower G11719. G11719 has an active status, but orange for—"

He stopped talking, lost in the troubleshooting data that flowed across the screen. After seeing that I was no help to what he was doing, I mustered up the courage to cross to the nearest window. The sunset was behind us, but the view was still stunning. Sand undulated in waves as far as the eye could see, unbroken by manmade structures. The last rays of sun painted the sands gold, highlighting every dip and curve.

I gradually made my way around, opening a third treat to savor as I did. By the time I had circumnavigated the room and wandered back to River's side, he had settled himself on the ancient, rickety stool and was raking his hand through his hair.

"Has your meter given any new signal at all?"

I held it up and waited the necessary time, but still an unhelpful tower icon popped up.

"Nope."

He sighed. "That's what I was afraid you were going to say. I don't know if this tower is the wrong type, or plain-old broken, but doing any-thing more is beyond my capabilities." He gri-maced as he said it, an apologetic look on his face.

"River, why do you look like I just stomped on your date collection?"

"Because," he groaned, "I wanted this to work. I wanted you to have some reassurance that everyone you know and care about isn't dead." He ran a frustrated hand over the back of his neck, before dropping it back to his thigh, de-feat written in the set of his shoulders. "I know how it feels, when everyone you care about is gone, and I don't want that for you."

"I'm sorry. This must be bringing back all kinds of bad memories for you." I took a step forward, laying a hand gently on his shoulder.

He looked up into my eyes—searching for what, I didn't know—and nodded. "I was nine when the Nightbloods wiped out my caravan. We were floating to a new water source, and—" He swallowed hard, looking away.

"Hey, you don't have to go into detail if it's too painful."

"No, it's way past time that I should tell you. What it was like after, with the Night-bloods—they're a hard people, Nyx. One man leads them—never shows his face—and the rest are almost all mindless sycophants. They would follow him straight off a cliff if he said the word." He paused, and his face grew angry.

"My party wasn't doing too well, but we still had water reserves. A few people had been left behind at the previous city—the elderly, the very young—but every other able-bodied person had been sent with the caravan. We could carry more water that way and split up to cover more ground. I was with the westward party."

He took a deep breath, and continued, "We got a call over our radios on the fourth day. Someone found water. They were mid-coordinate when the call cut off. Apparently, whatever water they'd found belonged to the Nightbloods, and they weren't willing to share," he spat.

"I don't know how they found the other three parties—they are technologically advanced, compared to most."

"Hence the water finder," I mused.

"Exactly. Anyways, they hunted down every party, and finished off the survivors left in the city. They only kept healthy children under ten, or women willing to marry one of their *warriors*. Like they're some kind of feudal society of yore." His words ground to a stop, and I could feel the hatred radiating off of him.

My stomach twisted painfully at his words. "And that's whose territory we're driving through."

"That's whose territory we're driving through."

"And your family . . . You survived, obviously. Were your parents still alive then?"

He closed his eyes for a moment, and I regretted the personal question. His expression was unadulterated sorrow when his eyes met mine again. "They killed my father in the initial skirmish. My mother was weeping over his body when they came for her. One of the warriors stepped forward to take her arm and she spat in his face. That was when he—" His voice broke, and I stepped forward to wrap him in a hug.

It was a bit awkward at first, because he was sitting, and I was standing. But he wrapped his arms around my waist and buried his face in my shoulder, and we fit together perfectly.

"I'm so sorry, River. God, I'm so sorry," I whispered it into his golden hair and held him until his shoulders stopped shaking. When he pulled back, he swiped away the tear tracks from his cheeks, and I caught a hint of embarrassment on his face.

I didn't know what to say to that—I'd never spent much time around anyone but Chace, and I'd only seen him cry twice my entire life—so, I offered him a Twinkie.

He smiled and took the cake. "Is this some kind of weird reward system? I cry like a baby, and you feed me?"

"Absolutely. Don't get used to it." I winked, and he laughed. Together, we found a spot on the floor with a good view and sat shoulder to shoulder, sharing snack cakes and watching the sun melt into the endless sea of sand.

Six

SKIRTING THE NIGHTBLOODS

S omething was wrong. I couldn't put my finger on it, but when I woke—still on the floor of the radio tower?—I felt itchy. River was at ease next to me, sprawled and drooling, with one heavily-muscled bicep thrown over his eyes to block the sun. Reaching down to finger my water droplet charm, I rolled silently to my feet in a crouch, then duck-walked to the nearest window so I could look out without being seen. All was still, with the pale sunrays making the sand look washed out at this hour.

I slowly made my way to two more windows, before I spotted it.

"River, get up!" I hissed between my teeth.

"'S early, Nyx. Slept like crap on this floor. Give me ten," he groaned but didn't pull his arm away from his eyes.

"No time, River. We've got company."

That got his attention. He lurched upright, golden hair askew, and started to surge for his feet.

"Stop. Stay low. They haven't seen us yet—let's keep it that way, if we can."

"Is it a single person, or—"

"Four SUVs. No idea how many passengers."

He swore under his breath and crept to my side before peeking out the window. "Okay, what's your plan for us getting down from here without being spotted?"

"Don't have one. We need to know what we're going to do at the bottom, first. They're still far enough out they might skirt the town, but I doubt it." I risked another peek, and they were still arrowing straight towards us, although . . . "Hey, does it look like those three are chasing the one in the front?"

We traded positions, me ducking down and him stealing a glance. "Yeah, they're all black, and the one in front is yellow. Shabbier, too, if I had to guess." We were side by side, shoulders pressed back against the cold metal wall, and I had no idea what tack to take.

"What do you normally do in these situations?" he asked.

"Normally I hide, if I know the terrain. But we were all over this place yesterday, and there isn't a single structure where we could hide the Bronco. If they find that, we're done. No wheels, no water . . . Four SUVs—even three, working together—and we can't guarantee how many people are inside. I think we have to run."

His eyes locked with mine, and I felt the most idiotic urge to kiss him square on the lips. "Let's do it," he said, a reckless grin crossing his face. For a moment I thought he had read my impulsive thoughts, but my surging adrenalin snapped me back into the present.

Without hesitation, we raced to the middle of the floor—abandoning the box of empty Twinkie wrappers—and began a wild sprint down the corrugated metal stairs. The wind buffeted us, the stairs creaked as our feet pounded relentlessly down and down, but we didn't dare stop or slow down. We had maybe a half hour before the four SUVs made the outskirts of this town, and then they'd be on top of us fast if we were still here.

Going down was easier than going up, and we hit the half-way mark in short order. It felt a bit like flying, the wind whipping my hair around my face as I bolted down, turned hard, using the handrail for leverage, and propelled myself down the next flight.

I saw the missing tread coming and called back to River as I leapt over it. "Watch the hole!"

"Got it!" He whooped as he cleared the hole effortlessly.

On the second to last flight of the stairs, I was swinging hard around the corner when the handrail gave way underneath my right palm. The metal crumpled, worn too hard by time and constant sandblasting to stand up to the force of my entire weight swinging on it. The sudden lack of an anchor sent me stumbling to the side, and my ribs slammed into the opposite railing, leaving me wheezing as the breath whooshed from my lungs.

"Ow, ow, freaking ow! My palm!" I snatched it from the jagged edge of the railing, but tried not to slow my pace as I pressed my throbbing palm against my breastbone and greedily sucked air in between my teeth. We had to make it to the Bronco, get moving, and then I could see how badly I was hurt. Maybe it was just a scrape.

At least the other railing had held and hadn't sent me falling twenty feet to the sand, I thought as every step jolted my aching ribs.

"You okay?" River barked, all traces of joy evaporated from his tone.

"Fine. Let's just get to the truck. I've got first aid stuff."

"Want me to drive?"

"No, I'm still faster, and I don't know if I can climb over the console right now to reach the kit."

"Okay, I'll take shotgun."

We fell silent as we cleared the final steps, and the two of us raced for the Bronco. Between my bruised ribs and River's regular running, he outpaced me quickly and ate up the ground between us and the Bronco, where we'd stashed it right inside the nearest row of buildings. The few industrial buildings remaining here had been completely empty, so we hadn't spent much time in them.

He had already dived into the passenger side and was hung over the back of his seat digging for the first aid kit by the time I made it to the driver's door. The wheezing hadn't completely stopped, and I had to stop for a minute and breathe through a stitch in my side before I could open the door and haul myself up with my left hand.

River saw my predicament and stopped digging in the back long enough to grab my right bicep and haul me the rest of the way into my seat. The motion pulled my damaged hand away from my shirt, and I felt a sticky trail of blood ooze down my chest as I used my left hand to drop the Bronco into gear. Not a scrape.

"Hang on, River, it's time to move," I warned him before I stepped on it. He braced himself with one hand against the roof as I slammed the pedal to the floor.

We were throwing up a dust trail as we skidded out of town and towards the open desert, when River flopped back to his seat, med kit in his lap. The white case had seen its share of abuse from flopping around in the back of the Bronco for so many years and was covered in dings and dingy-looking scuffs.

The original came with the truck, but Chace and I had expanded it whenever we could afford to over the years. Lesina joked that we were two of her best customers. Although, in hindsight, I'm pretty sure she said that to everyone who regularly bought her deodorant paste and tooth tablets. *I really hope she's still alive*, I thought as we crested a sharp dune, and the truck fishtailed on the way down the other side.

River opened the case and tossed through the contents quickly.

"Is it cut, or impaled?"

"Don't know, man, haven't looked."

He sighed. "Do you have a bottle of sterile wash?"

"No. Too expensive. I've got sterilization tablets, though. Green pouch?"

"Got 'em. Okay, I've got a wrap and gauze, let me whip up the sterilizer and then we'll see what else needs to be done. How are you feeling?" he asked as he worked. I spared a glance his way as we started up the next dune, and his hands were steady as he crushed a tablet in his fingertips and smeared it into the mouth of a water orb.

"Great, really spectacular," I retorted.

"I'm serious, Nyx. Are you lightheaded? Faint? Dizzy? Any tingling in your fingertips, toes, or blurred vision?"

"Err, no? I mean, my hand is throbbing so I can't tell if it's also tingling. But it hurts." I gritted out the last, not really wanting to admit it.

"That's good. What about anywhere else? You took a hard blow to the ribs."

"My ribs are definitely still attached, based on how loudly they're screaming."

He barked out a laugh. "Sense of humor's still intact—that's a good sign. Okay, this stuff's ready. Give me your hand."

I kept my eyes on the road as I peeled my palm away from my blood-soaked shirt, which tried to stick. I was pretty sure this shirt was ruined, unless I could get some dye and turn the whole thing red.

"Alright, hold tight—this is going to sting."

"I'm fi— Ahh, sweet camel humps, that sucks!" I hissed, trying not to snatch my hand out of his grip. "Dang, I want to punch you right now."

"Don't do that, I need to get these metal shards out of here so we can get compression on this and stop the bleeding."

"Oh, don't tell me you're going to dig around in there." I briefly closed my eyes, already dreading whatever he was going to do next.

"Okay, I'm not going to dig around in there. Brace yourself and try not to wreck us."

We crested another dune when I felt the tweezers meet my mangled palm. I bit my bottom lip, determined not to make a peep while he worked. Keeping my eyes welded to the sand in front of the Bronco, I kept the pedal down and didn't look back at the people behind us. Best case scenario, we never saw them, and they never saw us.

It felt like hours as River worked in turns, digging pieces of shattered metal railing out of my palm, then dousing the area with the liquid fire of sanitizer while I breathed through my nose in aggressive bursts. We'd crossed at least four dunes when he spoke again.

"This is the last piece, and it's the biggest. It shouldn't hurt as bad coming out since it's easy to grab, but you are going to start bleeding more. If you feel any changes at all in your vision, or anything else feels fuzzy or weird you need to tell me immediately. I don't want you to go into shock. Clear?"

"Clear." I ground the single word out, and closed my mouth again. He could say it wouldn't hurt all he wanted; I didn't believe that for half a second.

I felt it when the piece slid free, and I couldn't stop the grunt of pain that escaped my lips.

"You're doing great, hang in there. Almost done, almost done," he chanted as he doused my palm in sanitizer again. "There we go—I see some grit washing out, but I think it's clear now. Just gotta wrap it up. Have you got a preferred salve in here? There's a dozen of these little pots."

I finally took a chance and looked over at the wound, and immediately regretted it. My palm was red and raw, blood running in watery rivulets between my fingers as it mixed with the sanitizer and pooled into the lid of the first aid kit. There was a sizeable puddle in there, and I could see dark splotches of metal where they clustered at the bottom. "Yeah, there's a newer one in there—I got it right before we met. Ugh, what did she call it?" I swallowed hard, my mouth suddenly dry as cotton.

"It's fine, I'll find it," he said in a soothing voice.

My stomach lurched, and I forced myself to look away. *Sand, sand, think about sand. Dry. Boring. Clean. Oh, sweet oasis I'm going to hurl.* "River . . ."

"What is it? Talk to me." I felt him smearing something gooey over my raw palm, and the sensation made me want to heave again.

"I think I'm going to be sick," I gritted out between my teeth.

"That's okay. Just stop the truck. I've got you almost wrapped up and then I can drive." I didn't dare look again, instead taking my foot off the gas and letting the truck roll down into the valley between the next dunes under its own momentum. When we hit the bottom, I stood on the park brake to activate it, causing the truck to lurch to an inelegant stop.

"You're good, hop out," he urged, and I finally swung around and opened the door.

My feet touched sand, then my knees, and I heaved until my stomach was empty. Sometime during the process, River had come around, and was silently holding my braid out of the splash zone. I wanted to apologize, but all that came out when I tried to talk was, "Ugh."

"Shh, it's okay. Do you think you can stand?"

I shook my head, barely managing to push with my shaking left arm back up to sit on my heels. "I need a minute," I croaked, then spluttered a cough which made my ribs burn viciously.

"Do you think we have enough distance to wait out the others?"

My mind spun, but I knew the answer to that. I shook my head furiously and pointed with my good hand back to the truck. We couldn't stop.

He nodded; determination written on his face. Without hesitation he scooped me up and jogged around the other side of the truck. Once he'd settled me in and buckled my seatbelt—I was shaking too hard and dropped the clip when I tried to insert it—he shut my door and darted around to the driver's seat.

"Just rest, I got this," he soothed.

It was the last thing I heard as the sand blurred, and my eyelids slipped closed.

"Nyx, I'm sorry, but you need to wake up." River's hand shook my shoulder, and something about his tone reached inside my brain and woke me before the words even processed. *Wrong, something was wrong.*

"What is it?" I lurched forward in the seat, my chest and ribs bouncing angrily off the seatbelt, which was still fastened, and locked against my sudden movement.

"We've got company. I'm sorry, I'm not as fast as you—and apparently they are." He nodded back over his shoulder, and I cranked my torso around to look behind us, pissing off my bruised ribs in the process, and making the now-stiffened bloody shirt pull grossly at my skin.

"Crap, crap, crap. How long have I been out?" I straightened more carefully.

"Couple hours. I thought we'd lost them for a while, the dust trail got further back. They must have caught the yellow SUV, because the dust thinned out, and there's only two of the black SUVs now."

"I see that . . . It evens the odds some, at least."

"I don't think so, Nyx. This screams Night-bloods. They wouldn't have chased us if they didn't think they had superior forces. They won't ever go in unless they're sure of the out-come."

I swore. "We can't catch a break today. Okay, you lived with them. What's our best play?"

"I don't know, Nyx. They're looking for me. I—" He swallowed hard and gave me a grimace. "I don't know if they'll let me go. You being with me, well . . . you might be guilty by association."

"Not happening. Not today, not any day. I've got an idea." *Half an idea.*

Painstakingly, I dug behind the seat where some of Chace's personal items still hung out in the back seat pocket. I found a stained and well-worn ball cap and shoved it towards River.

"Put this on and keep it low. When we get over the next hump, you stop the car and get in the back. Stay low. No matter if they drag you out of the car, don't make eye contact with anyone and don't say a word."

"I'm not letting you deal with the Nightbloods alone, Nyx. You're still woozy, but even on your best day, they're *brutal.*"

"It's not up for debate, River. Stop here, now. Turn so we're perpendicular." I pointed, using every bit of steel in my voice I could muster as I gave the orders.

He grimaced, but didn't argue with me, cutting the wheel hard left and positioning us across the top of the dune. We were easy to spot, which was the point. After he threw it in park and climbed out, I cut the wheel hard right, in case we needed to get rolling again quickly.

By the time I'd lowered myself out of the Bronco and gingerly made my way around to the back, he'd already popped the hatch and climbed inside, making a space for himself amongst the supplies.

"Pass me my shoulder holster," I pointed with my chin, and he fished it from the pouch behind the passenger seat.

Without a word, he held it up and helped me get it over my injured hand. The backs of his fingers brushed my chest as he buckled it for me, and I chose to ignore that sudden burst of nerve-jangling energy that welled up in response.

"Thank you."

He leveled his eyes on mine. "Are you sure? I can stand with you."

"I'm sure, River; stand down."

His lips flattened into a hard line, but he nodded once quickly, shifted back into the hollowed-out area he'd made, and wallowed around until he was out of sight.

Hiding a grimace, I stretched up and hit the button to drop the rear hatch, and walked back to the driver's side of the truck. With the push of a button, my seat adjusted back to my settings and left the driver door open in case I needed to make a hasty exit. I heard a solid thump come from the back and craned my neck around to the back seat.

"You okay back there?"

"Peachy," River said drily, but didn't offer anything more.

Once everything was set, I propped myself against the rear door, shoulders back and one foot propped behind me on the running board. Painting on a trader's mask of cool indifference, I waited.

It wasn't long before I saw the two SUVs cresting the closest dunes. Three away, then two, and then the one opposite ours. They'd slowed, and stopped at the top of the closest dune, rather than pull down into the valley or try to fight me for position on this one. Still, I waited, unmoving.

For a few long moments, the two black SUVs stayed frozen; finally, the driver door of the lead vehicle opened with a soft pop, and I saw a pair of black combat boots hit the sand. The driver strode around the door and faced me, naked pistol in his grip.

I still didn't move, taking my time to size him up from booted feet, black linen-clad legs and chest, well-maintained pistol, and then to his face. He had an ugly sneer and a shaved head, loosely cowled in black fabric.

The outfit reminded me of Hema, except I couldn't imagine he'd held such a glacial expression behind his face covering.

Tired of waiting on me to speak first, the man called out, "Where's your keeper, little girl? We saw two people run down that tower. We know you're not alone, and we want to speak with him."

I raised one eyebrow slowly, intentionally, and lifted my chin to call back. "I have no keeper. You saw my kept *man*—Reed. If you want to talk, you'll do it with me."

He glowered and looked over his shoulder into the cab of his SUV. Whatever they said to him didn't carry, so I waited, trying to hide the shaking in my left leg that supported me.

"We need to see this man, nonetheless. We are looking for someone, and no man can go unchecked. Tell him to get out."

I crossed my arms over my chest, ignoring my aching ribs and buying a moment to think. They were looking for River. If he climbed out, we had at least a fifty-fifty chance of him being recognized; a ballcap wasn't much of a disguise.

Plus, I still had no idea how many people were inside those SUVs.

"I don't much appreciate having my property pawed over. Who are you looking for? Seems like you already caught one person today, and I don't see them anywhere. How do I know you're not just thieves?"

He took an angry step forward at the accusation but didn't come further. "You don't know with whom you speak, woman. I'm Karik of the Nightbloods, third in command. You are nothing, a bit of dust wandering along the breeze. We will search who we want, when we want. Tell your man to get out."

"Are you sure I can't just pay whatever tax you charge for passing through? I've got a brother to see, and you sand-jockeys are making me late." I looked down at my nails when I said it, feigning boredom, but I knew the insult landed.

He spun, turning his back on me, and making a sharp gesture towards the back of the SUV. That prompted two more men dressed in all black to jump out, landing heavily in the sand and coming to stand at his side. *Four in his car, four in the other?* I did not like those odds.

"You will still pay for passage, but not until after we see your man. If we have to, we'll drag him out ourselves." He nodded to his muscle; I sighed as they stalked down across the valley between the dunes, pinning frosty eyes on me the entire way.

Lazily, I reached back and double-tapped the glass with my palm. "Reed, step out here so we can get back on the road. These fellas want to see your pretty face. They might even want a kiss," I said sarcastically, and the one on the left glared angrily as he stopped in front of me.

I chuckled and shot him a wink as the back hatch opened, and River slowly—painstakingly, even—stepped down and came to my side. He had the baseball cap pulled low and hung his head as he limped to my side. I refused to let them see me sweat and pasted on a lascivious grin and swatted River on the butt when he stopped at my side. I cringed inside—I'd apologize later—but they needed to see what they expected, or else none of this was going to work.

"Okay, you've seen my grease monkey. Can we go now? How much is the tax?" I reached into the side pocket of the door, and with a quick bit of finger magic, slipped a fat gold chain from its hiding place. Quickly shucking the plastic baggie, I held it aloft so it could catch the sunlight. "Will this suffice? Twenty-four karat. Reed, put those arms to good use and toss this over to the boss man." I patted him on the bicep like a puppy, and pressed the chain into his hands, all while he kept his eyes trained on his boots.

"Not so fast, we need to see his face. Take the cap off and look up." The leader called, and I tensed as he began walking across the sand to join his goons.

Still moving slower than molasses, River reached up and pulled the cap free. I noticed his hair was sopping wet and slicked back from his face. But that wasn't the most surprising thing; no, the surprise was the purpling bruise below his left eye, adorned with a seeping cut and blood trailing over his cheek and down his neck.

I schooled my expression and looked back over at the three goons. One of the enforcers standing in front of us held up a tablet he'd pulled from his pocket, and they glanced back and forth between River and the image there.

"Could be him, but it's hard to say," the one on the right groused.

"This far west and with a woman, it's doubtful," the mean-mug on the left disagreed. "Besides, his hair's too dark."

The leader frowned, but didn't weigh in. "What happened to his face?" He pinned a suspicious stare on me.

I snorted and popped my hip out exaggeratedly to the side. At least one set of eyes diverted to my assets. "He got lippy. What do you *think* happened?"

He narrowed his eyes but handed the tablet back to his muscle. "It's not him, he's some Sidewinder trash. Look at the tattoo." He grabbed River's arm and jabbed the semi-fresh ink hard enough that River winced. Then he sneered at me once more. "Next time you cross Nightblood territory, don't bother running. Better yet, don't come back. Snap them for the database," he ordered and strode away.

The one on the right with the tablet gestured to River. "Turn to the left."

River didn't move or respond, just kept staring at his boots.

"You deaf, or just stupid? Turn your head!" he barked, and River slowly lifted his eyes, the unbridled rage simmering there enough to make my blood run cold.

"Reed, do what the nice men say so we can get back on the road, hmm?" I prodded, glancing quickly between the two black-clad men to make sure they weren't getting any ideas I wouldn't approve of.

The one on the left was tired of waiting. He reached up and grabbed River's chin and the back of his skull and wrenched his face around to the left.

River snarled at the manhandling, but still kept silent. The other guard snapped a photo with the tablet, then gestured with his chin for the other side. The guard took pleasure in wrenching River around the other way and jamming the blunt tip of his thumb hard into the swelling under River's left eye in the process.

He hissed out a breath of pain as they snapped the photo, and I'd had enough. "Hey, you can take your photos, but there's no need to damage my *property*." I stepped into the man's personal space, and shoved a palm against his chest, forcing him back a step away from River.

He turned ice-cold eyes on me and stepped forward so that we were chest to chest. I glared right back at him, planting hands on hips. It may not have been smart, but I'd never been accused of being smart. Being too stubborn to die, *that* I'd been accused of more than once.

Almost too fast for my eyes to track, his hands flew up. One landed on my shoulder, the other wrapped in the end of my black braid. I threw my hands up against his shoulders, but he was stronger. In an instant, he slammed me back against the side of the Bronco. The back of my skull met glass with a painful thud, and the burn in my scalp let me know he still had hold of my hair. The hand on my shoulder pushed me painfully against the flared metal of the door, and his buddy stepped forward to snap a photo of the side of my face. One side complete, he used his braid-wrapped fist to forcibly turn me the other direction.

"Got it," the other guard stated, unfazed by his buddy manhandling me. "Just need ninety seconds for the scans to process."

"Mm, it's not much, but it's time for a little fun." The guard holding me leaned his head forward, a cruel twist to his lips making my stomach turn as the hand pressing my shoulder traveled down my arm and made a cruel grab at my ribcage.

I gasped at the intense pressure of his fingers digging into my side, and he smiled wider as he tugged my braid back, exposing the column of my throat.

"Get your hands off me," I snarled, no longer playing along. I shoved with my left hand, but his shoulder didn't budge.

He chuckled and dropped his face down to the crook of my neck, running his nose along my skin. The sensation sent worms wriggling across me, and I stuffed down the panic rising in me with every second I was held against my will. I distantly heard River growl to my side, and the other guard reprimand him, but every bit of my focus was trained on the guard holding me. He shoved his knee forward, trying to spread my legs, and that was my limit.

"If you wanted to play, you should've just said so," I purred, and he mistook the sound of my voice for enthusiasm. He leaned back a pair of inches to look from my pursed lips to my neck and then further down, where I'd wriggled my left hand up and began playing with the black fabric which rested against the side of his jaw.

"Oh yeah, you feeling *playful*?" he asked, his voice going gravelly with interest.

"There's only one way to find out," I said, slipping my bandaged hand under the head covering, and dancing my fingers along the side of his neck and up to tease his earlobe.

His pupils went wide, and I didn't hesitate as his head lolled back another inch to pull the pistol from my chest holster and ram it under his jaw hard enough to snap his head back and leave a chin shiner.

His wordless yelp alerted his companion, and I hung on tighter, fingers wrapping around the back of his neck, shoving the barrel of the gun deep into the tender skin of his throat.

"On your knees!" I barked, all teasing gone.

"You sand-snorting witch! They're going to kill you and drag your bloodless carcass behind us all the way back to camp," he hissed, anger blazing in his eyes as he struggled in my grip. I just ground the gun barrel harder, and smiled as he winced, ignoring the throbbing of my palm, and the wet squelch of blood beginning to seep past the bandage.

His buddy tried to step forward, but River swept his leg out, knocking the man flat to his back in the sand and dropping a knee to his chest.

My eyes snapped up at a commotion as four men piled out of the second vehicle, and then six black-clad men were running, sand spraying up behind their boots.

"What's the plan, Nyx?" River's voice was edged with concern.

"If they don't want their friend here's brains next to his pride in the sand, they'll back off and let us leave." I wrenched the man around between me and his oncoming comrades and hollered across the sand. "Stop right there! Not a step closer or you'll be cleaning his brains off your shiny boots!"

They slowed down, but continued creeping forward, testing my resolve. Without a second's hesitation, I shifted my grip on my prisoner's neck to keep him in control and lifted the pistol to point at the nearest man's boots. My shot buried itself an inch and a half from his pinky toe.

He didn't make a sound, but he snatched his foot back and crouched low, his own weapon trained on me.

"You're going to start believing me, or you're going to start getting new holes!" I said as I dropped the barrel of the gun back to my captive's neck. "I'm tempted to give *you* a new accessory, just on principle. Give you a little taste of why people in power shouldn't take advantage of others." The imprints of his fingers on my skin felt burned into my flesh. I wanted to scrub them off—feel *clean* again—but I couldn't. Not yet. I kept my focus trained on the now-still soldiers.

"What do you want?" the leader, standing with his arms crossed next to the lead SUV, called across—interrupting my internal struggle.

"I want you and your goon squad to drive back where you came from, and forget you ever saw us." I kept my voice even, my trader mask slipping easily back into place.

The man squinted his eyes at me like I was a pile of camel dung under his boots, and my anger began to boil again. A repetitive *chirrup chirrup* sounded from the tablet where it lay discarded in the sand, distracting me before I could poke at them again.

River's prisoner made as if to grab for it, but River blocked him with a well-placed boot in the sand. Bending over—while leaning heavily on his prisoner's sternum—he picked up the discarded tablet.

"Their search is done," he said with a frown, as he swiped to turn on the tablet display, showing his mug shots. An alert popped up, which he read and then showed to me.

A4: *Potential match. Retain for questioning.*

I don't think so. I was still scowling at River when the tablet let out an ungodly screech in his hand. He quickly swiped side to side, switching from his mug shots to mine. He passed it to me, and I saw that another alert had popped up, this one with an angry red striped pattern around it over my face.

A1: *Release target and return to base immediately.*

What in the actual hell's bells? Why would they get an alert on me? Unease roiled in my stomach, and I passed the tablet back to him. It said to release me, but . . . *why?*

"We need to see that message," the man under River's boot insisted. "That's an alarm, which means at least one of you is in the system."

River tapped rapidly to clear the popup over his name, and swiped back to mine, where the release message still blinked rapidly. He raised an eyebrow in question and nodded towards the man held on the ground.

"Give it to him."

River lifted his boot from the man's chest and passed him the tablet but stayed alert in case he needed to be restrained again.

His deeply tanned face paled, and he called out immediately to his leader. "Karik, it says she's registered A1, and to return to base immediately."

Their sneering leader looked shocked, and the men idling with weapons ready between us shifted uncomfortably on their feet.

"You can't be serious! This witch needs to pay. Nobody gets to humiliate a Nightblood," my prisoner rasped out.

I snorted. The handsy one apparently didn't think getting bruised up under his fingertips was *payment* enough. I kneed him in the back to shut him up.

"You heard the smart one." I nodded to the man holding the tablet. "Time to let us go, and scurry on home to your boss."

"Release my men, and we will discuss it."

"Reed, let that one go, and grab some zip ties from the back of the truck, please." I was trying hard not to sway on my feet where I held him, but my fingers were beginning to tingle, and nausea was becoming my overwhelming state of mind. I needed these Nightbloods away from us ASAP, so I could crawl back into the truck and pass out again.

River hefted the man up by his forearm, and as soon as he'd begun jogging back, the men in the valley joined him in retreating to their vehicles. River then spun on his boot heel and dug out a fistful of zip ties. We worked together to restrain my mouthy guard with a series of zip ties from his wrist up to mid-bicep while the tablet was passed from man to man, disbelief painted on some faces, anger on others. Once a final zip tie was secured around his ankles, I pushed him over sideways into the sand with more than a little glee.

The deliberations across the way seemed to have concluded, as the leader made a circular motion with his left hand, and the guards one by one jumped back into the SUVs. The one I'd fired the warning shot at looked cranky as he climbed back into the second vehicle. I resisted the urge to wiggle my fingers in his direction. No need to push my luck—especially since I had no idea why I'd suddenly gotten lucky. I wasn't going to look that gift camel in the mouth.

The leader was slower to follow, in no hurry to move this *lovely* interaction along. "You may go, and we will not pursue you. We will pick up our man after you've gained some distance." He waved a bored hand towards his scowling comrade, who was in turn cursing my name and spitting sand out of his mouth.

I turned to climb back into the truck, wondering how I was going to make it without showing off my injuries, when I felt River's presence looming behind me, blocking their view.

"Thank you," I murmured as I hauled myself into the truck with the support of one of River's large palms, pressed firmly against the back of my thigh, when I faltered. As soon as I hit the seat, my whole body began to shake. I could feel the echo of my rapid pulse in my throbbing palm, and a sheen of sweat accumulating along the nape of my neck. I was in surprisingly poor shape, for a hand injury. How much blood had I lost? I gave into the temptation to look down, where blood had dried to my skin as I slept, and was flaking off all over the truck with every movement.

River jogged around to the passenger side, and hauled himself quickly into the seat. He fished a water orb from the back net, and pressed it into my good hand. "Drink this. You need to hydrate extra after blood loss."

"Sure, right after you tell me what happened to your face." I gave him a pointed look as I took a sip and tried to ignore how badly my hand shook as I handed the orb back to him to close. Staring out the window, I watched as Karik climbed back into the driver's seat and flashed his headlights twice. I guess that was our cue to beat feet.

Dropping it into gear, I quickly rolled down the window and tossed the golden chain out into the sand next to the trussed guard. He spat another curse as I stepped on it, spraying sand over him in farewell, and we rolled quickly down the dune.

"There's only so many ways to change your appearance on short notice while lying in the back of your truck. I improvised, oh wise *keeper.*"

I shrugged one shoulder as I watched the two SUVs quickly disappear in my rear-view mirror. By the time I crested the third dune away, they'd hauled their man out of the sand, and were clipping his zip ties. By the fourth dune, I could see them kicking up dust in the opposite direction, back the way they'd come.

Finally, I could exhale. I was still paranoid enough that I kept driving another half hour; then my eyes got too blurry and I had to let River take back over so I could fade into the welcoming blackness of sleep.

Seven

The Sand & The Sea

I t was two days of round-the-clock naps, only waking to eat, drink, and confirm for River that I was, in fact, still alive, before I felt normal again. When we sat on the truck's tailgate and River unwrapped my bandage the next morning to take a look at it, he blew out a relieved breath.

"It's healed, and there's only one small scar." His voice was incredulous as he ran his fingertip gently over the pink, puckered tissue on my palm. It was tender, and different, but not life changing. Thanks to him.

"How'd you learn all of the medic stuff, anyways?" I asked, hesitant to pull my hand out of his. "You asked a lot of pointed questions when

I got hurt, and you knew exactly what to do to doctor me up."

His smile was sad, but he didn't look up or stop tracing the lines on my palm with his fingertip when he answered. "My mom. She was a medic for Falcon's Brook, before the Nightbloods destroyed us. I was just a kid, but she let me assist her every day. I was her little shadow, passing her things and holding tools."

"The bloody stuff didn't bother you?"

"No, it never did. Some kids' parents work on metal, some work on electrical—"

"Some work on their backs," I muttered under my breath, and he chuckled.

"That too. Mine worked on people. It never seemed odd; it was as natural to her as breathing, and she taught it to me the same way. I don't think I could do surgery or dose more complicated medications like she did; but the basics? I've got those down." At that he smiled again, and when he finally looked up at me, the warmth in his eyes knocked the breath from my lungs.

I felt that same warmth unfurl in my chest, calling me to him like the sirens of old called hapless sailors to their deaths, bashed upon the rocks hungry for a taste of the sweet elixir of love. Would I be crushed on the obstacle that was River? And, more importantly, would I care, so long as I got him in the bargain? Every day we spent together, the call of him grew stronger. So far we'd both resisted, but I'd caught him stealing glances when he thought I wasn't looking.

He was interested.

I was interested.

The heat between us right now was palpable, even amidst the usual desert swelter.

And yet . . . I hadn't pursued him. It was unlike me, to waffle on something I wanted. I would lunge into uncertainty for any shiny thing, without a second thought. I'd survived countless brushes with death, attacks, attempted thefts, the streets as a child, and countless other threats over the years, and still I never hesitated to catapult myself headlong into a challenge.

So, what was different about River? I still didn't know. Hopefully I'd figure it out soon, or I was going to go nuts. Realizing that I should probably say something back, I rattled off the first thing that came to mind.

"Well, I'm glad you've got the basics down. If I'd been alone, I don't know what I would have done."

"I'm glad you didn't have to find out." His grin turned cheeky, and I shook my head at his ebullient arrogance. Just like that, we were back on solid ground; comfortable, surface ground.

"You know what I want to find out today?" I said, changing the subject.

"What?"

"How much further west we have to drive to hit the ocean. According to the GPS, we're close. But I don't know how long it's been since this thing updated, or how much evaporation has changed the coastline. We could be minutes or days away."

"Eh, that's half the fun, not knowing."

I rolled my eyes. "Sure, that's half the fun. You're crazy."

"Crazy can be fun. You should try it sometime." He winked as I slid down from the back of the truck.

"Well, now that I've been cleared by my own personal medic—"

"Better than your *kept man*," he teased.

"You are never going to let me live that down, are you? I had to play it off that way, or I'd have had no reason to keep you hidden from them."

"I know, I just like watching you blush when you think about smacking me on the butt."

I paused at the corner of the truck and looked back at him over my shoulder. "You know, if you keep bringing it up, I'm going to start thinking you liked it." It was my turn to wink at him, and his jaw dropped in surprise at my uncharacteristically blatant flirtation. I stifled a laugh as I hurried to the driver's seat, and pulled myself in.

It wasn't much for bravery, but it was a start. And I had a feeling that with River, he wouldn't make a move unless I did first.

The day wore on much like the rest had before it, until, according to the Bronco's GPS unit, we should have been driving straight into deep water. Instead, the tires bumped along over sunbaked ruts, making my teeth clack together painfully with the washboard effect. At least I was back in the driver's seat. Being weak and defenseless was foreign to me, but I appreciated River standing in the gap while I'd healed from my wounds.

I checked the rearview mirror, something I'd been doing much more frequently than usual after our run-in with the Nightbloods. So far, there had been no further sign of them once their dust trail had disappeared behind us.

"I'm starting to question the whole drive to the ocean plan," River gritted out between clenched teeth, the vibrations from the packed ground making his voice wobble humorously.

"Can't imagine why," I responded, sounding equally ridiculous. "My teeth are not enjoying this."

"Aren't we supposed to be there already? Oof—"

We hit a particularly large groove, causing us both to bounce up against our seatbelts and snatching the breath from River's words. However, after that the ground pattern changed, the rivulet-like patterns being replaced by diamond-hatchwork cracks.

They were still unpleasant, but more of a general gravelly bump than a washboard. "That's a bit better." I glanced over at River to make sure he hadn't bitten off his tongue. He looked peeved—but not murderous—so probably not.

"Should we adjust course? Head a little more north? I'm sure we'll still hit the ocean eventually."

"Let's give it another day. The temperature has actually dropped—" I toggled the dash controls to bring up the temp display, "Ooh, five degrees. It's only one-oh-two now."

He sighed and gave me a longsuffering look. "You want to drive over this crap for the rest of the day?"

I shrugged, not willing to give up my excitement at the possibility of seeing the ocean. "At this point, it's going to be a rough ride regardless. May as well go the direct route."

"Fine," he grumbled, and dropped his head back against the seat. It bobbled with every crack we crossed, which was with every rotation of the wheels. He scrunched his eyes closed anyways, studiously ignoring the sand-paper-like quality of the drive.

If he was content to pretend it was fine, I was content to let him. The dropping temperature was a good sign, and I had a hunch we were close. I didn't know why—though the unusual terrain had something to do with it—but I just felt it, somehow. We had to be close. And who knew—no one had been this way in years. Maybe there was potable water, or plant life? Or animals—preferably that weren't trying to kill us.

I still got sad thinking about the wolf I'd had to shoot. Pushing the morose thought from my mind, I focused on the road ahead, keeping my eyes sharp for any sign of the only body of water left on the planet. Even if it was probably poisoned.

As the afternoon wore on, I spotted a dark smudge on the horizon. It almost looked like a stain, bruising the edge of the sky. But as we drew closer, it grew larger, stretching across the entire horizon as far as I could see in either direction.

"River, I think that's it." I breathed the words reverently, my mind boggled at the sheer width of it.

"That *can't* all be water. Maybe it's rocks covering the ground. Plus, it's not the right color. Isn't it supposed to be blue in this part of the world? I can't tell what that is—gray, maybe?—but it's not blue."

"I don't know, at this distance it's hard to tell. They say it's tainted from the meteors. Who knows what it looks like now?" My excitement grew, even as the rough ground continued to make my teeth clack in my head.

Within another half an hour, we'd covered enough distance that I was sure it was the ocean. It was moving, retreating and advancing, and the ground had started to change again. It was no longer a cross-hatch of dry, cracked sand tiles. Now, it was smoother, and the bumps dissolved easily under my sand tires. I sighed in relief as the endless beating of the morning faded into a distant memory, fascinated as I was by the strange body of water in front of me.

With the ground smoothing out, I was able to speed up and cross the last distance in just a few minutes. About fifteen feet from the edge of the ocean, I pulled the Bronco to a stop on the gray, sandy beach, parallel to the water line.

We sat and stared at it for a long moment, silence and awe rendering us immobile. When I pulled the handle to open the door, the sounds of the water reached us, as well as a cool breeze.

I could smell salt, and something bitter that I couldn't identify in the air.

I leapt down lightly, my knees cushioning me against the resistance of the damp sand, and my boots sunk in much less than I expected. Despite our distance from the water, the sand here was packed hard, moist and clumpy as I walked closer to the edge. River was right behind me, not one to miss out on a new discovery.

It was both everything and nothing that I expected, when I came to a stop at the edge of the ocean. Much like the pictures in books, it had a life and movement all its own. There was an ebb and flow, but instead of a rich, deep blue, the water was cloudy, and a purplish rose color. The sand beneath us was gray, not white, and littered with sun-bleached shell fragments that crunched underfoot. And every so often, the motion of a wave would cause a reaction, and an explosion would happen out in the deeper water, followed by a smoking, fizzling aftershow.

"Well, I think they were right that it's non-potable." River ran his hand through his hair as his eyes roved over the foam-tipped waves, a grimace turning his normally plush lips into a pained slash across his handsome face.

"Yeah . . . it hardly even looks like water." I squatted down, tempted to touch it as the foamy crest lapped inches from the toes of my boots before slowly retreating back across the ashy sand. "At least it's cooler, here. I could get used to that," I said as I stood, propping my hands on my hips.

"It's still something to see, though. Can you imagine how it used to be? Miles and miles of blue, sparkling water?" He shook his head. "The stuff inside the orbs doesn't even seem related to all this."

"No, it really doesn't."

We stood shoulder to shoulder, and for some time we were content to watch the toxic water as it splashed and burbled, forever out of reach.

Eight

CAMPFIRE

T hat night, we drove a few more miles up the coast, and found a nice high spot to pitch our tents. We'd briefly discussed whether the air was safe to breathe and decided to risk it. Everything we both knew supported that the water wasn't safe to drink, but the noxious gasses had dissipated in the early years after the comet strike. I didn't know the science behind it, but it had been studied extensively in the beginning, back when people still had university-trained teams of scientists and hope that the ocean was salvageable.

Here in the after, we didn't have either. But we did have two tents all set up for the evening, and plans for a cozy campfire. Once we'd parked, we scavenged quite a bit of driftwood, sunbaked and bleached nearly white from years of uninterrupted UV rays. River collected it while I dug a small sand pit to contain it. I'd never had a fire before, but we'd both been intrigued by the idea of fire-roasted dates and cactus pads. It might suck, but how often would we get to try it?

It wasn't the kind of opportunity you passed up, even if you didn't need more heat. So, River piled it up in the center of my sand pit and used a flint and steel from the Bronco's emergency kit to shoot sparks into the pile. It took longer than I expected—having never made a fire before—but River kept at it, and within five minutes a tiny shower of sparks had grown into a tidy fire, nestled at the center of our mound of driftwood.

"Oh, it's green!" I leaned forward in shock to get a closer look. As the flames licked along the different logs, the orange tendrils took on flecks of green, blue, and even the occasional lavender flame.

"That's cool," River said appreciatively as he plopped his butt into the sand right next to me. His shoulder rubbed against mine, and a frisson of excitement sparked low in my belly. We'd been teasing and testing each other for the better part of two days and each new interaction had me anticipating what would happen next. Would he start the playful banter? Would I? Would he initiate the physical contact, for once? Would we do more than brush shoulders and offer a consoling hug? Did he want to? Did I want to? I was a well of endless questions.

However, I was surprised to find as I stared into the mesmerizing flames, that I felt *ready* for more. Nervous? Yes. There was a pit of anxiety the size of my fist nestled in my stomach with a label of "unknown" emblazoned across it. But . . . excitement, too. What would it feel like, to have his lips pressed against mine?

I leaned my shoulder into his, suppressing a shiver at the contact. We watched in companionable silence as the fire blazed higher and hotter, eventually taking root and covering the wood. I guess that was some sort of sign of readiness, because River positioned a rock at the edge, and began laying out peeled cactus pads on it. Once they were positioned to suit him, he offered me a skewer of driftwood-speared dates, and we each held one out towards the flame.

Almost immediately, a toasty, sugary smell began floating through the air, making my mouth water.

"So, have you ever done this before?" I asked.

"Nope, first time. But I have seen cooking before. When people around the city were sick, my mother would make up pots of soup from meal packets. She used a little stove, though. This always sounded fun." He glanced over at me, a smile showing off straight, white teeth.

My gaze lingered on his lips longer than necessary, fixated on him like he was my next glass of water. *Deeply*. Forcing myself to look back up at his eyes, I scrambled for something else to say. "It's cool that your mother was a doctor. It's clear you learned a lot from her."

"Yeah, she was an exceptional woman. Brilliant, and she gave the best hugs, too. I swear they were magical."

I couldn't help a return smile at that, even though deep down, I had no idea what that was like. Even when I'd lived with Jaen, she had never been maternal. She fed me, and clothed me, and kept me out of sight of her keepers, but beyond that, we'd mostly coexisted. She was often vacant, staring off into the distance and gesturing with one hand for me to step back. From the road. Another child. Her. What would my life have been like, if I'd had a mother like River's? I couldn't fathom it.

"You were lucky to have her."

"I was. She was one of a kind. Apparently all the women in my life are going to be as rare as mythical creatures. You're basically a unicorn, yourself." He winked at me before leaning forward to flip the cactus pads over on the rock, sending steam rising enticingly from their edges.

I rotated my little stick-skewer of dates dutifully, not letting them get too close to the fire and scorch, and pretending not to notice as he licked sticky date from his fingertips.

"So," he started, "tell me about Chace. How old were you when he started looking after you?"

I smiled, memories of my only real family floating to the surface. "I was seven. Jaen was passed to a new keeper, and he didn't like that she was taking up his tent with a child that wasn't his. Sharing water with me, feeding me. My very existence seemed to offend him. He suggested that I be sold to a friend of his, and the very same night Jaen packed up my clothes, snuck me out of the tent, and deposited me across town on the streets next to Chace." I reached down and lifted a water orb for a sip, surprised by the sting of tears at the painful memory. Jaen wasn't perfect, and her setting me aside like that hadn't made sense when I was seven. As an adult, it had a whole new meaning.

"That must have been hard on you both. At least she didn't sell you, though. I can't imagine that would have been a better life." He shuddered, and rested his hand on my knee, giving me a supportive squeeze. I ignored the bolts of electricity racing from where his palm touched me straight to my overactive heart, and focused on the words.

"Looking back, I am grateful, of course. I can't imagine that anyone willing to buy a seven-year-old girl would have had good intentions. But at the time, all I could see was that she'd abandoned me. I had no food, no way to get more water. I was scared a lot, even with Chace. He wasn't that much older, and it was hard on him. To his credit, though, he never once complained or tried to pass me off."

"Good man."

I snorted. "He was still a kid, but he did right by me." I swigged my water once again, my throat painfully dry all of a sudden. "That's why I have to find him."

River squeezed my knee again and ducked down to catch my gaze from where it had sunk to the sand. "Hey, we *are* going to find him. You and me. Hopefully he doesn't run me off in a fit of protective brotherly rage."

I rolled my eyes and looked up at him. "And why would he do that?"

"Because he might not like me kissing his sister, if he's been protecting you that long."

"Well, he's in luck. You're not kissing his sister." I poked him lightly in the chest, awkward at the memory of the earth-shattering kiss we'd shared . . . and then he'd left. It had battered my ego, even though I'd die before I'd admit it to a soul.

He reached up a hand, and trailed his fingertips upward along my jawline, tucked a stray strand of hair behind my ear, then traced down the sensitive line of my neck. The motion sent an avalanche of shivers through me, and I let my eyes sink closed briefly.

"I'd like to change that," he whispered, and my eyes flew open of their own accord, searching his.

He was rock steady, warm and sure, and for a moment, I felt sure I knew what it was like to drown. To be so consumed that you sank to the bottom, and there was no air anymore; just me and River and those perfect, all-consuming eyes. When I sucked in my next breath—turns out, there was still plenty of air—I managed to respond. "Would you, now?"

"I would. But see, I've heard it's complicated being a woman these days. It seems like that sort of thing should be your choice. So, I've been waiting, and I'll keep right on waiting, if that's what you want, but it seemed like I should at least tell you how I feel."

"No." I shook my head lightly, stopping him in his tracks. He straightened a little, and his face clouded with doubt. I reached my hand up and rested it on his cheek, then brushed my thumb over his lips. "You don't need to keep waiting. I—"

He didn't hesitate another instant, swooping forward, cupping my face in his palms. They made me feel safe, protected, as his lips pressed against mine, warm and alive, and softer even than I'd remembered. Suddenly I was burning up from the inside out—desperate to have more of him, feel more of him. I yanked my dates from the fire and dropped them in the sand so I could run both hands over his chest. He slanted his mouth over mine, deepening the kiss, and my pulse sped to a rapid staccato beat. I couldn't say how long we stayed locked together, only that his lips on mine were all-consuming, feasting on me and swallowing me up, body and soul. I never wanted it to end, because I was sure I'd never have another moment so perfect to hold onto.

Eventually we both pulled back, and I found my fingers laced around the back of his neck, while he had one hand tangled in my hair, the other supporting him in the sand as he leaned into me like a starving man. He rested his forehead against mine and closed his perfect blue eyes. His thumb traced gently along the nape of my neck, and I couldn't suppress the shiver that rocked through me.

"That was—" he started, and stopped again, sending a lightning bolt of insecurity through me. I bit my lip and waited, as it felt like the future of our relationship hung on whatever he said next. "Incredible. You're amazing, and I already knew that—but this confirms it. You really are a magical creature. Although, I think I was wrong before. You're not a unicorn; you're a siren." He pressed a chaste kiss to my forehead as I snorted.

"I haven't lured you onto the rocks yet," I pointed out, heavy sarcasm in my tone as I reluctantly removed my hands from his neck and dropped them down to my lap.

"No, but I'd follow you anywhere," he said with complete sincerity, "even if you never wanted to kiss me again. But I really hope you do. Grilled cactus pad?"

I chuckled at the sudden change of subject, even though I was reeling from his admission. He dropped a steaming cactus pad onto a metal camp plate, and pressed it into my hands, easy as you please. There was no hint of awkwardness between us, even though we'd just shared an earth-shattering kiss. But, that was River. Steady and unflappable, no matter what life threw at him.

"Looks good, thank you," I said as I sniffed the cactus.

"Here's hoping, because we both abandoned the dates, and I think if we ate them now it'd be with a side of sand." He held up a crusty, sad-looking skewer of dates with a mournful look.

"Sorry, there were more pressing matters." As I chomped down on my cactus, I wasn't the least bit sorry about that kiss, though. I was already looking forward to the next one.

Nine

Surrounded

E ven the best things come to an end, and when the fire burnt down to coals, we covered it in sand and crawled into our tents. When the next morning dawned, we packed up and got back on the road heading north, the ocean lapping the beach to our left. Thanks to the flatter terrain right next to the water line, we were able to drive quickly, traveling along the drier edge of the smoothed sand, so there was no chance of getting caught by an incoming wave.

We nibbled sand-free dates and jammed out to the radio, singing our favorites at the tops of our lungs, windows rolled down to let in the ocean breeze. It was a hopeful time, and I was happy. We were finally making real progress towards Chace. We'd made it past the Night-bloods with River still at my side—albeit with a few bruised ribs in the process—and that kiss we'd shared had been spectacular. Everything was good, despite the nagging worries of Coyote Springs. One day I would know what happened, but it wouldn't be today.

I'd like to blame that happy cloud for why I was less observant than usual; the new-to-me sounds of the ocean for why I didn't hear them coming. Whatever the reason, it wasn't until a louder-than-average explosion out in the ocean drew my gaze left that I spotted an orange motorcycle in my side mirror.

"River, six o'clock!"

He craned his head around and swore. "How long has he been back there? He's close!"

"I don't know," I admitted reluctantly as I scanned the horizon. Then it was my turn to swear. "He's got company." I nodded right, and River craned his head around to find what I'd seen. Three more bikes, painted orange and gaining on us rapidly.

"Where did they come from? It's wide open out here. You'd think we'd have seen them," he said, frustration evident in his tone as he scrabbled in the back seat pocket for a weapon.

"It doesn't matter now, all that matters is that if they try to stop us, we're prepared. They're giving me gang vibes, but not Nightbloods."

"No, definitely not Nightbloods," River agreed. "At least this time we can see upfront that there are four. Better odds."

"Yeah, but we don't know if there are only four. Keep an eye out the back, and I'll do my best to make sure they don't catch us." I did my best to sound confident, but deep down I was concerned. On a flat straightaway, they wouldn't be able to force us to stop. But this was their terrain, and with four bikes they had a lot of options to mess us up. Even if I took to the dunes, those bikes would be faster than the Bronco, and able to catch air off the peaks. They'd catch us much faster if we deviated to the dunes. Which made me wonder, why weren't they trying to drive us that way?

All I could do was keep the pedal down and stay alert to whatever they were planning. I reached for the sound system, turning the knob all the way down. River set my chest holster on the center console, after strapping knives to his upper thighs and setting a few spares in his lap.

For a few tense minutes, nothing changed. River held the wheel while I strapped on my holster, but the bikes kept their distance. They were definitely riding in formation, three on the outskirts, one directly behind. They didn't *want* us in the dunes. I edged closer to the water's edge, to see if they'd react.

It was slow, but they repositioned. The one at six o'clock—he was the leader, in my mind—swerved to stay directly behind us, and the other three adjusted to close some of the new distance between themselves and the leader, but not all. A three-car gap had widened to about a four-car gap.

Five minutes turned to ten, and ten to fifteen. The tension between my shoulder blades was strong enough to pop a water orb, and River wasn't much better off. He rode sideways in silence, back to the console so he could keep all four bikes in his line of vision at all times, and I could stare straight ahead and try not to grind my teeth.

"There, they're making a move!" River's voice was calm, but it ratcheted up my heart rate, nonetheless. I cast a quick glance in the rearview and saw the three bikers off to our right pulling into a tighter formation, angling toward our rear bumper as the one directly behind us surged forward, gaining ground quickly. The inside man swooped past the leader, quickly gaining on our left rear fender.

"What are they doing?" I asked under my breath, zoning in on the path ahead. What I saw made me squint. "What . . . what is that?" I pointed forward and River took a beat to look with me.

"Looks like something's blocking the path. Can't tell if it's an old building or a rock face."

"Whatever it is, we're not going to hit it, if that's what they're after." I tightened my grip on the steering wheel and ran through the options in my head. The sand was packed firm here from the water, unlike what I was used to in the Wastes, making handling a bit different. I did not want to run one of the bikers over—whatever they were after, I still didn't want to murder someone over it—but I also wouldn't let us be herded directly into the side of a building.

I began to slow, but none of them tried to get past us. Instead, they caught up quicker, revving their engines and shouting, like sheepdogs nipping at our heels. One even popped a wheelie, and I caught sight of a white slash of teeth in a deeply tanned face as he grinned and fell back a bit. The lead rider shouted something, though, and he popped back into place like a demented mole.

"Roll down your window, River."

He cast a quick glance over his shoulder at me. "What are you thinking?"

"Still working on that, let's just see how they respond to a little negotiation."

He hit the button, and his window rolled down lazily, just like any other time we wanted to catch a cross-breeze.

The rider closest to the window sped up, drawing level with the window and swerving dangerously close to the side door.

"Back off! We don't want any trouble!" I shouted, and the man threw back his head in a cackle.

He pushed up the visor of his helmet and shouted back, "Great, stop and give us all your water! We'll let you go."

"Is he *serious*?" River asked, shooting me an incredulous look.

"Apparently they're straight shooters," I groused, not happy. While I might be able to sell them on only taking the water we had inside the truck without mentioning the tank underneath, I didn't want to give them any of it. We had half the trip to go, and no idea what we'd find when we got there. Plus, there was no guarantee the city was still where the map led. Hundreds of years changed things.

I mulled it over, keeping an eye on the rapidly growing obstacle ahead of us. It wasn't a building, but a thirty-foot-high rocky shelf, with something I couldn't make out dotting the sides. It was solid and running headfirst into it would mean death. Of course, so would giving these bullies all of our water. Luckily, neither one was about to happen.

"Grab two of the half-empty jugs from the back seat, and then wait for my signal."

"You're not seriously going to give these nut jobs our water, are you?" he asked as he reached into the back and started hefting the different jugs to see which ones weren't completely full.

"Oh, we're going to give it to them, but they're not going to like it." I tilted the wheel right, swaying towards the furthest forward driver. All four of them reacted. He dodged slightly but began yelling and swerving towards the passenger door, trying to urge me back onto a straight path. The ones behind edged a bit more forward, squaring up the box we were in, and the one on the front left tightened up on my side door.

River sat up, holding two good sized jugs.

"This is a lot of water, Nyx."

"Good, hopefully that's all we'll need. On my count, toss both of those out your window at the same time. Don't give them a warning and aim for the front tires of those two bikes."

"Okay, what about the other two?" he asked as he tightened the lids down hard, making sure none of the water took an early exit.

"Oh, I'll handle them," I said with an eyebrow waggle. "Get in position. We're running out of runway, here." I nodded ahead, and he quickly spun in the seat, so his back was to the dashboard, and he could keep an eye on both his riders.

"Three, two, one, now!" River didn't hesitate; I waited until I heard the twin thuds, immediately followed by hollering as the bikes and their riders met the packed sand, and used the distraction to swing the wheel left. The rider of the bike next to my window had a skull-cap-style helmet on, with no visor, so I saw his eyes widen as my fender came into contact with his bike, bumping him over into the surf. His scream of alarm was cut off as the frothy purple liquid closed over his head. Three down, I sought out the lead rider who'd been guarding our left flank.

He'd fallen back, rather than allowing distraction over his comrades to leave him swimming. He didn't slow as he rode past the fallen riders, instead coming back to the center position on our tail.

Three down was enough, though. The jutting rock was just ahead, and I hauled hard right on the wheel and made for the dunes. The Bronco skidded, sending hunks of damp sand flying and making a whining sound as the tires tried to grip the spongy ground. I held my breath as we made the turn, carefully mediating how much pressure I put on the gas pedal and praying to anyone who'd listen that we didn't spin out.

The Bronco didn't fail me, though, and after a handful of tense heartbeats, her tires caught and she straightened. We zoomed along, and right outside my window I could see ancient clumps of hard coral dotting the sides of the rock, which was scraped and embedded with the remnants of past victims' vehicles. There were even some chunks of metal hanging off busted clumps of coral.

This wasn't the first time this crew had pulled this little water heist.

Glancing back into the rear-view, I saw our last motorcyclist was still with us, though he'd fallen back about ten feet and was wiping smears of sand off his visor.

"The one in the water's up, and he looks pissed. The two on my side are both alive, but one of them is still down. Seems like he's hurt, and his buddy's going to help him."

"I can live with that. I really didn't want to shoot them or run them over."

"Me either. There's enough death out here without us killing each other," he said. The words were light, but I could hear the tension as he tracked the final rider behind us. "What's the plan for boss-man?"

"Wait him out. Alone, he can't mess with us without messing himself up, too. Plus, I've been thinking; these guys have to have a base out here. Can you grab the atlas, see if there might be a city? If they're anything like the 'Winders, they'll back off as soon as we're in the safety of the city."

"On it." He pulled the well-worn leather sheaf of maps from the gap between the seats, and spread it out on the dash, quickly scanning our GPS location to find the right one.

I kept my eyes on the landscape, trusting him to do his job, while I did mine: keep us alive.

"There's three options. Dead north up the coastline where we were already heading, due east, and one southeast, maybe an hour."

"Which do you think?"

"I don't know, Nyx . . . I'd say southeast, but, if I'm wrong and we have to backtrack, we've gotta drive back through these guys' territory, and they're gonna be ticked. If we go north, that's where we're heading anyways, but it's smaller. East—"

"It's east, it has to be," I said, quickly scanning as his finger moved over the ancient pages.

"Okay. East it is." He paused, folding the atlas carefully. "Care to explain why?"

I shrugged, not sure how to explain what I knew by instinct. "It's the Wastes. We've been driving due north for a while. We just came from the east, so any cities further south of here, we'd have seen some dust trails. Especially if they've got a biker gang running the show, rooster tails would be all over. We haven't seen anything, so it's not that one. Due north is tiny. It's east." As I explained it, the feeling of rightness settled into my bones, and I stepped on the accelerator. He leaned back in his seat as he folded up the atlas and tucked it into its usual place.

The flat, wet sand gave way to crosshatched misery before long, though I noticed a set of tracks where the sand was a bit smoother and did my best to stay there. The motorcyclist still trailing us—his buddies hadn't reappeared, yet—picked the tread closest to the rock shelf, though even it was starting to flatten out toward what must have been the coastline in the past.

We drove for an hour, and I was pleasantly surprised to find that the miserable bumpy terrain gave way to loose, sweeping dunes much sooner than it had to the south. We both let out sighs of relief as the teeth-rattling stopped, and the smooth *shhh* of sand shifting underneath us returned.

"Nyx, look there." River pointed ahead and to the right, and sure enough, I spotted a couple of slow dust trails rising from the city in the distance.

I whacked his arm excitedly before twining my fingers into the loose fabric of his shirt. "Yes, we chose right!" A quick glance behind showed the rider was still tailing us tightly, so we had a ways to go. But that was okay, we had nothing but time.

As I released River and settled back into my seat, an odd *chirrup chirrup* sound emitted from my water meter.

I glanced down, confused, when I saw a steady green tower symbol display.

Ten

Phone Home

"River, look!" I jangled my wrist in his direction, and he held my arm still so he could see.

"We must have driven into range of a tower—that's great! Now the question is, how do we use this thing?" He turned my wrist forward and back, as if my water meter was going to suddenly sprout an instruction manual.

"Well, I don't know. He said just click it, if I didn't install it in the meter, but he didn't give any instructions on using it *in* the meter."

"Maybe you should just take it back out?"

"Yeah . . ." I held the wheel steady with my knee as I felt along the bottom edge of the meter for the pinprick-sized hole the comm rod had slid into. As my finger brushed it, a static sound emitted from the meter, and I froze. "Maybe not?" I pressed my finger over the hole and tried speaking. "Hello, this is Nyx. Is anyone there?"

I locked eyes with River as we waited, tension seizing both of us up as we listened to unbroken static. The silent moment yawned long and empty, and I clenched my jaw against the disappointment.

"Maybe you have to take your finger back off to let them respond? Like a walkie-talkie?"

"A what?"

He shook his head at my ignorance. "Just trust me, try taking your finger back off."

I lifted my finger, letting my hand fall back to the wheel, and the static died, leaving silence in the car besides the quiet hush of our breaths, and the low hum of tires crossing sand.

"Okay, scratch that, let's just give them some time. The equipment could have been damaged . . ." He trailed off, the unspoken *in the explosion* hanging heavy in the air.

Leaving my right hand on the wheel this time, I used my left pointer finger to cover the hole as I drove. "Sidewinders, this is Nyx calling in on the comm you gave me. Is anyone there? I would like a status update," I tried again.

"Hold for two," an unfamiliar voice came through, and I nearly jumped out of my seat. I shot a quick glance at River, who gave me a thumbs up.

"Can you confirm—is this the Sidewinders of Coyote Springs?" I tried again.

"Affirmative, Nyx," 'Conda's dry tone rang out, and relief washed over me from head to toe.

"Well, I can honestly say I never thought I'd be relieved to hear *your* voice."

"I'm hurt, Nyx. We share a special kind of loathing. Have you already made it to Bastion City?"

"No, 'Conda, we're still headed north. We saw the explosion and wanted an update. Did anyone make it? Hoss, Maisie, Marl, Hog, Lesina?" I rattled off names, and stopped before I choked on *the street children*.

"I'm hurt—you weren't even worried about me," he mocked, and I wanted to reach through time and space to strangle him. Before I could retort, though, he continued.

"Hog's fine, and the hotel lady has already taken up residence in the best digs in town up there. Something about a *special* set of coordinates she was given? King's not happy about that."

A wry grin twisted my mouth as I looked at River, and I didn't even try to keep my satisfaction from my tone. "Too dang bad. And the rest?"

"I don't know a Maisie. Can't say."

I rolled my eyes. "Her keeper's Bandy."

"Oh, uh, he's back in Coyote as part of the cleanup crew. She's probably there."

My heart sank. "Cleanup crew?"

"Yeah, we had to send people back. There wasn't a lot left after the bomb, but we need to salvage what we can. Freaking high post was ground zero." He cursed angrily.

"What about the low post? Did Hoss make it out?"

"Mm, I don't have a report about him, one way or another. He's not here, I know that much."

The festering pit of dread bloomed in my stomach, and the horrible knowledge that Hoss was likely dead stole my breath. I had been holding out hope that my coordinates had saved him and Marl, but it looked like I hadn't done enough.

"Anything else I should know?"

"Yeah, your mission's even more critical. We need a trade route with the BC. Get to it, and don't call again until you get there. We're trying to rebuild here."

"Gee, thanks. I'm touched to hear your deep concern for my brother's wellbeing," I mumbled as I removed my finger from the meter, letting the static die.

"Hoss could be fine. Just because he hasn't made it to Wolf Well doesn't mean he's dead," River said soothingly. "He was a good guy; he

probably turned around to try to help survivors."

Maybe, maybe not. That seed of hope could crush me if it turned out to be false, so I couldn't afford to let it sink into me; I had to keep functioning, because I saw the skyline of a small settlement ahead, and two more dirt bikes arrowing straight at us, shooting up rooster tails as they sliced through the dunes.

Eleven

Red Riders

As we drew nearer, two dirt bikes turned into four, then seven, and finally the rider who'd trailed us the whole way peeled off, making a wide U-turn and spitting up a rooster tail of his own as he fled back the way he came. We weren't free of a tail for long, as the seven riders quickly formed a perimeter around us and escorted us into the small city.

Much about it reminded me of Coyote Springs, but there was also a lot that was different. The heart of the city was smaller, with tents completely ringing the city here. And they weren't well maintained, from what I could tell as we drove past. Holes provided a window into the lives of the citizens on the outskirts, and what we could see wasn't much. Though . . . the bikes were well maintained, if patched together. They had a solid mechanic here, at least. *And some sort of working radio tech.* I thought back on the irritating conversation with 'Conda, but quickly shoved it down, dragging my attention back to my surroundings. We were only moments inside the city before the riders forced us to a stop outside of a large striped tent, a red-helmeted rider kicking down the lead bike's stand and approaching my window.

To my surprise, when the helmet was pulled free, it was a woman shaking a long mane of russet hair loose and gesturing for me to roll the window down so we could talk.

"What are your intentions for visiting the collective?" Her tone was all business, and her eyes were sharp as they skated over me and River in swift appraisal, lingering on River longer than I liked.

"Just passing through and hoping to shake an annoying tail." I gestured with a nod back to the way we'd come, and her eyes narrowed angrily. "We do have trade goods, though, if you're interested."

"How many riders?"

"Four, we took three of 'em down a few pegs," I admitted with a shrug. Better to lay all the cards on the table up front. "We appreciated the help ditching the fourth." It was an afterthought, and she knew it. It was always wise to start on good footing with the locals before trading began, though.

She snorted, and I caught the briefest hint of a smile at the corner of her mouth, but it quickly dissolved back into stern calculation.

"Not sure you needed any *help*, but we don't get a lot of trade out here. We'll be happy to see what you've got."

My mind immediately went back to the threadbare, holey tents, and I cursed my luck that I'd sold all of my good, new ones to the Sidewinders. They were probably ash, now. *Depressing.*

"I didn't catch your name." I lifted an eyebrow in question.

"Sasha. You?"

"Nyx, and River." I reached a hand over and squeezed his forearm quickly, before dropping my hand back to the wheel.

"Pleasure to meet you both. You can park here, and we'll show you around." She turned back towards her bike but paused, adding over her shoulder, "Sorry about the un-welcoming committee. Steve can be a real camel's hump sometimes."

"Err, Steve?" I asked.

She sighed wearily, and looked down as if embarrassed before admitting, "He's my idiot brother."

"Ooh, that sucks," River half-cackled from the passenger seat. Sasha gave a resigned shrug, then paced away from the truck to wait for us.

I shot him a *shut-it-up-so-we-don't-of-fend-these-people* look, but he grinned back, unfazed.

"She already knows it sucks; didn't you see her face? Come on, maybe they've got something better to eat here than your sawdust bars."

"*Meal* bars," I insisted as I hopped down from the driver's side and clicked the lock.

"You keep telling yourself that," he teased with a wink as he joined me outside the Bronco and we made our way toward where Sasha waited for us at the end of the nearest tent row, "and I'll try to sweet talk someone out of something that's *actually* tasty."

I rolled my eyes but didn't complain. "Just don't get *too* sweet," I muttered, a flare of jealousy bursting unexpectedly at the idea of him cozying up to somebody else. I stuffed it down as he cocked a questioning eyebrow in my direction. *Simmer down, Nyx. River's with you because he wants to be.*

"So, where are you two from, if you don't mind sharing?" Sasha asked as she held the tent flap open for us. I hesitated, unable to see much of the dim interior and unwilling to walk into a trap.

"Coyote Springs," River jumped in, covering for me.

She rocked back on her booted heels and scratched her dust-smeared cheek. "That far?

Huh. I bet you've got some stories. Nobody's gotten through Nightblood territory in a long time. Not since I've been in charge, at least."

I tucked that tidbit away to digest later as we stood on the threshold, at an impasse about going inside. "It was quite a trip," I agreed, before quickly addressing the safety concern. "Our trading posts back home are all open air. Do you have somewhere less enclosed we could handle our business together?" I gestured to the small cobblestone-lined square I could see about halfway down the middle of the city.

She dropped the tent flap and narrowed her eyes as she considered my request. "In the past that sort of request might have lost you a finger, but given the fact that you were chased to our doorstep, I'll choose not to take offense this time." She bobbed her chin at a burly man with a mohawk and three nose piercings who stood off to our left. "Cade, can you show them over to the square? I'll get Squeak and meet you there. Oh, and show them where the water is, in case they'd like to cash in some credits."

He nodded and stalked off down the road without saying a word or waiting for us to follow. River and I both strode after him, and I had to hustle more than I would have liked to keep up with his longer strides. I noticed for the first time that his right hand was missing, the arm ending at a smooth stump mid-forearm.

River laid a hand on my shoulder to slow me to a comfortable pace and whispered, "I thought we were making nice. Why didn't we go in?"

"Because we didn't know who was *already* in there. Steve's her brother. Maybe he's actually in charge and the rest of his goons were in that tent."

He pursed his lips and threw a weighty glance back over his shoulder. "You really think it was a trap? Sasha seemed nice enough. Is this one of those things where you use your trader magic to read people?" He used air quotes around *trader magic*, and I briefly considered punching him.

I rolled my eyes instead of giving into the violent urge. "No, I don't *think* it was a trap. I think I didn't stay alive as long as I have by walking into tents with people I didn't know."

"Touché."

We crossed the rest of the distance in silence, taking stock of the small city, and cataloging any possible exit routes or complications we could spot from the road. Cade pointed to a small structure with a hand-painted "water" sign without comment, and I cataloged the location for later. It would be great to fill up again, in case things didn't go to plan with Bastion City.

My first impression still rang true when we reached the town square, and inside of it were some ancient wooden benches, a couple of scrub bushes—potted, of all things—and a mother with two small, thin children who scurried away at our approach.

Well, Cade's approach. They didn't stick around to see us trailing behind him. He stopped and crossed his arms over his chest next to one of the benches and glowered at us silently. We stopped a few feet away, but we didn't have to wait long for Sasha to join us, trailed by a pale man with light brown hair and pinched features.

She didn't waste time. "Squeaks, this is Nyx, and River. They're here from Coyote Springs with trade goods. Can you update them on the water cred rate, and tell them our top five most desired trades?"

He glanced nervously at Cade and then steepled his fingers, reciting a generous water credit rate to the fifth decimal place, and then just as effortlessly began listing their top trade needs. "Organic matter for the replicator, tents or tent fabric, good quality steel, silver, and of course unique food items are always a welcome addition to our stockpile." He stopped his recitation, and immediately hunched his shoulders, visibly withdrawing from the interaction.

"Thank you, Squeaks," Sasha clapped him on the shoulder, ignoring his obvious discomfort as she honed in on us. "Do you have any of those items, or something similar?"

I drummed my fingers on my thigh, mentally running through our stock. "We have some things I think you'll like. Can I ask–why silver, and are you looking for any particular quantities?"

Cade shifted, and my eyes darted to his imposing form before settling back on Squeaks, who shifted on his feet anxiously. Sasha nodded approval to our question, so Squeaks answered.

"Silver is a necessary ingredient in burn cream, something of which we're always in short supply. Proximity to the ocean, which is caustic, the Nightbloods' territory, and the regular sweeps by the Bastion City citizens means our people are frequently injured, and in need of wound care. This area is naturally poor in precious metals, making our own attempts at sourcing silver inadequate."

"Ahh, I see. Thank you, Squeaks." I pursed my lips and nodded, debating how much of my jewelry and how many precious metal bars I was willing to part with. The exchange rate was the best I'd seen in a while, but small high-value trades were hard to come by, and I was reluctant to part with a large quantity in a single location. That was my *head north* fund.

But . . . they needed it for medical treatments.

"Can we have some time to gather the items we'd like to present?" I addressed Sasha, who nodded.

"I'm sure you understand that we'll have an escort assigned to you for the length of your stay."

"Yes, I understand. Though, you haven't said—what is this place called? I'd like to mark it on my atlas."

"This is the Rock. One of three encampments the Red Riders collective cycles through."

"Wait, you guys aren't stationary here?" River beat me to the question.

"No. Unfortunately it's a dangerous territory, and to avoid being wiped completely off the map, we have to stay mobile. Every citizen has an evacuation vehicle, and tents are assigned with each settlement based on size and need." She raked a hand through her red hair, agitated about something. "We rotate through three separate encampments, based on our intelligence monitoring of Bastion City's radio feeds."

Well, that explains the advanced radio tech and the well-maintained motorcycles.

"Wow," River said, casting a speculative glance my way.

"Well, we'll prepare our best offer, and meet you . . . here?" I prodded, trying to stay focused on the task at hand, even if these people were in a precarious situation.

"I'd prefer to meet you in the trade tent, but you seem opposed for some reason." She arched an eyebrow and stared me down, testing me.

I raised a hand, waving lightly to diffuse the tension. "I meant no offense. We don't know each other well; it's unwise to enter unfamiliar, dim tents."

She rolled her eyes, and the motion made her seem young, younger than I'd originally thought for a leader of an entire city. *Especially one with problems on this scale.*

"Just let your escort know where you'd like to trade. If you don't want to stay, you're welcome to leave as soon as the trade's through." She nodded to Cade and stormed off back the way she came, her shoulders tight.

River glanced back and forth between me and Cade in indecision, so I nodded down the road and started walking. Cade followed, ten paces back. Word must have already spread from the other riders about our presence because I spotted dozens of dusty little heads poking from the cracks between the tightly packed tents, tracking our progress with wide eyes.

Some scattered as we passed by, scurrying backwards so we couldn't see them, but a few brave kids stayed, and one even waved. He was a tiny thing—maybe four years old—and I had to work to keep my return smile as I saw the huge, painful-looking burn scarring his cheek.

Thick, purple webbed scar tissue crossed from the corner of his left eye past his ear and disappeared under a shaggy mop of brown hair.

"Hey, buddy!" River called, going out of his way to wave and catch the boy's attention. The little guy lit up like a lightbulb and puffed out his little chest at the attention.

"Go on home, Spencer," Cade rumbled from behind us, and the little fellow trotted off obediently.

"Do we have anything these people need, Nyx?" River asked, his eyes following the child as he slipped away between the tents.

"We do, the only question is how much can we spare?" I twisted my lips regretfully. It didn't sit well with me to hang onto food and silver that could be lifesaving, but a nagging voice at the back of my head said that we didn't know what lay ahead of us.

"I hope we can spare a lot. I know you're suspicious, but this place reminds me of my childhood home. Skinny kids, poor people—but tight knit. We looked out for each other, and the only read I get from Sasha is that she's trying to make the best of a crap situation. Not like the Sidewinders, or the Nightbloods, or heck—even her brother, Steve."

"I know, River. I know. We'll figure something out."

He nodded. "I'm willing to trade all of my dates. That was on their list. I don't have any fabric or metal besides my pocketknife, unfortunately. I wish I knew where to get some silver."

"I've got an idea," I admitted, swallowing hard and fingering my water meter. As soon as I'd seen the little guy's face, I knew the burn issue was real. They needed that silver more than I needed an extra security blanket. We'd never intended to head north on easy street, after all.

Chace would understand.

We rounded the back of the Bronco, and I popped it open so we could assess our tradeable goods more carefully. While I always knew what I had on hand like a permanent mental log, River was new to this. He didn't remember the nitty-gritty details of every single stop we'd made.

In the end, we had a sizeable pile. Dates, cactus pads, cactus seeds, random metal objects salvaged from the last few stops. I hesitated, but in the end I also tossed a box of twinkies on top of the pile, imagining the smiles from all those kids when they tasted the sugary goodness. I could spare a box. I was uncomfortable digging out all of my stashed jewelry with Cade standing ten feet away watching—that was just asking for a midnight five-finger-discount—but I pulled a few baggies from the back that were accessible without being obvious that I'd hid them inside the car panels themselves.

River's eyes widened as, one by one, I flipped through the baggies of jewelry, tucking the ones which didn't contain silver back away without comment. Once he realized what we were doing, he helped me sort the stash while I hid the non-silver pieces back away.

Once I'd gathered all I could reach and tucked the remaining baggies back out of sight, I turned to River and asked, "Cover me, please."

He casually shifted and stretched to block my actions from our guard while I climbed up into the back of the Bronco. Underneath a floor panel, I quickly picked out the lone silver bar I had from the underground jewelry store. It was heavy and solid, nothing like the thin little sticks of gold. I tucked it right into a cargo pocket on my thigh, and walked back out of the truck, hunched over to keep from whacking my head.

"Do I want to know?" River asked mildly.

"I'll tell you later, if this goes well."

"I look forward to it."

Twelve

The Trading Table

S linging the leather satchel full of small silver pieces over my shoulder, I grabbed one of the milk crates full of our trades, and River hefted the other, then slammed the back hatch shut. We shared a nod, then walked over to where Cade waited, the same sulking expression on his face that he'd had the entire time.

"We're ready. And you can take us to the tent," I told him.

He grunted and started walking, slower this time since we were burdened with stuff, but he didn't volunteer to carry any of it. Not that I'd have let him. Nobody laid hands on the goods until they were on the trading table.

He strode straight to the same striped tent as before, but this time it had both flaps open and was well lit inside. I could see Sasha and Squeaks engaged in a conversation behind a battered folding table which spanned the entire width of the tent. Cade took two steps inside, took up a post against the gaudy tent wall, and resumed his bored expression.

Appeased by their efforts to make the tent appear safer for our business, River and I walked in without comment, and began laying out our trades on the table. They watched in riveted silence as River led with a large container of his dates, I laid out a small selection of items we'd picked up at the last city we'd scavenged, the big coffee canister full of cactus clippings and seeds, and then began laying out the silver jewelry. The final thing to come out was the thick silver bar from my pocket, and it landed on the table with the satisfying *thunk*.

Squeaks stepped forward as soon as we stopped spreading out items, and immediately began turning over each item and tapping away at his tablet with the speed of a scorpion scuttling across the sand. He let out a series of *hmms* and *ahhs* as he worked, but Sasha paced in silence behind him. She cast frequent glances over his shoulder but didn't interrupt his evaluation.

When he got to the pile of individually bagged jewelry pieces, he hissed through his teeth. "Is this all real?"

"As far as I know, yes. It was scavenged like the rest, but I have no way of verifying it outside of a trader's machinery. I pulled out everything that appears to be silver per your request, though I know they used other metals in the past with similar coloring. It may not all be of use to you, and I'm happy to keep whatever isn't silver. As well as the stones, assuming your equipment is capable of separating the silver without damaging the gems."

Sasha's eyebrows flew up, and she jerked her chin in a gesture to summon Cade over. "Have Leith and Ray bring the splitter from the storage trailer. Tell them to hurry."

He nodded once, but hesitated. "Do you want me to send another guard?"

"No, I think we've reached a point of trust, don't you?" She leveled an appraising gaze on River and me, and we nodded.

Cade jogged off without further delay, his boots sending clumps of sand flying with each step.

Meanwhile, Squeaks had stayed busy working on his trade value estimate on the tablet, and he pressed it into Sasha's hands. She scrolled through his notes and passed it to me.

The number of water credits they were offering at the bottom floored me, and I tipped it to the side to show River.

"Is this including the jewelry already? We're not sure it's all silver."

Squeaks shook his head. "This only accounts for a conservative estimate of four ounces of silver, based on roughly half of the bar."

"Only half?" I asked, passing the tablet back across the table. He looked to Sasha, who sighed, and leaned forward on her elbows, letting the table prop her up.

"Only half unless you're willing to trade for something besides water credits. Unfortunately, we're broke."

It was our turn to stare in shock as she laid it all out for us.

"We rotate between three locations—it was four, until a very recent bombing. As such, we have to travel somewhat light, and our population doesn't grow much with the way we're sandwiched between two larger forces. Most of the people here are descendants of the people who originally were born here. Which is fine; newcomers are new mouths to feed. Lately, though, the death marshmallows have been targeting us a lot harder than usual, and—"

I cocked an eyebrow at the odd turn of phrase, but River nearly choked he laughed so hard. "Death marshmallows?"

"Oh." She rolled her eyes. "Yeah, that's what we call the soldiers who patrol the perimeter of Bastion City. The suits they wear are *ridiculous*."

My mind zoomed right past the ridiculous nickname, and on to the problem. They'd been targeted by the city, *and* been a target of the recent bombing—perhaps the same run that hit Coyote Springs?

"Sasha, we're not entirely broke. We do have an extra ten percent—" Squeaks raised a finger, his jaw set in determination.

"Absolutely not!" She rounded on him with the anger of a feisty scorpion. "That ten percent is for the children, Squeaks. I don't care *what* someone comes in here to trade. We do. Not. Touch. The children's fund, capiche?" She jabbed a finger into the table with each word, driving her point home.

"What's the children's fund?" River asked, gaze flitting between the two of them with rapt curiosity.

"The children's fund is the water that's allotted for the children of the Red Riders. We haven't lost any children to dehydration since its inception two years ago. Ten percent of everything that comes into the government gets earmarked for their care, parents or no. We protect our own."

I had to clench my jaw to keep it shut as she explained. A children's fund, and no dehydration deaths in two years . . . when more than half the kids I'd been on the street with as a child were long dead. If it weren't for Chace, I'd have been dead, too. This woman was doing something good here, and the internal struggle over what to do about this trade just got a hundred times harder.

"What can you trade beyond water credits?" I asked, my tone sounding sharp and short even to me, and I hid a wince at the tell. I always stayed deadly calm; why were these *good* people sending me into a tailspin?

Squeaks stepped forward, steepling his fingers. "While it all has to be authorized by Sasha, we have several highly talented citizens who might be willing to aid you or help you restock for your travels. Where are you going from here? If you have a set path marked, I can offer you some more tailored possibilities."

I ran my tongue over my teeth, stalling as I debated how much to tell them. River leaned forward and rested his hands on the table, glancing at me for only a second before he began to lay it all out. "We're heading for Bastion City. Her brother was taken, and we don't know if he wants to be there."

Sasha's back straightened near-imperceptibly, and her tone was icy as she said, "Do tell."

She kept a white-knuckled grip on the table, her jaw ticking angrily as River relayed how we'd followed the map here all the way from Coyote Springs, the bombing, and even the run-in with the Sidewinders. By the end, incredulity had replaced spitting anger as her overriding emotion.

"They just let you go? That's impossible. The Nightbloods take you, or they kill you. There is *no* in-between. We had a patrol get captured two days ago, and all we found was the transport vehicle, abandoned and half-scrapped."

"We found it pretty impossible, too. But it happened. And we're heading for the city. Assuming the marshmallows don't get us."

The corner of her lips quirked, and then a thoughtful look passed over her face. "Cade, can you please go get Bramily and Louie? Tell them their services may be needed for our visitors."

Cade nodded, and jogged out of the tent, silent as usual.

"This is probably super rude, but what happened to his arm?" River asked, keeping his tone light.

Sasha answered in a matter-of-fact tone, "Saving his daughter from a flipped vehicle in the middle of a BC raid. He hasn't let it slow him down, and I wouldn't expect you could overpower him because he's a hand short. I've seen him put plenty of cocky attackers on the deck."

"Oh, no, I wouldn't dream of attacking him. I mean, unless he attacked me first, obviously, I was just curious. You do seem to have a lot more medical needs here than where either of us came from." He grimaced and ran a hand through his hair. "We saw a little boy, Spencer—"

She nodded, a grim expression on her face. "He was in the same transport as little Vinna. Cade got them both out and to safety, but not without extreme cost."

"I understand. I'm sorry to pry."

"No offense taken," she said. My hackles rose at the appraising gaze she ran over River once again. With someone else's eyes roving over him, it felt like his masculine perfection glowed like a beacon. Though frankly, that could have just been my jealousy talking. I took an unconscious step closer to him, and her eyes snapped back to me. Before I could say or do anything to make it even more awkward, Cade jogged back in with a thin man hot on his heels, and a woman trailing a few paces behind, a giant pack slung over her shoulder causing her to huff and puff as she traversed the cobblestone street.

The man slowed as he saw strangers at the table, looking around curiously, and the woman stepped in a few moments later.

"Don't offer to carry anything—I've got it, *thanks*," she drawled sarcastically.

The man startled and looked to his left where she stopped. "Don't act so uppity, Bramily. None of us offer to help because we know what's in those bags." He slapped her enthusiastically on the shoulder and took two pointed steps away from her.

Bramily rolled her eyes as she walked forward and dropped the bag with a thud that shook the long trading table. "Men. So squeamish around explosives. They think they're tough but drop a little C-4 and they scatter like cockroaches." She rolled her eyes and leaned in close to whisper, "It's incredibly stable, unlike the woman who makes it. Won't blow without a detonator, but don't ruin my fun by telling them that."

"I wouldn't dream of it," I said drily. "Is there C-4 in that bag?"

She waggled her eyebrows and gave me a wicked grin. I resisted the sudden urge to step back from the table, stable or no.

"How can we help, Sasha? Do you have a tech issue?" The thin man spoke up, clearly used to Bramily's eccentricities.

"Possibly, Louie—that's up to Nyx and River. They have some trade goods that would be very useful to the collective, but we're unfortunately coming up short. We thought your services might serve as an alternative trade option, given they're heading straight into the gaping maw of the beast."

He blew out a surprised breath. "Bastion City?"

"The one and only," she confirmed.

"What do you need from me?" Louie was all business, the polar opposite of Bramily, who was elbow deep in her bag, lifting up chunks of putty explosive, and flipping them back into the bag as if taking haphazard inventory while muttering under her breath.

"Well, we all know you can't trust anything that comes out of the Bastion, but this is their first foray into their territory. I was thinking a radio tuned to the Bastion's private channels would go a long way towards fostering goodwill and helping them with their mission of retrieving her stolen brother." She nodded in my direction, and Louie gave me a sad grimace.

"My condolences. I'll be happy to provide a radio. So far I've isolated four of their comm channels, but not all of them. You might be able to get better signals from inside, if you make it that far."

"We *will* make it that far. And I'm happy to report back with whatever we find, if that's helpful to your collective."

"I'd appreciate that. We keep our distance as a rule but having inside access . . . it could be a game changer for us. If we could figure out a way to get it in undetected." His expression grew wistful at the possibilities.

"They're taking on Bastard City, eh? I can *definitely* help with that, although if you'd told me they were going full-frontal, I'd have packed the good stuff." She flipped the flap of the bag closed, as if the contents were no longer interesting. "If you give me an hour, I've got enough T-4 in the lab to blow the roof off that joint."

River shot me a concerned look, and she waved him off. "All you men are the same. It won't hurt *you* so long as you don't eat it or stick a detonator in it. The good stuff is highly toxic, which is why I only bring it out when strictly necessary for a bigger boom."

"Do you guys have a munitions replicator? I thought nobody left on earth had that technology?" River prodded.

Bramily snorted. "Don't need a replicator, when the original recipes are all right here." She jabbed a finger toward the side of her head, then turned her attention back to Sasha. "How much do they need, boss-lady?"

Sasha deferred to Squeaks, who had been tapping away furiously at his tablet. "According to the exchange rate and the estimated value of the goods they've offered us . . . here's the proposal." He slid the tablet back across the table, and River, Sasha, and I all leaned in to see what he'd put together.

They were offering all except their children's fund in water credits, plus a radio valued at thousands of credits, and a hefty quantity of plastique explosives. I leaned back, considering the offer.

It was fair, but I wasn't at all sure explosives were the way to go. I didn't want to kill anybody inside the city; it was supposed to be the last hope of humanity, from what I'd seen on Chrysanthe's locket, after all. But if what these people said was even a little bit true, and they *were* responsible for the recent spate of bombings . . . they'd stopped looking out for the interests of humanity somewhere along the way.

"I'm not sure I want to lead with a bomb—"

Bramily cut me off with a snort. "Girl, you don't *lead* with a bomb. You use a bomb to blow out a back-door exit when the lying snakes don't want to let you out. If you happen to take down a few load-bearing walls in the process, well, the more destruction the merrier." She grinned, the expression more a vicious baring of teeth than an expression of joy.

I looked at River to gauge his reaction and found him thoughtful. He met my eyes, steady as a rock, and we both pondered in shared silence.

In the end, I turned back to Sasha, and stuck out my hand to shake hers. "We accept. I'll never say no to a potential back door. My only request is, please put in some of the non-toxic stuff too. Just in case we need a *smaller* back door."

Bramily rolled her eyes, but quickly looked over the order Squeaks had put together and began neatly stacking blocks on the table without arguing. If I didn't know better, they could have been modeling clay. At least I had some newly vacant hidey-holes I could stash it in until it was needed.

"We have an empty tent, if you two would like some time to unwind, and then we'd love to have you as our guest for the community meal this evening," Sasha said, dragging my attention away from Bramily the fire bug. "Cade can stand guard, and let you know when it's time to eat."

"That would be great," River said, genuine cheer in his voice.

"Do you have a laundry facility, or someone who does it for credits? I'm happy to pay for cleaning."

"Absolutely. Cade can take you by Analiese's tent, too, and show you where to collect however much of your water you can hold."

"Thank you, I appreciate it."

Thirteen

COMMUNITY

After a quick stop at the Bronco to drop off our billion water orbs—I was already missing the containers we'd sacrificed to get past Steve and his crew—and to grab our spare clothes, Cade led us to an unassuming, orange-tinged tent. The sounds of little voices filtered out, and he stopped near the closed door to call inside.

"Analiese, you've got a laundry customer." His voice was deep and rough, as if his throat had also been damaged somehow in his accident.

A lovely, fine-boned blonde woman pulled back the tent flap, and all the air left my lungs in a whoosh. I must have staggered a step, because River's hand on my arm snapped me back to the present. *My mother was dead, and Analiese was twenty years too young to be her. She was not my mother, even if she looked uncannily familiar.*

"Cade, always lovely to see you," she said with a genuine smile, before switching her searching blue gaze on us. "I don't believe we've met; you must be new here. Welcome." She nodded, even the simple movement graceful and dignified.

River looked at me—since I usually took the lead—but my tongue still wasn't working. He smoothly introduced us. "We were hoping to get some laundry done before we leave tomorrow . . . though, you appear to have your hands full!" His shocked chuckle pulled my attention past her linen-clad legs and into the tent beyond, where fifteen children under the age of ten all sat giggling and shoving, making owl-eyes in our direction.

"Oh, yes. Those are my students. I'm honorary teacher for the collective, but school has nearly ended for the day." She gave River a warm smile and turned her attention on me.

They have school here?

"Do you have laundry as well?" She had already taken River's clothes and gestured to the small bundle tucked under my arm.

"Oh, yes. Thank you. It's wonderful that you teach the children; we didn't have that back in Coyote Springs."

She accepted my laundry and dropped it into a woven basket just inside her tent flap. "Yes, I know most places don't have any sort of formal education anymore, but here we feel that it's important. If our knowledge is lost, then our hope for the future is, too."

"You're right. I'm impressed." I gave her a cursory smile. "We'll let you get back to it."

"Will we see you at the community dinner this evening?"

"Yes, we'll be there."

"Wonderful. We'll talk then." She gave Cade a familiar wave and ducked back into the tent to shush the tittering kids. They were night and day different from the sad, dehydrated children living on the streets in Coyote Springs. The little bit of water I'd been able to spare from my scavenging efforts for the children back home suddenly felt so insignificant.

I swallowed hard and kept my head down as Cade led us towards the outskirts of their tent sector and stopped in front of a medium-sized tent. There was only one hole, and it was too high up to impinge on our privacy, so I counted it a win.

River went in first, and I followed, a sigh escaping my lips as the somewhat cool, dark interior enveloped us. The thin spear of light from the hole landed on two single cots standing against the far wall, a rickety wooden chair next to them, and a battered chest next to that. Otherwise, the tent was empty.

I watched in silence as River crossed the tent, opened the lid of the chest and poked around, producing a metallic rattling with his rifling. He pulled out a compact lantern and shut the lid.

"This is a pretty nice setup, to just be sitting here empty," he observed, taking in the sparse furnishings. It was more than we'd ever had in our travels so far. "There's even a couple plates and cutlery sets in there."

That explained the rattling. "This place is very different. It's not *fancy*, of course—I've had nicer stays at Marl's—but not for free. They're trying to look out for each other. Educate the kids, they have a water fund . . ."

"It's nice to see isn't it?" he said with a grin and dropped heavily into the chair. He let his booted feet splay out in front of him, and I envied his easy comfort in whatever situation we landed in. I was also tempted to curl up against his chest and forget the massive obstacles still in front of us for a little while, but with lingering jealousy still in my veins from earlier, I wouldn't feel right leaning into those instincts. "If we weren't going north, I wouldn't mind coming back here, and joining these guys. Assuming everything's how it looks. Heck, we might even be able to help them find a place with water, like we did for Coyote Springs. You know, we could take the water meter, and find a more permanent place for them, outside this little strip of territory they're stuck in." His eyes were lit with enthusiasm, but all I felt was the characteristic grit in my eyes from a too-long day, and exhaustion.

"Maybe, River. Maybe after. For now . . . the obstacles in front of us are too big for me to see past." I flopped down onto the cot, toeing off my own boots and settling back on the creaky green fabric.

"I get it. I was just dreaming. These people are so opposite of the Nightbloods . . . It'd be nice to do some good for once." He rested his head on the thick tent material and closed his eyes.

"It's a good dream," I murmured, eyelids already lowering. *It just isn't my dream.* Unease coiled around my stomach like a venomous snake, threatening to poison the fragile thing growing between me and River.

I fell asleep quickly, dragged under by dreams of a cottonmouth snake twining up my left leg before sinking its fangs deep in my calf, then slithering off and leaving me to die. A man lifted it from the ground like a pet, but I couldn't quite make out his face.

"Dinner time, get a move on!" Cade rasped through the tent, jolting me from my fitful sleep.

River rubbed the heel of his hand over bleary eyes as I sat up, checked for scorpions, and slid my feet back into my boots. Since we hadn't brought any of our possessions besides what we carried in our pockets, we walked right out and trailed Cade to the center of the small city, where about a hundred adults gathered with numerous kids weaving in and out between them as they played a game of tag.

A little girl barreled out of the crowd, arrowing straight for Cade. He met her halfway and scooped her up to sit in the crook of his arm, and planted a big kiss on her dirt-smeared little cheek.

"Dad, who are these people?"

He cast a furtive glance our way before answering. "Just travelers passing through, baby."

"Don't travelers have names?" She cocked her head to the side, pretty blonde ringlets touching her shoulder as she examined us.

He sighed. "Nyx is the woman, and River is the man."

"Hi, my name is Vinna! You should stay here instead of passing through. There's nowhere good to get to, anyways. That's what the grown-ups say when they think the kids aren't listening." She wriggled to be let down and then zoomed back off into the crowd, chasing another girl about the same age. Within seconds, they'd disappeared into the throng, only an effervescent trail of giggles trailing in their wake.

"Don't mind her; the older kids talk. You won't have any trouble finding the Bastion from here. It's only a couple days' drive, and due straight north." He shook his head, as if questioning the tenacity of little girls who thought they knew so much from such a young age.

"She's adorable. Is your wife around?" River asked, searching the crowd for a woman who might be coming to greet Cade, too.

Cade pressed his lips together in a thin line and walked away, abandoning us to the crowd. Vinna's mop of blonde curls reappeared, and he scooped her up again without breaking stride and cut through the crowd like a dirt bike through the dunes.

"Uh, I think I may have just stepped in it," River whispered, watching Cade's retreating back.

"I think you just *jumped* in it," I agreed. We stayed where we were on the fringes of the gathering but weren't alone for long. A man in red motorcycle leathers stalked over and took up Cade's abandoned position, with Louie the tech guy hot on his heels.

"Oh, Nyx, River—I'm so glad I caught you before the dinner began. This is Hank, one of the other guards." The red-clad man gave us a perfunctory wave but didn't interrupt. "I've been thinking over the radio situation ever since we talked this afternoon, and I think I've come up with a solution." He held up a device no bigger than my pinky nail, as if it explained everything.

Our expressions must have conveyed our bewilderment because he rushed to explain. "This is a waterproof implantable signal transmitter. I was able to modify it so that it can function as a two-way radio. But it's small enough, and with an essentially inert state when not in use, it should make it through any scans the Bastion may do on you—assuming they actually let you in at all, of course. If you were able to get this in and transmit to us from inside their walls, well, that could be a huge breakthrough." His eyes gleamed with excitement, and River rubbed his hands together anxiously.

"Tell it to me straight, man. You said it's waterproof. Where *exactly* do you intend to put that thing?"

Louie laughed, and elbowed Hank as if River was the funniest guy he'd ever met. "Don't worry it's not too invasive. It goes right inside your mouth—well, whoever's mouth is willing to volunteer." His gaze flicked rapidly between the two of us, as if he was holding his breath for an answer.

River chafed the back of his neck with his palm. "I have a feeling I'm going to regret this, but I'll do it. If it'll help, I'll wear the radio. Is it going to hurt?"

Louie didn't waste any time stepping forward and pointing out little spiky feet protruding from the small device. "Pain should be minimal. These calipers will clamp onto one of your back molars and remain in place until you choose to remove it. There's a button on the side you can press with your tongue, to start and stop transmitting, as well as to trigger the removal sequence. I can write out a guide for you. Open up, please." He pulled a pair of long, menacing looking forceps from the satchel on his side, and carefully pinched the device between the tips.

I cast River an, *are you really sure about this* look, but he tipped his head back and opened his mouth. The long tweezers slowly disappeared inside his mouth, taking the tiny device—about the size of a tooth, now that I realized its destination—with it. I held my breath as he rotated his hand, and then all of a sudden, River jerked and grabbed the side of his jaw, working it side to side.

"Okay, that definitely hurt a little," he groused.

"Sorry, I stretched the truth. But it should fade quickly, and then be like you're not wearing it. I would avoid any acidic foods, granted those are unusual these days." Louie dropped the tweezers back into his satchel, and then dug out a handwritten set of instructions. "This will tell you how to work through the modes, so you don't transmit until you're ready. It also includes instructions on how to remove it, though best case scenario you don't need to do that until you are outside the city. If it were found, I can't imagine they'd take it well."

"This seems like a bad idea," I interjected. "We're trying to go in on good terms and find my brother. If you already have four radio streams, what difference is this going to make, besides putting River at risk?"

Louie sighed. "I understand your concern, and I've made every effort to make this device untraceable. But our lives out here are difficult, and our people suffer. Sometimes, it's just from the struggle of eking out sustenance, and that I can live with. More often than not, though, it's not the struggle to survive the Wastes; it's the struggle to survive *other people* and I'm not okay with that. If I can do anything which helps these people, I'm going to try. The more we know, the more we can avoid their plans to wipe us off our patch of sand. Maybe we can even strike back." His frustration grew to an angry tirade at the end, and I could see that River was in agreement. His eyes shone with determination as he turned to me.

"Nyx, it's fine. I want to help. This is a good thing."

I could tell he was trying to convince me, though I felt far from reassured. "If you're sure," I said through gritted teeth, not willing to argue the point surrounded by strangers, many of whom had turned to stare as Louie's voice rose in anger.

Sasha strode through the crowd, a frown tugging down her eyebrows in the middle. "Everything okay over here, Louie, Hank?" She cast a quick glance around, clearly looking for Cade, and coming up short.

"Yes, everything's fine. I'm sorry to make a scene, it's just—"

River clapped him on the back of the shoulder, a wry grin on his face. "Don't apologize for being passionate about this. Your people are important. You *should* be passionate."

Louie shot him a grateful look and ducked his head as if embarrassed. The sudden camaraderie made me anxious, and I turned to Sasha.

"So, you guys do communal dinner?"

She nodded. "Once a week. You showed up on the right day. Come on, I'll show you." She wove through the crowd to the center, where a brawny man had wheeled up a large cart. It had been cobbled together from scraps, with metal sections covered in peeling paint fastened to split wood, sitting on the most cracked and bleached set of wheels I'd ever seen. But on top, a newer countertop sat covered in bowls of, well, I didn't know what. But it was green. There was also a large tray heaped with compressed cubes, seemingly from a replicator, and something gooey red in bottles off to the side. There was a smaller table set up there, too, with child-sized plates of . . . dinosaur patties?

"What is all of this?" I asked, gesturing to the food I had no hope of identifying. I watched as person after person walked up, and the man behind the cart carefully measured out scoops of the green substance, piled up the same number of cubes, and squirted the red goo on top of the greens. With a nod, the person took their plate, grabbed a kid's plate, and walked off. An orderly line was forming, and I was staring unabashedly.

"You've never had chlorella before? It's a bit of a strong flavor, but incredibly nutritious, and one of the few things we can grow regularly, even while moving from place to place. One of our engineers was able to work with some data from a city escapee on how they grew it, and they cobbled together a setup inside a trailer. It takes about a week to grow enough for everyone, but we hope to have community dinners more often as we grow our setup. The rest is just meal cubes, and the secret sauce. Oh, and the protein patties for the kids. None of them will touch the green stuff yet."

River and I exchanged a quick glance, and then went to the back of the line with Sasha. The system was efficient, and in a matter of minutes people were settling down all over the square in groups, chatting and eating the odd meal. The server handed us all plates, and we followed Sasha to a shady patch against one of the building's exterior walls. She folded her legs and gracefully sank down into a crisscrossed position, so we followed her lead.

She scooped up a large spoonful of the chlorella and shoved it into her mouth without preamble. I took a smaller scoop and sniffed it as it hovered closer to my face. A tang of salt and earthiness mixed with something I couldn't place. I took a small bite, not wanting to appear rude, and was instantly grateful I hadn't taken a larger one. Salty, musty, and just *eww*. I forced myself to swallow and took a rapid swig from a water orb in my pocket as my eyes began to water.

"The red stuff burns," I hissed out through my teeth.

River's entire face was turning red, and tears gathered at the corners of his eyes as he nodded effusively and gestured for me to pass him the orb. He must have forgotten to grab himself one earlier. He drained half of the orb in one gulp.

"What *is* that?" I asked, once I could speak normally again.

Sasha laughed so hard she snorted and covered her mouth. "You've never had hot sauce before? We all love it."

River and I both shook our heads, and I snatched the water orb back from him to take another sip. My mouth was *still burning.*

"Our replicator belonged to a fancy restaurant, so it can make a pretty good variety of things, even with the limited organic material we have to feed into it." She shrugged. "I guess it's an acquired taste."

"I'll say," River choked out.

One by one, other members of the Red Riders collective came and sat around us, some asking questions about life in parts of the desert away from the purple ocean, and others asking how we'd made it through Nightblood territory. We asked some questions of our own about the strange green plant, and what technology they'd used to grow it.

It was gross still, but in a weirdly addictive way, so long as you avoided the hellfire sauce.

Fourteen

Tick, Tick, Tick . . . Boom

We were listening, enraptured, to one of Sasha's guards tell us the story of how he'd nearly lost his bike *and* left leg in a Night-bloods attack on his first ride with Sasha, when an eerie tone pealed out through the compound.

Sasha swore, and a split second later, everything erupted into pure chaos. Children screamed, adults bolted in seemingly every direction, and all of the people who'd been so casually lounging mere minutes earlier were on their feet. River and I jumped up as well, confusion not stopping us from leaping into action.

"What's happening?" I yelled as we bolted after Sasha, who was sprinting straight towards
the city center.

"Bomb threat! Everyone to evacuation vehicles! Move, move, move!" she shouted, but her
tone was even and commanding amidst the
chaos.

"Sasha! Sasha!" A little boy came running
alongside us and tripped over a loose stone. I
barely heard him over the din of frantic people
yelling to each other, but by the time I turned
my head, River had already caught him and
swung him up to his shoulder without breaking
stride. His face read pure determination, and I
knew we wouldn't be bolting for the Bronco and
heading out into the Wastes on our own.

We cleared the center of the streaming
crowd, and Sasha froze, glancing around as she
sucked in the dusty air. "There!" she muttered
and darted to the right, past where the abandoned food cart sat, and I spotted a trio of children, all under the age of six, huddled together
and crying.

"Jace! Lena! Ria! To me, to me!" she bellowed
and waved her arms, causing the little boy to
look up, tears streaking his cheeks. They didn't
move, though, and I could see they were frozen
in fear. I thought Sasha was going to plow into
them, but she skidded to a stop at the last sec-

ond and scooped two of the three up. Without hesitating, I grabbed up the third.

Once she saw that we all had a kid in arms, she led us through the maze-like tent side streets, towards the east. I was hassling I was breathing so hard by the time she reached the edge of the tents and slowed, looking for something. There was a line of vehicles—half bikes, half SUVs, a handful of trailers being pulled behind the larger ones. As soon as she spotted the one she was looking for, she took off again at a dead run.

The largest SUV was a mottled-orange color covered with wavy lines, in an attempt at camouflaging it against the dunes of the Wastes. As soon as we drew near, the back door swung open wide and Cade leapt out, taking the boy from my arms first and shoving him in, then the older boy from River's arms, and climbed back in himself. Once Sasha packed her two kids on the other side, she slammed the door shut and banged twice on the top. It took off like a shot, whoever was driving not wasting another second. Sasha had already started crossing the clearing, sending vehicles out left and right as she did her head count and gave them the signal.

"River, we have to go."

"Crap, where's the Bronco?" We both turned and shielded our eyes as we gazed back at the near-empty encampment. We took off at a run, but I was lagging.

"River, here—" I dug the keys out of my pocket and tossed them to him. His startled gaze met mine, and I huffed out, "I'm not keeping up. Go get her started and meet me halfway if you have to. If the Bronco's still in the city and it gets bombed, we're as good as dead. GO!" I urged, still chugging forward at my slower pace. He sent me one last uncertain look, and then turned and took off, leaving me behind as if I was tied to a cactus.

I kept my head down and ran as fast as I could, in the rough direction of the Bronco. My world narrowed to the pounding of my pulse and the breaths sawing in and out through my mouth. My calves burned, and finally I made it to the main thoroughfare into the town. I'd angled to the shortest path, knowing River would get the Bronco and pick me up. Sure enough, I heard the tires grabbing on the odd road as the Bronco cleared the corner and surged into sight. River slammed the brakes and skidded to a stop right in front of me, and I moved as quickly as I could to the passenger side and hauled myself in.

As soon as I was in—not even belted, yet—he punched it again, and headed south, straight out of town. When we cleared the last tent, he cut the wheel so hard left, it felt like my side of the Bronco levitated, breaking free of the grip of the sand on its tires for one terrifying moment.

"Eeeeeeah!" River hollered as the tires touched down again, and we cut east, the same direction the rest of the Red Riders had headed. All but a few of their motorcycle riders were already on the move, scattering into the dunes in all directions, rooster tails flying up in their wakes like a hundred sand serpents roaring briefly to life.

I caught my breath as we hit the top of the first dune and went slip-sliding down the other side. "River, you've got to ease up a bit. We're going to be fine, but you can't flip us going down the other side. If we hit a razorback ridge at that speed, it's all over," I gritted out through clenched teeth as I clutched the handles over the glove compartment and above my right shoulder.

"Sorry, this is usually your territory!" He had a white-knuckled grip on the steering wheel, and the tense line of his shoulders was clearly visible through his thin white shirt.

"You're doing fine. Take a couple deep breaths, and ease off the gas just before the peak of the next one. Don't stop—we don't want to slide. But you want a visual of the other side before you punch it again."

Crhrhrhrh—the sudden radio static made me jump. "Come in, Collective, come in. Bomb threat confirmed, target unspecified north-western location. Repeat, unspecified north-western location. King Louie out." The static from the console nearly made me hit the roof, it startled me so badly.

"What is this?" I snatched it up—it was a hand-held radio with a piece of paper fastened around it.

"Don't know, it was on the hood. Tossed it in and hit the gas. There's a bag, too." I looked down, and sure enough a black vinyl bag rested on top of the console.

I pulled the paper off the radio and found a hand-scrawled note.

Don't use the tooth radio until you're inside. Godspeed.

He'd taken the time in the middle of a bomb threat to give us a way to contact them. I quickly unzipped the bag, and found all of the stones due us from the silver jewelry, neatly stored in a small case, a couple capsules the size of my thumb of something green, plus more plasticized explosive—this labeled differently than the C-4, with an instruction booklet laid on top.

"What's in it? I didn't have time to check," River asked, eyes glued to the next dune we were climbing.

"Everything they owed us, to the penny, and our clean clothes."

"They're good people. I wish we could do more." He clenched his jaw, the muscle twitching as I stared. I made a snap decision.

"Come in, King Louie. Come in, Louie and the Collective." I spoke and then let the button go. I was proud that I didn't even roll my eyes when using his ridiculous call sign.

River arched a brow and looked at me quickly before turning his attention back to the front windshield.

A loud crackle from the speaker made me jump. "—Come in, Lady of the Night."

River cackled at the impromptu handle, and I grumbled before pushing the button. "Don't make me regret this, Louie. Anyone on channel, take note. Latitude 37.636264126842946, Longitude -112.67220281534073." I rattled the coordinates off two more times, and then added one last message before I let the button go. "Tell them Nyx sent you."

"We read you loud and clear, Night Goddess. Safe travels." I rolled my eyes at the ridiculous name and dropped the radio into the cup holder.

"What was that?"

"The coordinates to Wolf Well. I don't know if they'll figure out a way to get there, but anywhere's got to be better than stuck between hell and a hot place."

"Amen to that. How long do we keep going this way, do you think?" he asked.

"Let's give it another hour. Then we'll turn north." Deep down in my gut, I had an ominous feeling as I leaned forward and punched the co-ordinates for Bastion City back into the navigation system. We'd made it through Nightblood territory unscathed, but had we passed through a den of thieves only to crawl into bed with the devil himself?

Fifteen

The Bubble by the Sea

We took turns, swapping off every few hours, and drove through the night. It sucked, but we were unwilling to let our guard down when we hadn't heard a boom, or gotten any kind of call that the threat was cleared. By mid-day, however, our candles were both burnt down to nubs, and we succumbed to our need for rest. Bathroom breaks aside, we stayed in our seats, laid as flat as they'd go, and snatched a few hours of stationary rest.

You wouldn't think it was possible under the glaring sun, but eventually the exhaustion won, daylight or no.

I woke to a setting sun and rubbed the grit from my eyes. The purple and gold melting into the orange dunes was beautiful, but I instantly spotted something amiss.

I elbowed River, and smirked as he sat up grumbling about pushy women. "What is it?"

"What does that look like to you?" I pointed to the horizon, where a black smudge darkened the sky, and a haze mingled with the vibrant colors of impending night.

"Smoke," he said grimly.

"That's what I was afraid of. Why are these people bombing everyone all of a sudden? I lived more than twelve years in Coyote Springs, and never once saw hide nor hair of these people, and now . . . ka-boom every time we turn around."

"I don't know. I was under the impression that the Nightbloods were the biggest bad in the desert. At least, they were in the southern desert. These guys . . . they've got tech on another level, if they've got aircraft *and* bombs big enough to wipe cities off what's left of the map."

"But *why*? What are the desert dwellers doing that's hurting them? Are they just out to be the last humans? Because give us another twenty or thirty years, and they'll probably achieve that without the bombs."

"Maybe they want the water." River gave me a grim look from his seat. "They wipe out all the other people left on the planet, they've got more water. They're ensured more time."

"They're supposed to have this amazing technology! Why do they need what little water is left scattered in the desert? Shouldn't they be able to find sources not in use, instead of just killing everybody all over the place?"

"I don't know, Nyx. I really don't know."

"I'm not looking forward to finding out. If they bomb their neighbors, do we have a chance in the Sahara of them letting us in?"

"I've been wondering that, too. But unless we want to give up and turn around . . . we're going to have to find out."

"Planting 'the good stuff' on the side of one of their fancy buildings is sounding better and better by the minute."

He snorted. "We haven't seen the city yet. Maybe they're not as fancy as we were led to believe."

"Maybe, but I have to say, that would be disappointing." I unstrapped my seatbelt and popped the driver's door open so I could slide down and stretch my legs.

River followed suit, stretching his arms up high overhead, the golden light bathing him distractingly. I looked away quickly when he dropped his arms, not wanting to be caught staring.

When I looked up again, I caught him staring and he looked away with a blush, scuffing his palm over the nape of his neck.

"Checking me out, huh?" I was only half-joking, but I didn't know how to do this with a man. I took charge in every area of life, but in this . . . I didn't have years of experience to draw on. My mother had been weak, a servant of men. A *possession*. That version of intimacy made me sick. I had to find a way to build a connection while still remaining *me*.

"Maybe. You got a problem with that?" he teased, turning to hold my gaze in a challenge.

"No, not a problem. Just an observation." I stepped closer, putting a teasing sway in my hips as I passed the front of the Bronco.

His eyebrows shot up, and he fingered a small scar on his left bicep, as if unsure what to do with himself at my blatant flirtation. *Should I back off?*

I paused, uncertain where this game would lead. I didn't want to push him away or mess up what we had between us.

As if sensing my internal argument, he took a step forward, then another. Stalking me, he was an alpha male with tantalizing heat in his eyes. A shiver coursed over my skin, and the corner of his gorgeous mouth tipped up in a grin. He closed the final foot of distance between us and reached up to cup my face between his palms.

"You are stunning; a goddess in the flesh. And I was checking you out. I'd have to be blind not to." He swept his thumbs over my cheekbones—the motion soothed my height-ened nerves, while his eyes held me in their entrancing grip. He studied me all the while, checking my reaction. When I didn't pull away, he leaned in, and slowly, slowly brushed his lips to mine. My eyes fluttered closed, and I was lost to him. The stress and worry of the world washed away, and I was swept up in the sweet press of lips on lips, fingertips on shoulders, hands slipping into hair.

After a short eternity, we separated. I blew out a shaky breath as he tipped his forehead down to rest against mine. His soft whisper broke my reverie.

"Every time I think you can't possibly get any more incredible, you do."

I slipped my arms around his waist and gave him a squeeze, struggling to find the words to encompass how much I was feeling. It was just a kiss, and yet, it felt so much deeper to me. Like we'd connected on another level entirely.

"You're pretty incredible yourself," I mur-mured, hiding my face in his neck. It felt insuf-ficient, but it was all I had in the moment.

We stayed there, clinging to each other and hiding from the world together, as we watched the sun melt into the horizon.

After a late evening together of shared meal bars and tucking into our respective tents to sleep, we woke with the sun, ready to finish this last leg of our trip. I was so ready. We were close enough I could taste it, and this nervous energy seemed to permeate the air around me. I knew Chace was close. I just had to get into the city.

The city that kept kidnapping and bombing everyone for no known reason. No big deal. I huffed out a breath as we crested another identical dune, right at the edge of the ocean's hard pack. We could still see it but didn't have to drive on the horrible bumpy part of the sand. The anticipation was *killing me.* The idea that we were this close, and still might not make it in to see Chace, and make sure he was safe, was unacceptable to me. I mean, I wouldn't blow River up, but I had been serious about blowing a hole in one of their walls if they wouldn't let us in.

Though, the idea of hurting innocent people inside those walls made my stomach sour. We'd try the nice way first and hope they didn't blow *us* to kingdom come.

I drummed my fingertips on the steering wheel, gazing listlessly out at the purple ocean about three hours into our drive, when River sucked in a breath.

"Nyx, look there! Is that a wall?" He pointed out to the right, but we were already descending the dune, and I didn't catch it. Every muscle in my body tense, I stepped on the gas pedal, leaning forward as if that was going to let me see it half a second sooner. Even the continuous hum of the tires digging into the sand grated on my nerves as we crested the next rise.

Then I saw it. Still quite a ways in the distance, sat a clear dome, shimmering under the baking sun. I could see hints of metallic supports spiderwebbed beneath it, and inside the sphere was a structure with massive, gray stone walls. The edges of the dome spread out a ways around the structure on all sides, touching and disappearing into the sand below.

I frowned and stopped the Bronco, squinting at the strange city. "What is that around it?"

"I don't know, but it kind of looks like a really big soap bubble. And that image just makes me want to pop it, which they probably wouldn't appreciate."

I snorted. "Probably not, but I didn't exactly appreciate them blowing up Coyote Springs. Or those kids back there in the Collective. *Or* whatever poor unsuspecting saps they blew up yesterday. So, we'll reserve judgment on whether or not we'll be popping their bubble."

He didn't say a word, just offered me a fist, and I tapped mine on top in a *booyah* gesture.

"Even if we took out the bubble, those are taller walls than I've ever seen. We're still far,

but this place looks huge. Bigger than I expected."

"If it's the last hope of all mankind, I was expecting pretty big."

"Yeah, but pretty big is five to ten times the
biggest building back in Coyote Springs. Or literally any town I've ever scavenged. But that's .
. . practically a medieval castle."

"I don't think those were actually very large by
modern standards," he argued.

I slugged him lightly on the arm, and he was
kind enough to humor me and pretend it hurt.

"You know what I mean, River."

"Fine, yes, it's a soap bubble castle. Maybe
there's a king in there looking to grant us a boon
and make us lords and ladies."

"Okay, now you're just being ridiculous." I
stuck my tongue out at him, and took my foot
off the brake, turning us towards the city. With
each dune we crested, it only grew bigger, and
my tension rose to match.

"What if they don't even let us get close
enough to ask to come in? They could blow us
up at any second," I whispered when I couldn't
take it anymore.

"Nyx, look at me."

"I'm driving."

"Well, stop for a minute. Please?" He rested a
hand gently on my forearm, and when we hit
the belly of the next trough between dunes, I

shoved the shifter into park with much more force than was necessary.

River was calm, turned sideways in his seat to face me. I couldn't bear to hold his gaze, the emotions in my chest too much to handle while looking into those endless blue eyes. "I know you're scared, and you have every right to be. But this is why we came here."

I picked at a loose thread on the knee of my pants and tried to swallow down a stubborn lump.

"Don't let them get into your head before we even make it to the gates. You are the smartest, toughest woman I've ever met. If anyone can get inside those gates, get her brother, and figure out how to stop these idiots from bombing everybody left on this stupid, dried-up rock, it's *you*. And I have no doubt whatsoever that we will make it to those gates, and through those gates. None."

I pressed my lips together in a hard line, and quickly flicked my eyes up to his. They were full of sincerity, and I quickly looked away again.

"River, that's sweet—"

"No, Nyx. It's not. It's not sweet; that was last night, holding you close and watching the sun set. This? This is hard fact. We are spitting distance from the people blowing up the entire freaking world. And I don't know about you, but I'm *pissed* and want to know why. I really think that you are the only person who has a shot in hell at getting into those gates."

I looked up, already shaking my head. "If we don't make it—"

"Since when do you, who has stared down the meanest sons-of-camel-humps that run the desert gangs on more than one occasion, doubt yourself? Nyx, you've all but spat in the face of the people everybody else cowers and hides from. You're fearless, and you *have* been this whole time. What's changed? Why the sudden doubt? Because I don't have any."

"River, of course I have doubts! There's just no other option. There's no choice but to be tough, when the other option is to lie down and die. That's no option!" I raised my voice, getting angry that he wouldn't just let me wallow in my insecurities.

"Bull. Crap. You and I both know that people lie down and die, every. Single. Day. We've seen them, we've pitied them. That's not us. We don't quit. We fight, even if it's stupid. So don't lie to me, Nyx. What's wrong?"

I clenched my fists several times, resisting the urge to do something stupid like punch the steering wheel. "We're wasting time," I ground out, hoping he'd drop it.

"If you don't talk to me I'm going to go stand on the hood so you can't move this truck until you do."

"I snorted. Try me. I'll drive away *cackling*." I glared his direction, begging him to call my bluff. It might be cathartic to dump him off the top of the car. Not hard, just a little spill to take my mind off what we were about to do.

He grinned, not at all threatened by my bravado. But still, he waited, that frickity-fracking *earnest* expression on his face.

A minute ticked by, and then two. My resolve to keep the fear in slowly crumbled to nothing, and I looked down at my hands as I spoke. "If they kill us before we make it inside, Chace is going to think I gave up on him. The closer we get, the more I know in my soul these people are not the goody-two-shoes Chrysanthe thought they were, all those years ago. Maybe they started that way, but now . . . can you imagine her knowing the very people she used her gifts to help save are being *blown up* every day?"

"She'd be appalled," he agreed.

"Exactly. So, there's a good chance they're not going to let us in. And I can't die, not like this, with Chace thinking I gave up on him. If we find him first and then something goes wrong, at least he'll know I came for him. But to make it this close—" Instead of continuing to botch the explanation, a sob choked me and, to my utter horror, a tear escaped and rolled down my cheek. I dashed it away and looked out my side window, trying to hide my shameful reaction from River. He thought I was some fearless woman, and I was crying like a child, an hour from the goal I'd dragged him weeks through the desert for.

His seatbelt clicked, and then I heard his door latch click open. I didn't look, too ashamed to be crying to see what he was up to. Knowing him, he was probably going for a jog until I got myself back under control. I bit my bottom lip, sucking air in through my nose and trying to stop the steady stream of tears leaking from my eyes.

I was jolted out of my self-inflicted misery when my door clicked open, and River demanded, "Take off your seatbelt."

"What?"

"Just take it off."

Lost to my misery, I clicked the button to release it, and let it slither off of my shoulders. River reached up into the Bronco and guided me down until my feet touched the sand, and then wrapped me up in his arms. I sank into him, burying my face in his chest and tucking my chin down, still trying to hide.

He rubbed my back, and for a moment I just sucked in gulps of air, trying to collect myself.

"We are sitting ducks like this. We need to get back in the truck and keep moving."

"If they decide to blow us up, it won't make a lick of difference if we're in the truck or not," he said, his chest rumbling under my cheek.

That was true, I supposed.

"Nyx, did you think for even a second that Chace willingly left you?" he asked, still gliding his hand up and down over my back.

"No, of course not. He would never."

"Don't you think that Chace knows if it was within your power to get to him, you'd fight like a demon to do it?"

"I guess so. I mean, I would hope he knew."

"Nyx, I've known you a couple months, and I know. He's known you your whole life. He *knows*. And it's probably killing him that he can't get back to you, too."

I looked up at that, not having thought of it that way before. He cupped my cheek with his free hand. "No matter what happens. No matter if we make it inside, get blown up before we reach the door, or find out he's not here. No matter what, *he already knows*. You don't have to worry about that. We just have to go over there and see if those camel kissers took your brother." He jabbed an accusing finger in the direction of the enormous fortress.

"You're probably right," I whispered, letting the words sink in.

"I'm absolutely right. And I can't stand to see your confidence shaken like this. He wouldn't want this any more than I do. He would want take-no-prisoners Nyx to storm the freaking gates and tear the place down with holy fury in her eyes."

I chuckled, the sound small compared to his booming enthusiasm. But he was right. It was time to storm the fracking gates and take no prisoners. Well, we were going to take back one of *theirs* . . . or we were going to take them out trying.

I looked up, meeting his gaze with renewed determination. "Let's go."

Sixteen

De-Con

T he closer we got, the larger the dome loomed, to the point where I couldn't believe that a structure that looked so delicate from a distance could in fact be so imposing. We couldn't see perfectly through due to the spiderwebbed support structure inside the glass, but we could clearly see a severe gray wall, which had to be at least four stories high. We drove around, looking for an entrance and saw that the structure stretched into a long rectangle, oddly juxtaposed to the swooping bubble encasing it. It reminded me a bit of a medieval castle pictured on one of the romance books I'd found in the underground mall. I found myself getting distracted looking up, up, up, trying to see the top as we drew closer.

Movement inside the bubble drew my attention back down to ground level, where soldiers in puffy white uniforms streamed out of a large, arched gate at what must have been the front of the city. It was flanked by sandy ground, but that bit of ground was congested with more desert scrub plants than I'd ever seen in one place. Cacti, scrub bushes, and odd, spiny trees filled most of the space surrounding the interior structure. There was a well-worn path from the gate, and they marched in two lines from the entrance to the exterior wall of the bubble. I pulled to a stop a few feet from the dome as the soldiers formed up just inside.

"The marshmallow nickname makes a lot more sense now," River mused from the passenger seat. He had a weapons holster on, and he thumbed his favorite knife handle where it stuck out of its sheath.

They were white and puffy, but somehow I doubted there'd be a sugary sweet center on these people. Flat expressions greeted us as we exchanged a quick glance, and I debated how to proceed. I didn't have to debate long. A loud announcement boomed around us.

"Step out of the vehicle and remove any weapons. If you fail to comply, you will be fired upon."

"They are just pure joy and sunshine," River muttered. "You ready?" He glanced at me, his hand resting lightly on the door latch.

"Yep. Let's go meet the bastards who stole my brother." I clenched my jaw as I popped open the door and slid to the ground. My chest holster was on, but I hesitated to throw my gun into the sand. Instead, I made a show of sliding it out with my thumb and pointer finger and tossing it into the driver's seat. River likewise ditched his knife, and we both shut the doors. As soon as I hit the button to lock the Bronco with our weapons inside and dropped my arms back to my side, a seamless-looking panel of glass lifted smoothly up from the sand, and the two lines of soldiers streamed out straight towards us.

The motion was both fluid and precise, and somewhere in a detached part of my brain, it reminded me of the stream the nomad had shared with me, all those weeks ago. I dug into that detachment as the first soldiers to reach us grabbed me and River by the upper arms and dragged us towards the breathtaking glass dome.

Hopefully it wouldn't become our glass coffin.

They dragged us through the opening, and the panel of glass swept gracefully down behind us, sinking into the sand with a soft hiss as it resealed. I didn't get a chance to watch and see how it worked, though, because they pulled us relentlessly forward, to the gate in the front of the fortress. The smells inside the bubble were unreal, and many of them I couldn't place. There was also a strange moisture caressing my skin, something I'd never experienced before. It reminded me of the foggy bathroom, after I'd finished my one and only shower, except it was cool, unlike the scalding heat that was ever present in the Wastes. Or maybe it was even closer to the bone-deep humidity of Armand's greenhouse.

They were silent, and the intense questioning I expected didn't happen. *Yet.*

I slowed as we approached the gate. The great, unbroken gray city walls overhead loomed up, up, *up* in a way that stirred an animal fear inside me. Some primal part of me wanted to revolt, run for freedom and open air before they could shut that gate behind me, too. I breathed through my nose, chanting in my head over and over, *You're here for Chace. You have to get Chace. Chace is here.*

It helped, but it still felt like the panic was trying to claw its way out of my throat. The man on my right didn't like that I slowed down, and jerked on my arm, sending me stumbling. I regained my footing and didn't fall, barely.

"Hey, there's no need to be so rough. We're all friends here," River insisted from a few paces ahead, his own guards pushing him on when I'd slowed.

None of them spoke, however, or acknowledged that he'd spoken. Instead, they ushered us through the gate, into a sterile white hallway, and towards a small room off to the side. A strange blue light radiated from it, and there was no furniture inside that I could see. A creak and a popping sound overhead made me jerk my head up, and my resolve nearly broke when I saw the gate coming down. I cast a desperate look over my shoulder, to where the Bronco sat, forlorn and abandoned in the sand, and I'd never so much longed to get behind the wheel and drive away as fast as her tires would carry me.

But I didn't, and they didn't slow. River and I were shoved into the blue-tinged room, and the door slammed behind us. Inside, there were no windows or other exits, and as far as I could see no ventilation access.

"This is not going how I thought, River," I murmured, sure they were watching us somehow, even if all I saw were bare walls. The eerie blue light glowed straight from the surface of the walls, making them hard to look at.

"They're definitely not very welcoming. Or talkative," he agreed. We stood side by side and River reached up and squeezed my shoulder. It would have been even worse if I'd been alone.

"Hello, and welcome to Bastion City!" A too-chipper voice sounded all around us, and we both spun to identify the speaker. However, a woman's face had appeared on every single wall of the room, as if the room itself was a screen. Her confident smile did little to tamp down my apprehension. We faced the largest wall, and took in her perfect face and blinding white, straight teeth as she spoke again.

"I'm Brenda, and this is the decontamination room. The microbiome inside the Bastion City Dome is incredibly diverse, unique, and also fragile. As a result, all people taking trips outside of the dome—or new visitors to the dome—must undergo decontamination. This is a process by which we remove harmful bacteria and chemicals which you might not even know are hitching a ride."

A photo of a cowboy on a saddled horse in the middle of a green, sprawling field popped up on the screen, and I snorted. Seriously?

The photo blinked out of existence, and Brenda's face popped back up. "As much as we love a good cowboy, those hitchhikers could really damage the delicate ecosystem fostered inside the dome. There are over four thousand species from around the world represented inside, and the balance is delicate. We appreciate your cooperation in keeping our home bountiful, beautiful, and blooming. Please follow the directions on the screen, and you'll be out of here in two shakes of a lamb's tail!" Brenda waved, and her picture was replaced with a picture of an ewe and lamb, grazing in a mountain valley surrounded by lush vegetation, the likes of which I'd never seen. A numbered list popped up next to the paradise sheep, and I quickly scanned it.

"Remove all of your clothing and place it into the decontamination basket, stand with your arms and feet spread, and close your eyes until the full decontamination cycle has processed," I read aloud.

"Uh, we're just supposed to strip in here? They could all be standing on the other side of the door, watching us." River frowned and walked forward to poke the wall. It glowed yellow now, the instructions blinking on the walls as if urging us to comply with a smile.

A minute of silence passed in which we both searched the room high and low for another alternative, but other than a white chute where we were supposed to drop our clothes, there was nothing. Even the door was recessed into the wall so tightly, there was no way to pry it open, and no knob on this side to jiggle.

I tapped my fingers restlessly on my thigh and met River's worried gaze with mine.

"What do you want to do?" he asked.

"I don't think we have much choice. These people have all the power in here, and I don't think they're going to let us out unless we co-operate."

"Doesn't seem like it," he agreed.

"So, I guess we have to strip," I said, biting my lip.

"You know, I envisioned us getting naked together once or twice, and this is *not* how it went," River said drily, and I could feel my face turning red even as we turned our backs to each other.

I slowly pulled my belt from my waist, the *swoosh* of it pulling through the loops exacerbating my nerves. A soft *thwump* in the basket told me River'd ditched some article of clothing, and I moved faster, trying not to envision a dozen marshmallow soldiers on the other side, watching us and snickering. I pulled the Bronco's key from my pocket and dropped it on the ground at my feet before tossing the pants into the basket. As I pulled my shirt over my head—the final thing I had left on to cover me as long as humanly possible—leaving nothing on my person except the familiar weight of Chrysanthe's locket around my neck. I reached for it, but my hand stopped short, and I found I couldn't part with it. The walls changed colors and the basket sank down into the floor, disappearing without a sound. It was seamless, and if I hadn't seen it happen, I never would have believed it.

The red blinking light freaked me out, so I closed my eyes and stuck my arms out, as instructed. I counted in my head, trying to think of anything besides whatever was about to happen. *One, two, three* . . . A soft hissing sound filled the room, the quiet sound firing goosebumps all over my body. *Four, five, six.*

Then, the mist hit my skin, and the uncontrollable shaking started. *Seven.*

Eight.

Nine.

I blacked out before I could count to ten.

Seventeen

MILITANT

I woke slowly, as if rising up through thick, heavy sand. It was an absurd thought, because sand was light, sifting freely away like nothing. Inconsequential. But waking was hard.

"Nyx, come on, come on. Nyx. Please, Nyx." Someone patted my cheek. Then harder. I wanted to frown, but my face muscles weren't moving right. The voice soothed me, though I didn't know why.

A large, strong hand gripped my shoulder, gave it a shake. The warm press of fingertips felt nice on my skin.

Wait. Why could I feel it on my bare skin? My mind whirred, trying to catch up. I always had clothes on. What had happened to my clothes? Panic rose, and the memories crashed through the haze, dragging my eyes open in a rush, to stare at a bleached-white ceiling, marred only by River's panicked face dangling over mine.

"Nyx! Thank the sweet oasis." He breathed out a relieved sigh. "You passed out halfway into the decontamination spray. I don't know what was in that crap, but I puked my guts up for ten minutes. You didn't even stir. Are you okay? Do you feel all right?" He ran his hands down the bare lengths of my arms, then brushed my hair back from my forehead, and cupped one cheek with his hand.

My eyes wandered down from his tanned face and crystalline eyes to the baggy white t-shirt and gray sweatpants he was wearing. My own arm was bare, but on further inspection I realized he'd covered me up with my own enormous t-shirt and a pair of sweats, draped over me and tucked carefully around. Warmth suffused my cheeks, and I realized belatedly that he was still waiting for me to respond.

"My head feels fuzzy," I slurred, and frowned again in concentration. "That sucked," I said, trying harder to enunciate.

The corner of his mouth turned up in a half-grin, and my heart did a little flip that was entirely inappropriate for our current crappy circumstances. I wedged an elbow underneath me, and tried to sit up, but everything spun and bucked like a drunken see-saw.

I closed my eyes again and breathed through my nose, trying not to puke.

"Hey, take it slow. It is not a fun ride to come off of."

"How long have I been out?" I asked through my teeth, keeping my eyes wedged tightly shut and willing the world to stop spinning around me.

"I don't know exactly, but it feels like more than an hour. There's no way to tell in here. After the decontamination spray, the stuff on the walls just went back to blue, and no one's come in or opened the door. They did send in water orbs, though, if you think you can take a sip?"

As soon as he said the word water, thirst overtook me like a desert sandstorm. My throat was so dry it hurt, my lips felt cracked, and desperation to drink overtook me like I hadn't felt since—well, since I'd found Chrysanthe's locket and been misted with the green powder of death.

I tried again with the elbow and managed to lever my torso up off the floor, desperation giving me the power to push through the nausea. "Yes, please," I rasped, using my other hand to hold the shirt up to my chest as it tried to slide away.

I cracked one eye and watched as River reached over and plucked an orb off the bare floor, cracked the top, and passed it to me. Carefully, I lifted my palm from the floor, and accepted the water. I lifted it to my mouth and drank it greedily, the cool, fresh liquid like a balm to my poor, desiccated throat.

I drained it all in a single, long pull, then passed the empty orb back to River. He chuckled, and offered me a second, only half full. I eyed it for a moment, then shook my head.

"That one's yours. We don't know how much longer they'll keep us in here."

"True, but you just passed out. Whatever was in that stuff didn't agree with you, and this is all we have. You should drink it." He pressed it into my hand, but I set it down next to him, clenching my molars and giving him my most defiant look.

He sighed and shook his head. "Stubborn woman."

"Self-sacrificing man." The words slipped out, but the truth of them rang in my chest. He would sacrifice it all for someone else, and never think twice.

River rolled his eyes and dropped his gaze to the hand clutching the shirt against my chest. "Do you need help getting dressed?"

"No, just turn around again." I made the twirly motion with my finger, and he complied without argument.

I tugged the shirt on over my head—the thing was large enough it swallowed me and fell down to mid calf. I was fully covered even without the pants. When I slipped my feet into the pants and hauled them up, I was grateful that they were closer to size, and at least had a drawstring. Once everything was in place, I tugged out the ends of my braid, ran my fingers through snarled hair a few times, and pulled it back into a tight, fresh braid.

Between the water, clothes, and fresh hair, I was feeling back to myself again.

"Okay, you're good."

River turned back around and offered me a hand up, then passed me the Bronco's key to slip into my pocket. The strength of his much larger hand wrapped around mine was comforting as well as exciting, and a herd of camel-sized butterflies stampeded in my stomach. I hoped he couldn't see on my face how much I reacted to him these days.

He pulled me off the floor as if I weighed nothing, and I used my other hand to steady myself on his shoulder. My knees were a little shaky, but I felt solid enough. He smiled at me as we stood face to face.

"You have no idea how happy I am to see you upright and okay, even if you are too stubborn for your own good," he said with a soft smile.

"Too stubborn to die is not a bad thing," I argued.

He huffed a laugh but didn't pull his hand away. I swayed towards him as if magnetized, and his eyes dropped once more to my lips. He leaned forward, as if he felt the pull too as a bright white light sliced through the blue glow of our decontamination cocoon. We both whipped our heads around to the right, where the soldiers waited in their puffy white suits once more. This time, though, the helmets were down, and I could see the faces of the men—and one woman, towards the back—that had thrown us in here like so much dirty luggage.

"Come with us; the commandant would like to speak with you two." The man in the front—their leader?—was black, with close cropped hair and straight, white teeth. He had no expression, save a hardness in his eyes that screamed, *If you protest, I will take you out.*

I quickly scanned the other seven soldiers in his unit, and while they were all of various heights, complexions, and ages, the hardness wove through each of them like tainted fabric.

I drew myself up, and stepped forward, not willing to show any more weakness than what I'm sure they'd already seen through some hidden camera. "We'll be happy to speak with the commandant." I met the lead soldier's gaze, and he gave me a minute nod, turning to lead the way back out into the hall. The soldiers parted, none touching us this time. They surrounded us instead, marching in perfect sync down the wide, barren hallway. There were a few twists and turns, and we passed other groups of the marshmallow soldiers, none talking, none smiling, all moving like well-oiled machines on a mission.

Finally, he stopped at a conference room door, and lifted his water meter to tap a panel to the left of the door. He then spoke into his wristband, "Commandant, Excursion Team One has secured the unexpected arrivals. They are ready for you."

There was no reply for a long moment, and the leader stepped back, heading the formation of eight surrounding us like he was the tip of a spear. We stood there in the hall in unmoving silence for a minute, then two, and not one of the soldiers twitched or spoke. I glanced over at River to see if he was as creeped out as I was, but he was busy taking stock of the individuals. Looking for someone he thought he could overpower?

I remembered the woman at the back and turned around to see that she was indeed the very end of the formation. When I caught her gaze, her eyes narrowed, and she gestured with the barrel of her gun for me to turn back around.

I didn't get the impression that there was much leeway in these soldiers' lives. Hopefully, if Chace was in here, he wasn't part of the military force. I couldn't imagine him doing well under this level of stricture.

The door in front of us cracked open, revealing a middle-aged man in a sharp white suit, no hint of color except his assessing brown eyes, raking over me and River disparagingly. He turned those eyes to the leader.

"Thank you, Gabriel. A flawlessly executed mission, as always. You and Nanette can attend. Everyone else, at ease." He waved a hand in dismissal, then turned sharply on his heel and retreated back into his office. Gabriel turned to us and nodded that we should follow.

River waited for me to step ahead, and I took the lead. Chin up, eyes sharp, trader face on. I stepped into the office and found that the space was dominated by a floor-to-ceiling window, overlooking the scrub area outside. Though, rather than random spiny plants like we'd seen on the way in, a carefully-arranged arc of blooming cacti in varying heights stood outside, bringing in light and color that I hadn't noticed anywhere else in this place.

The other three walls of the room were completely bare, their flat white surfaces pristine and free of scuffs or wear marks of any kind.

The commandant crossed behind his desk and sat, leaning back in the chair and steepling his fingers as he looked at River and me. He didn't say anything, but the expression on his face made it clear that to him, we were nothing more than unwanted tumbleweeds to clear from his pristine city.

There were several molded plastic chairs arranged in front of the desk, but I stood and gripped the back rather than sinking into one. River took up a similar position to my right, but crossed his arms over his chest, causing his muscles to pop. One of these days I'd remember to ask him if that was habit or an intimidation tactic.

The commandant didn't waste time. He tapped his fingertips together a few times and spoke. "So, why are you here, and what do you want?"

"We believe that a relative is inside these walls. We've come to find him."

His eyebrows rose, and his fingers stilled. "Is that so?"

I nodded.

He pursed his lips like he'd tasted something foul. "And how did you come to know of this location?"

"Another relative sent us." I thought of the locket tucked under my shirt, and how Chrysanthe had given a password for her family.

It might have been stretching the truth, but I'd do what it took to get Chace, whether that was beg, borrow, cheat, or steal—I had a feeling Chrysanthe wouldn't mind in these circumstances.

"What relative could you possibly have inside who'd give you the location? There is no communication from our populace to the outside, except via the excursion teams. We've checked our records, and no one on any excursion team has come into contact with either of you. Therefore, this is a baseless claim."

He lifted his hand and gestured for the guards to come forward. "As such, you will be removed from the premises. If you return here, you will be shot on sight. If you tell others this location, they will likewise be shot on sight. You will have two hours to leave our sensor radius, or else we will fire on your vehicle."

I threw up a hand in the universal sign for *back up, buddy* towards Gabriel, who'd already taken a determined step forward. "Hold up, if I'm lying, then how do I know about Kokinos?"

Gabriel took another step forward, but the commandant lifted two fingers, and the soldier stopped in his tracks. The commandant narrowed his eyes, and I held my breath as he considered us. When he leaned forward, I had to strangle down the triumphant crow trying to fly out of my mouth, because I knew I had him. I didn't know *why*, but we weren't getting booted out of this place and that was all that mattered. *I'm coming for you, Chace.*

When he finally spoke, it was drawn out with all the menace of a diamondback rattler's hiss, "Do tell; how did you come to find out about that?"

I reached into the neckline of my shirt and lifted the locket out by the chain. "Like I said, a relative. And I would like to speak to Chace Brandt, as soon as possible."

A muscle in his jaw ticked, and it took all of my willpower to keep my trader's mask firmly in place. I didn't break eye contact, didn't move, didn't twitch, just stared him down and held my ground in silence.

"Take them to the C Barracks and post a guard. We need to check the veracity of this wild claim, and I must confer with the leadership panel before we decide what to do with them. Dismissed." He raised two fingers again, and both of our guards stepped aside to open the door, and ushered us out.

I was counting that a big fat win.

If the outside of the Bastion City was a jaw-dropping wonder, the inside gave me the heebie-jeebies and reminded me of photos I'd seen in a book on haunted mental institutions. While it was clean and, in theory, ghost-free, it looked more clinical than homey by any stretch. We twisted and turned through near-identical hallways long enough that I wasn't certain, but I thought we were on the far side of the building from where we'd parked outside the bubble. I was attempting to keep a mental map in case things went sideways and we had to get out of here on short notice, but it was difficult when the whole fracking place was identical. *Institutional.*

C Barracks was stark white, like everything else in this city, with a single green letter C for identification beside the door. The top of the oversized door was a window with fogged glass, but I couldn't see any shapes moving behind it. One of the other soldiers jogged ahead of our group to press a palm to a scanner, then pulled open the door to the barracks. I had to repress a groan when the inside was yet another white hall, this one filled with doors spaced at regular intervals.

Gabriel led us down the hall to the very back, and pointed to two doors, side by side. "One room or two? There's a double bunk in each."

"One," River spoke up immediately, and I cast a sideways glance at him.

Gabriel nodded, and pointed to the one on the right, against the wall. "This is you, then.

There will be two guards posted outside at all times. Meals will be delivered three times a day, no substitutions or seconds, so don't ask. Your water quota comes straight from the tap; there are glasses in the dorm. Should you be here more than three days, someone from bio-systems will train you on how to properly handle the composting toilet. Otherwise, we'll notify you if you're needed by the commandant again." He stood at parade rest, hands tucked behind his back, and eyes trained on us.

"Okay, then. Looks like we're on vacation for a few days, River." I strolled forward and pulled open the door but paused and looked over my shoulder at the soldiers, still arrayed in formation. "Do any of you know a man by the name of Chace Brandt?"

They stared straight ahead, none of them deigning to answer. I searched their faces carefully, but there was no sign of recognition on any of them. With a sigh, I walked into our new vacation-slash-jail-cell, River hot on my heels. The door swung silently closed behind us, and my stomach felt shriveled to a pit. We were in it neck deep now, and there was no turning back.

To my surprise, that afternoon we both slept. The room was unremarkable, a set of bunk beds with—shocker—white linens, a desk, chair, and a small bathroom. There was a slim floor-to-ceiling window set in the back of the room, showing us a narrow slice of the diverse plant life and the bubble. As suspected, we weren't looking out over the Bronco, but I couldn't confirm our direction, either.

When several hours later there was a double-rap on the door, I sat bolt upright and reached for my chest holster—which of course, wasn't there.

"Coming in, don't be naked!" a young, feminine voice shouted as the door swept open.

I leapt off the top bunk, and River sat up in his, not as quick to get moving as I was. A short, thin woman with brown hair backed into the room, hauling a bag along the ground, and balancing a tray over one shoulder.

"Thanks, guys, no need to hold the door, or help at all," she said, her sarcastic tone biting at the posted soldiers. They didn't respond, or turn, or blink. "Phew, you two got a real lively bunch out there. I'm Morgan, your keeper."

I just stared at her, unsure what to say.

"Oh, not you, too! Come on now, that was a good one. Why doesn't anybody appreciate my humor around here?" she muttered and kicked the bag to get it moving a little faster.

"Sorry, I was asleep; my brain isn't running at full speed yet. Did you say you're our *keeper*?"

She sighed. "It was a joke. I've been assigned to bring your meals and attend any needs while you're not allowed out. You know, you're the sad zoo animals but instead of everyone being allowed to come by and gawk, you just get to see a tiny strip of Spine City." She gestured to our window, and the cacti outside. "No? Nothing? Huh. I might be losing my touch. Anyways, hopefully it doesn't take long for you to earn your freedom. But, you two seem like the type that get into trouble, and frankly I don't like lifting heavy food trays. Dinner's up. Hope you're not too hungry. They keep us on tight rations around here. Although, rumor is you two came from the big empty, so you should be used to eating light, right?" She cocked out a hip and inspected us. "You do look different. Most lifers here look about the same, so it's easy to spot the transplants." She shrugged. "Where do you want the food?"

"Here, I can take that." River was on his feet, signature smile in place and crossing the room to lift the tray from her shoulder. "Thank you for bringing this. You're the first person who's spoken to us. Well, besides the commandant, and he wasn't in a welcoming mood."

I snorted at *that* understatement.

Her eyes widened. "You saw the commandant? So, you really are from outside, then? What's it like out there? She abandoned the bag of laundry, and perched on the edge of the desk, feet swinging.

"We are," I said. "It's hot and dry, mostly."

Morgan rolled her eyes and River snorted at my abrupt answer. I don't know why. It was *true*.

"Well, duh. But I mean, how do you *survive*? What do you eat? How do you find water, when supposedly there's none left outside the city? We all know there's some, since they've brought in transplants this year. But . . . nobody in the laborer class is allowed outside the dome. You're not creepy ocean-drinking mutants, are you?" She wrinkled her nose, and I once again questioned her age. She couldn't be more than fifteen.

River chuckled. "No, nobody that we know of is able to drink ocean water. We're actually from further east, so we've never even seen it until recently. It's pretty cool, even if it is purple and poisoned."

"You've seen the ocean?" She breathed out the question reverently.

"Yes," I interjected. "We've seen the Wastes, the ocean, two—wait, no—idiot brother Steve still counts—three gangs, and more abandoned cities than you can count.

Her eyes were as round as plates, and she clasped her hands together. "Could you tell me how you find water out there? The outside is *death.* If everyone wasn't so afraid of the outside . . . never mind." She shook her head, and refocused. "Could you teach someone how to find water?"

"That depends," I said cockily, intentionally popping out my hip in a mirror of her earlier pose and resting a hand on it as I looked over at River.

She narrowed her eyes, not buying my masterful setup. "On what?"

"If you can get us out of this room. I've got somebody I need to find."

Eighteen

Rebuff

Morgan left us in a hurry, a determined look on her face, and a promise to move things along on her lips. River and I unpacked our clothing—it was all there, and cleaner than it had ever gotten with Marl's laundry techniques, so, silver lining—and pulled the top off the tray of food she'd brought.

She wasn't kidding about small portions. Interestingly enough, there was the same green stuff we'd had with the Collective, and to my shock, *fresh produce*. At first, I didn't recognize any of it, but when I poked one of the small red things with a fork, it popped and seeds and juice oozed out, much like I'd seen back in Chrysanthe's mansion greenhouse.

"River, I think this is a tomato." Excitement rose in my chest at the sight. If these people were growing fresh food . . . they had water, and far more science than anyone outside. The bubble must do *something* good, besides look pretty.

"What's a tomato?" he asked, pinching the little red fruit between his thumb and forefinger before taking a tentative bite. His eyebrows flew up, and he scrunched up his mouth. "It's tangy. I'm not sure I like it."

"I'm not a hundred percent sure. It looks like something I saw once, in the same place I found the—" I stopped, and glanced around the room, conspicuously free of visible cameras. Though, the absence of *seeing* something meant nothing in this place. "Never mind. I've seen tomatoes before, but they were much, much bigger." I held my two fists up side by side to demonstrate how large they'd been in Armand's greenhouse.

"If they're growing fresh food, they've got a lot more inside these walls than we dreamed," River said in an awe-tinged tone.

"Yeah, but dates are better." He sat the remaining half of his tomato back on the plate and poked at the green stuff with his fork. "She wasn't kidding about *small portions*. You think everyone gets this little, or is it because we're prisoners?"

I shrugged. "Doesn't really matter, does it?" I stabbed my pile of greens and took a bite. The taste was still weird, but it was food, and I'd learned not to be picky in my long childhood of hunger and scrounging for scraps.

"I mean, yes and no. If they've really got this little to go around, why kidnap people? Presumably they visited more than just Coyote Springs." He grimaced as he chewed his next bite, but my mind was off and running. He had a good point. Was there really this little, or was it a control thing? We couldn't exploit their weakness if we didn't know what it was.

"We'll keep an ear to the ground."

He nodded and took a pointed sip from his water glass. "They have to be on tight rations. They have water metered per inhabitant. But, if water's not currency here—since they're presumably giving us room and board for free, right?—then how does their society even work?"

He was right, there was water rationing technology built onto the faucet in the bathroom, and we had to scan our palms to get any out. It even displayed how much there was left of your allotment for the day, on a display just inside the wall. I was using thirty percent less of my daily quota than River used of his, which confirmed that my hydration really was staying elevated longer than it used to, as I'd suspected. I still wasn't convinced they *had* to ration, though.

We talked through various scenarios as the sun sank and darkness fell over the strip of desert we could see out our window, but Morgan never returned, nor did we get summoned by the guards. As I lay on my back in the top bunk, listening to the soft sound of River's breathing as he slept below me, unease churned in my stomach.

I didn't like to be caged, and I didn't like being inside these walls and unable to find my brother. The little voice in the back of my head wouldn't shut up about the what ifs. What if he's not even here? What if they shoot you and toss you out of the bubble like so much trash? What if they leave you in here until you go crazy? What if, what if, what if. I tossed and turned, and finally succumbed to my exhaustion as the sky began to lighten in the distance.

Pounding completely unlike Morgan's polite double-tap woke me, and I couldn't contain my groan. My head was muzzy and throbbing, and I felt like I'd only been asleep for five minutes. I squinted out the window and realized that might not have been too far off reality.

River beat me to the door and pulled it open. A low, masculine voice rumbled, and I heard River respond. When the door clicked shut, I rubbed my eyes with the heels of my palms and waited for the news.

"We've been asked to speak with the leadership panel about our unsanctioned visit to the Bastion." River stopped right next to the bed, eye level with me even though I was in the top bunk.

"Okay, that's good, I guess. Progress."

"They want to see us now."

I sighed and shoved up off my back towards the foot of the bed. "They better want to see us after a tooth sanitizing tablet and a bathroom visit," I grumbled.

He chuckled, not put off by my grouchiness. "If you hurry, it should be fine. Though, I don't know about you, but I didn't think to bring any tooth tabs."

I groaned again and let my feet slap against the floor as I landed. "This city just keeps getting worse."

After five minutes of freshening up in the bathroom—which *did* contain a weird but effective goo called toothpaste—River and I were back in our own clean clothes and marching down the twisty hallways with our heads held high in the middle of Excursion Team One's formation. I was once again trying to fine-tune my mental map of the place when I spotted Morgan out of the corner of my eye, tucked just inside an intersecting hallway. She caught my eye and gave me a thumbs up. I elbowed River and used my eyes to point her direction, but she was already slipping out of sight.

We didn't have to go as far as the commandant's office this time; Gabriel's team stopped us just outside a different door. One of the men knocked rapid-fire on the door, announcing our presence. Within a single heartbeat the door was pulled smoothly open, and the soldiers parted for us to go in first. River nodded for me to take the lead, and I didn't hesitate. The first thing I noticed inside was a long, shiny wall of windows overlooking the lushest landscape I'd ever seen. Tall, towering trees, thick ropey vines, and even lush, low ferns warred with vibrant grasses to conquer as much of the available space as possible.

My step faltered, and I stared in utter disbelief out the window for a long moment, temporarily forgetting the people we'd come to meet. When I snapped back to myself, I noticed the looks on their faces ranging from amusement to irritation and all the way around to boredom. There were exactly thirteen of them if you counted the commandant, and they lounged around the room in artfully clustered chairs, all canted towards two seats in the middle of the room. It was meant to look casual, but it was clear we were going to be in the hot seats.

Unlike last time, the full complement of guards filed in, and lined up in a row behind us. They had neutral expressions on their faces but turning my back to armed enemies made the skin between my shoulder blades itch, nonetheless. I opted to stand in front of my assigned chair, and slowly gazed around the room, searching for potential allies and enemies.

No one had spoken yet, but body language could tell you a lot if you paid attention. The woman in the back corner was leaned away, arms crossed over her chest. She wasn't a fan of ours. A man in the middle of the room was avidly scanning our clothing—which stood out like a sore thumb in this room of pristine white—a curious look on his face. Curious could work in our favor *or* see us in a lab tested like rats; I'd have to keep an eye on him. I didn't get to finish my perusal before the commandant cleared his throat, drawing all eyes to him. He sat on the far end of the room, his chair's back squarely to the wall, one ankle casually tossed over his knee, and his suit jacket unbuttoned.

His sharp eyes belied the casual air he was putting on. "Thank you all for coming and thank you to our traveling guests for agreeing to meet with us."

As if we'd had a choice. I kept the retort sealed behind my teeth, where it couldn't get us into trouble before we'd found my brother.

"This meeting is unnecessary, as usual. We have a protocol for outsiders, and this isn't it. What I want to know is why you're wasting our time, when you should have simply executed the plan that's already been voted on in the past," a man at the opposite end of the room droned. Ahh, he was part of the bored contingent. Clearly we were imposing on his time.

"I'm acutely aware of the protocol, Josef. I felt that this situation was unique and brought along . . . extenuating circumstances." He held out a flat hand, as if serving them this reasoning on a platter.

"Well, let's hear it then. We've got duties to attend to." My eyes snapped to the studious woman in the middle of the room. Her facial expression was nearly as tight as her black hair, tied severely into a bun.

"Of course, Margaret. These travelers have come a great distance, and do not hail from our local area of the desert. In fact, the sand samples from their clothing prior to laundering have confirmed the story that they come from far to the east, well outside of our monitored range." He steepled his fingers, letting that sink in. "The reason that brings them, however, is even more unusual. They believe they have a familial connection to a member already inside of the Bastion, and this is what brings us here today. While our standard protocol would not allow them to remain, familial connections can supersede those decisions."

"So, which one of us are they related to? The man could be one of Dietrich's, I suppose. If you ignore the height difference. And the blonde hair. And the good looks." The man who'd been so interested in our clothing snickered.

Commandant Kieran raised a hand to stop the tittering and speculation. "Nyx, please inform the leadership panel of the code you were given to gain access to our illustrious city."

Unease, swift and all-consuming, reared its head. This was where the tire tread met the dunes. "Kokinos."

Silence, complete and eerie, filled the room.

The angry woman from the back right corner stood, her expression murderous. "There has to be a leak. There's no way. How could these two sand fleas know anything about a top-secret project that's been closely guarded. Our allies are not going to be happy to hear—"

"Celeste! Enough!" the commandant barked, and she stiffened, red hot fury creeping up her neck as she slowly sank back into her chair.

"Have you confirmed this wild claim?" The bored man on the left—Josef?—leaned forward, resting his elbows on his knees. It was probably not a good sign that we'd caught his attention.

The commandant scowled. "There is a procedure that must be followed, which is why you are all here. We need to take a vote on whether the *typical* procedure for outsiders is followed, or whether we make an exception, and verify this claim. I move—"

"Wait. Just hang on a second," I interrupt the commandant, and I can feel the weight of every person's eyes in the room settling on me at once. "You still haven't confirmed whether my brother is even inside your city. Chace—he's the reason we've come, and if you'll give him to us, we'll happily leave." I said the words with conviction, even as I had to fight not to let my eyes stray back to the beauty and wonder not ten feet away from me. If we left, I'd never see it again—but it would be worth the sacrifice.

Mr. Curious in front of us spoke up again, a gleeful expression on his face. "Is he one of the recent transplants? If so, how was the Koki-nos connection not found during the intake process?"

"It's possible, but—"

"Quiet, everyone!" the commandant snapped again, and the room fell silent, this time with much irritated shifting from the rest of the leadership panel. I took the opportunity to steal a glance at River, and his baffled expression told me he was every bit as in the dark as I was. "Before any state secrets are revealed, we *must* vote on how to proceed in this highly unusual circumstance. All in favor of continuing with standard protocol?" He paused, and only one hand went up—Celeste in the back corner, face red and fuming still. Commandant Kieran shook his head in annoyance. "All opposed?" The rest of the hands in the room flew up as one, and the curious looks they were all sending us made my skin crawl.

"As I suspected, the standard protocol failed to cover this scenario. They will not be sent back out." He shot a smug look over at the man who'd questioned him at the beginning, and continued. "Now. The question is, how do we proceed? We must verify this claim, but there are consequences. According to the law—"

"You can't seriously want to offer these two *citizenship*? Not with everything going on! We just took in new transplants; that's already upset the balance enough!" Celeste shot to her feet again.

My brain whirled as they argued. Transplants? Were those the kidnapping victims? How many had they taken, and what balance was she referring to?

"It was necessary, Celeste. Everyone but you could see it. The drift was already starting, and within two generations—"

"Oh, poppycock! The drift has been the guillotine hanging over us from the beginning, and we've managed *just fine* until now. Look around, Stephanie—it's just an excuse to bring in fresh laborers, when what we needed is more discipline!" Celeste's raised voice grew shrill, and I had to hide my wince. "This is what happens! You think your decisions are without consequence, but these two, right here—these are consequences! If you people hadn't been so fickle, we wouldn't be having this conversation. Just you wait. This is going to cause a ripple, and we'll be dealing with it for a decade. Mark my words!" She shook her finger angrily at the other woman, who rolled her eyes and sat back in her chair.

"I am *not* stating that they should be automatically given citizenship. You are correct, Celeste, in that the balance cannot take two more individuals at this time without severe consequences. *However*, the law does state that the blood testing is voluntary."

Josef snorted. "You've got to be kidding. If there is any chance the connection is real, they can't be allowed to leave without us knowing. I'm telling you now, if you allow that, I'll call for a vote." Josef looked around the room, meeting the startled gazes of the other leaders one by one, and when I looked back at the commandant, he was glaring down his nose at Josef.

"You do that, and you'll regret it."

River cleared his throat next to me, and I groaned inwardly. Now didn't seem like a good time to draw their attention back to us. "I'm sorry to interrupt, but what is this blood testing, and why would we need to do it?" He had on his best friendly smile, and I'm pretty sure everyone in the room fell under his spell, except Kieran and Josef, who refused to be distracted from glaring at each other.

Mr. Curious scooched forward to the edge of his chair, and leaned in to stage whisper, "It's a blood test to check your DNA compatibility and relational ties to every single human inside the city. If you're found to be a match to this relative, you would have grounds for citizenship, assuming they're in good standing. Though you would have to agree to the rules, and they are extensive." He shot a look over at Celeste, before pasting a wide grin back on.

"Okay, thank you. And why wouldn't we consent to a standard blood test, especially if it helped us find the relative that much more quickly?" River asked, his tone soothing.

The man laughed. "I like this one. I think we *should* offer them citizenship. Look at those *eyes*. Anyways, some people object to the rules. All new citizens must choose a way to serve the city, for the greater good. For the men, it's fairly straightforward. We have a laborer program. Seven years' good behavior, and you're eligible for other training and duties. For the women, it's a bit different. The laborer program can be quite strenuous, so, often they are placed in our reproductive pool."

"I'm sorry, *what*?" I interrupted, not liking where this conversation had taken a sharp left.

"Oh, our reproductive program is highly structured, and all citizens have to submit to testing. Genetic diversity is absolutely crucial for population longevity, so no births are allowed outside of the reproductive program. There's no funny business—if your genes are what we need, you'll go through clinical fertility treatments, and embryos created and stored in cryogenics. You don't necessarily have to act as the gestational carrier, though most opt to remain in the program rather than attempt to join the laborers."

"I—I—" River reached out and squeezed the back of my arm gently, and I snapped my jaw shut. Forcing the trader mask back in place.

"Perhaps we should discuss this further privately," the commandant said, and gestured with his chin for the guards to escort us out. I didn't even protest, simply turned on my heel, and marched toward the door with my chin up. My mind was racing, and I would have given anything to get out of that room. Except—

I snapped out my arms, bracing myself against the door frame.

"Wait! Will you confirm if my brother is in the city? You must know, if you don't get new people often. He's four inches taller than me, sandy hair, blue eyes. A really sarcastic streak, if you tick him off. Surely you'd know. I want to see him. I won't consent to *anything* until I see him," I demanded, leveling my gaze on the commandant. That muscle in his jaw ticked . . . and my mind stalled as it clicked into place that I've shown them exactly how to force me into doing what they want. Blast it all.

Mr. Curious visibly deflated, slumping back against the chair and dropping his arms to the side dramatically.

"Take them back to the barracks. Now."

At the commandant's snapped order, both of my arms were gripped by determined soldiers, and they lifted me easily from the doorway and carried me down the hall by my arms. River trotted along behind, not waiting for the same treatment. "Put her down, please. She won't fight. Right, Nyx? They can put you down."

I closed my eyes briefly, stuffing down the anger at the useless babble and red tape, but then I nodded. "Yes, I can walk."

The soldiers didn't put me down, though. They carried me all the way back to Barracks C, and all the way to the middle of our room before releasing me.

After they left, the indents from their fingerprints on my arms throbbed, but I barely noticed it over the rage pulsating in my chest.

These people had my brother, and they were going to do everything in their power to make sure I didn't find him.

Nineteen

Laborer Class

An entire day passed in a furious haze, nothing to break it up except the turn of the sun, and Morgan's three visits with food. She kept it short each time, but promised that she was working on something, a way to get us out to look for Chace.

By our third day in the room, I was pacing a track into the white flooring, my boots leaving smudges on the pristine floor, and deep down a part of me was glad. They wanted to cage me like an animal, and I wanted to strike back. Even if it was a small, petty thing. I tried to throw a chair through the window, but it didn't even scratch. So unsatisfying. Then River wouldn't let me try again.

My head was not in a good place. River noticed, but he was very polite about how cagey I had gotten in such a short amount of time. It was like we switched personalities. While out in the desert, I was content to lie around like an oversized lizard while he ran laps. Inside the same four walls, though? I couldn't hold still, and he stayed stretched out on the bed relaxing with his hands propped behind his head.

The impressive display of biceps distracted me every now and again, but I wasn't willing to cross any physical lines inside this room, which could have had cameras. *I'll pass on the audience, thanks.*

When Morgan's mid-day knock for lunch delivery came, I was surprised to see she wasn't holding a tray at all. I rounded on her, and it took everything inside of me to keep my arms at my sides, where they belonged. This girl hadn't locked us in here, but watching her come and go while we remained stuck was almost more than I could bear. Her mischievous grin, though, caught my attention and stilled my pacing for the first time all day.

"How would you two jailbirds feel about a wee little lunch tour?" She pinched her fingers together, leaving only a hairsbreadth between them.

"What kind of lunch tour?"

"Well, my Uncle Vander is on the leadership panel. You might remember him—he's rather more expressive than the rest. He certainly had a lot to say about you two." She arched a dark eyebrow as she took the two of us in. "He seems to think you're an item, but I'm still not sure and I've been coming in here for days. He was very disappointed I couldn't confirm that for him, and, in exchange for this little favor, he wants details on your relationship status."

I spluttered at the out-of-left-field question, "What does our relationship status have to do with anything?"

She shrugged. "Personally, I don't care. They've been locked in meetings twelve hours a day discussing your fate, and they are hotly debating whether your relationship status will impact your willingness to join the reproductive program. According to my uncle."

I just stared, floored by this information. They were keeping us locked in here for the sole purpose of debating hypotheticals? Fury, hot and swift, replaced all the blood in my veins. I kept my face neutral, but only through a Herculean effort.

River appeared at my side as if by magic and slipped his arm around my waist, tugging me into his side.

"Why don't we get going on this tour, and we can give you something juicy to tell your uncle. Perhaps like . . . 'Nyx's brother's in here, and we found him?'" He pasted on a lighthearted grin, but there was a faint edge to the words that raked across my skin in a delightful promise.

River was always so calm, so controlled—so happy. People often mistook that for harmless, but I knew better.

Morgan didn't seem to notice River's change in tone, though she looked pointedly at his hand on my waist. "Well then, let's go suss out a brother."

She strolled back towards the door, flinging it open with all the enthusiasm of youth. The two guards outside were surly but didn't say a word as she led us out of the room. As we walked past and exited the main entrance to the C Barracks, a knot of tension between my shoulder blades loosened. A quick glance over my shoulder found our guards following us at a respectful distance of fifteen feet, weapons drawn.

"So, which council member is your uncle?" River asked as we followed Morgan through the twisting hallways.

"Oh, Vander's a chatter. He's also very flamboyant at times. Not a favorite of some of the other members, but he's shrewd. The flamboyance is to put people at ease and distract them from what he's really up to."

"Mr. Curious," I mumbled, and River chuckled.

"I think we met him. He didn't give us his name, but he was definitely the most animated of the bunch."

We made a turn and found a huge door towering overhead with light pouring through the fogged glass. Morgan paused dramatically with her hand on the knob and turned to grin at us over her shoulder. "You two ready for this?"

I nodded, and I assumed River did too, because she turned back to the door and pushed. It glided open smoothly, and thick, warm air engulfed us. I sucked it in, and it was thick and syrupy in my lungs. I didn't think about that long, though, because the beautiful forest-like area in front of us captured all of my attention. There are trees. Real, live, green-leafed trees with thick, ropey vines, and was that . . .

"Are those birds?" I blurted out, stepping forward eagerly.

"Uh-huh. There are over a hundred varieties that live in here. You won't catch sight of many, because they mostly stay in the trees. But there are chickens and turkeys that wander the grounds. It is against the rules to touch or feed them, though, unless you're on the lifeside preservation team."

"Understood," River said quietly. I glanced over and saw that he was just as enraptured as I was, taking in the beautiful ecosystem ahead of us. Suddenly that decontamination process felt justified, as anger and awe began to war in my chest.

These people had preserved something so precious, and yet they had no qualms against destroying the rest of humanity. *Why?* Why could they value this life, but the rest of humanity's lives so little? It wouldn't mesh in my brain, and anger won out.

Though every step further Morgan led us into the lush, humid landscape thawed my heart towards the place just a little. Hundreds of varieties of plants flourished everywhere I looked, from small green mosses and ferns clinging to the sides and clustered around the bases of the trees, to weird, bumpy patches that Morgan told us were *lichens* clinging to leaf-bare limbs.

A well-trod stone path wove through the thicket of trees—some reaching more than forty feet overhead—and into a grassy plain up ahead. When I looked back, the curve of the path had swallowed the dull white halls behind us; for a moment I could pretend that none of the bureaucratic nonsense existed, and that I was truly in a magical forest.

Within a few moments, the trees thinned and we stepped out at the edge of a wide, grassy field. From that vantage point, we could see the vastness of the space, stone walking paths curving beautifully and intersecting across the green, many of them leading to a ring of benches underneath the largest tree we'd seen yet. Fat, purple fruits dangled from it, and mint-green leaves bigger than River's hands cast dense shade underneath.

"What kind of tree is that?" I asked reverently, eyeing the fruits.

"Fig. She's one of the largest trees inside, after a pine and a redwood. The pine struggles, even though it's the second."

"Why is that?" I asked, saddened by the fact that even in this piece of paradise, the plant life wasn't all thriving.

"Something about the roots not being able to go as far down as is natural for the tree? I don't know the science behind it all, but the dome extends down under the sand, and is fully enclosed. There is piping down into the aquifer, but besides that we're contained. According to our history, it did well at first, but as it grew it lost health. The tap root isn't able to run sufficiently deep." She shrugged one shoulder. "It's not parkside. I won't be able to take you to the lifeside today, but, maybe if you agree to do your citizenship stuff . . ."

"There's another side?" River asked, the awe clear in his tone. He'd squatted down and was reverently running his fingers through the blades of grass nearby. I was tempted, but still skeptical of this arrangement and wanted to stay alert.

Plus, out in the grassy area I could see other citizens wandering through. Some alone, or in pairs. I scanned each face eagerly for my brother, but so far I hadn't seen him. Though, this place was bigger than I'd realized from outside. And if this was only one *side* . . . the vastness of the task of finding Chace rattled my nerves and got me back on track.

"Any idea where we might find my brother, or the newest group of people brought into the city?"

She dropped her voice to a low whisper. "Oh, I wouldn't know *anything* about your brother, but we might be wandering past a group of new transplants on the way to lunch. Keep an eye out, but don't try to approach them."

With that warning still hanging in the air, she took a hard right, following a more direct path across the lawn, past—to my utter shock—a pond, with brilliant white flowers and placid lily pads floating on the surface. Through it all, sunlight poured in from overhead, seeming to multiply and refract as it hit the glass panes of the dome far above. We came out of the park and onto a more mundane-looking sidewalk on the other side. This part of the city wall was lined with what appeared to be market stalls. There were no signs, simply people in white behind white tables, with tidy boxes and bins stacked around with lines of customers stretching back from their tables. It was clinical and strange, compared to the wild, sandy market back in

Coyote Springs, each of the vendors wearing different scavenged clothing, and hollering out to the passersby.

We passed the stalls, though, once again without stopping. Morgan wove through the crowd a bit more than seemed necessary, mumbling as she went. "Sorry. 'Scuse us. Taking a tour. Watch out!" She elbowed that last one, a towering man who hadn't been inclined to let us pass. He grunted and scowled but didn't stop us from brushing past. Or move, so we didn't *have* to brush past.

Morgan sped up and tossed a warning quietly over her shoulder. "Hurry, and keep your heads down. We're taking an unsanctioned detour." She jogged past a corner stall surrounded by tables and chairs and cut down an alleyway behind it. Palming a scanner, she let us back into the twisting hallways of the city's walls and the three of us broke into a run as soon as we were clear of the door.

"It won't take long for the guards to catch us, and I can't promise you'll see him, but his laborer class is working on the pressure system today, and that's back here. The quicker we get there, the better chance there is you'll be able to spot him!" She slid something out of her pocket, and checked, then darted down a side hall.

We followed hot on her heels, and my heart thrummed in my ears as I ran. He was here. She

230

hadn't said it outright, but, if she knew where his work group was, that meant *Chace was here.* We rounded two more corners at a dead run, and then Morgan skidded to a stop in front of us so suddenly that I nearly bowled her over. River grabbed the back of my shirt and helped me stay upright as I flailed and skidded to stop short of the teen's back.

One heartbeat, then another, and I followed her gaze through a glass wall, amidst a tangle of pipes and tubing, some of which were bigger around than my torso, to a cluster of a dozen people in jumpsuits off to the side. Armed guards caught my attention first, weapons naked in hand as they strode around the perimeter of the group. Then a man off to one side heaved up a large stone and trundled to the side with it balanced on his shoulder. A woman, with a smaller rock, did the same. A bright red stain on the back of her white, one-piece jumpsuit made me blink, and then again.

"Is that blood?" I whispered, horror and agony crawling up my spine like twin serpents.

"Probably. The women often struggle to keep up, and they try to persuade them into the reproductive program."

River growled beside me. "*Persuade* them? Are you blind? Half her back is drenched in blood. What the hell do they consider persuasion around here?" His angry snarl matched my feelings perfectly.

She looked guilty, but only shrugged and cast a nervous glance over her shoulder.

I scanned each straining, sweating—and often bruised—face desperately, both hoping and not hoping to find that one, familiar chord amongst the group that was Chace. A man at the front edge with his back to us straightened, a massive rock clutched in front of him, and he took laborious steps towards the pile off to the side. As he turned, his profile made my breath catch. The set of his mouth, the look of determination on his face, and that dishwater blonde hair . . . I took a step forward, squinting to be sure, but he was undeniable. My heart pounded, and my feet moved without my consent. I shoved past Morgan, who hissed at my back, "No, Nyx! Don't approach him!"

I ran, heart in my throat, up to the floor-to-ceiling glass wall, and screamed out, "Chace! Chace!" and pounded my flat palm on the glass.

My brother froze, his back stiffening as he dropped the boulder and turned, a jolt of awareness passing between us as our eyes met across the sterilized space. He looked awful—his hair was chopped short and a purple bruise covered his right eye and half of his cheek. He'd clearly been hit, and he looked like he'd *lost* weight, which I wouldn't have expected in a place like this.

He was still, and then he wasn't—bolting across the floor towards me, bellowing something. It took a moment to sink in, but rage twisted his facial expression as he charged towards me, away from the gawking workers and guards. "NOT MY SISTER! YOU CAN'T HAVE HER! NO! RUN, NYX! RUN!" The words finally sank in, and I pounded the glass, frantically looking for a door to the pressure room. I spotted it, all the way at the end of the hall, and gestured wildly towards it as I began to run. He adjusted course for the door, and I kept darting glances over at him.

The guards had recovered from their shock, and ran after Chace as he dodged and leapt under the towering pipes. He was still bellowing at me to run, hide, *leave*, but I ignored him, only focusing on the door. I needed to get to the door, throw myself into his arms and drag him bodily out of there.

He made it free of the tangle of pipes, but the guards were gaining on him. He was slower than I remembered, even pumping his arms and throwing everything he had into it. I reached the door and yanked on the handle, but it was locked up tight, a palm reader blinking placidly to the side.

"No, no. Come on. Morgan! Morgan, I need your hand!" I screeched, still yanking on the door. River had caught up to me, lending his strength, but the stupid door didn't even wobble in its frame.

Chace was close, only twenty feet away and at a dead run when I saw the first guard take aim.

"Look out! Chace, look out!" I screamed and pointed behind him, but he didn't waver. His eyes left mine and landed on a red emergency panel just inside the door. He angled towards it as the officer fired, whatever he'd shot glancing past and thudding into the wall. My breath caught in my throat. A faint tendril of hope twisted in my heart that Chace would make it to that panel, and that the door between us would fly open. *Come on, come on.* The second guard, however, pulled a blocky-looking weapon from his holster, and dropped mid-stride to his knees to aim lower on Chace's body. The thing fired, and a length of rope flew out, spinning through the air with cylinders on each end.

The rope hit the back of his calf, and Chace's entire body locked up as the weighted ends flew around and around, sticking to his leg like glue. His frozen frame dropped to the ground, not ten feet from the door.

"No, Chace! Come on, get up! I love you! Please!" The last word came out a broken sob.

His whole body was frozen and jerking, eyes rolling wildly in his head as the first guard loomed over him and lifted his weapon.

"No! Stop! Don't shoot him! Please!" I screamed and beat the glass door with my bare knuckles, the shrill sound splitting my own ears as tears coursed down my cheeks.

The guard didn't hesitate, lifting the weapon and shooting him square in the chest. Chace's body fell limp and his eyes rolled back in his head. His only movement was a periodic jerking, still coming from whatever that rope was around his ankle and calf.

"Chace!" I sobbed, shoving away the hands trying to pull me. "Stop it! Stop it!" I pleaded as River wrapped both arms around me, pinning mine to the side and hauling me away. The second guard walked stiffly over and kicked Chace in the thigh, before saying something into a comm device. As River and Morgan carried me away down a narrow side hall, he didn't move again. And then, we were through another door, and he was lost to my sight. The sobs racked my body all the same, and I dropped my head to River's shoulder, letting them course free.

Twenty

Regroup

Our guards caught us and hauled us back to our room. Morgan was dragged off in another direction, by a stern-faced black-haired guard gripping her by the upper arm. Gabriel and his team met us somewhere within the halls and formed up in their familiar circle around us as we were directed back to the C Barracks. I saw this in flashes, from where River carried me.

It didn't matter. None of it did. They'd just felled and shot my brother in front of my eyes. Nothing mattered anymore. Nothing but *revenge*. Underneath my sorrow, rage formed a simmering pit of hatred just below my breastbone.

We were taken back to our room, all the way in the back of the barracks, and Nanette was the one to close us inside. Our eyes met as she swung it shut, her hard gaze clashing with my burning one. She didn't blink as the door cut off my fury.

River carried me across the room, kicking off his boots along the way. Wordlessly, he sat me on the edge of his lower bunk, stripped off my boots, and pointed for me to lie down. I curled onto my side, facing the wall. But when I expected to hear him walk off to the bathroom, or maybe climb up into my bunk, he didn't. He scooted in next to me and wrapped himself around me. In the protective cocoon of his warmth, I cried.

No one came to our room that night, and by the next morning, ravenous hunger was our constant companion. Worry for Morgan—who'd only done what she'd done to help me—was running a close second to the anger over their treatment of my family. Surely no harm would come to a fifteen-year-old girl over this?

I didn't know, and once again I found myself pacing.

"I don't think he's dead," River murmured, watching me from his place on the side of the bed. I stopped, and turned to look at him, confusion warring with hurt in my chest.

"Did you not see the same thing I did? They electrocuted him, and then shot him point-blank in the chest. How could he possibly survive that?"

He shook his head. "I saw that, but whatever they shot him with . . . it seemed to be a drug of some kind. Not to be too graphic, but there was very little blood. I suppose whatever was in it could have killed him, but if they'd shot him with a normal bullet, there would have been more blood. I think they tranquilized him. I've been thinking about it all night. If they killed people every time someone acted out, how would they ever integrate new people?"

I chewed on my bottom lip, thinking it over. A seed of hope bloomed in my chest, and I began pacing with renewed vigor, despite the camel-sized hunger stomping around in my stomach.

"That still wouldn't be good, but alive is better than the alternative."

"I think he's okay, Nyx. Not happy—he *really* didn't want you here." Worry permeated River's tone, and I stopped to look at him, *deeply* look at him for the first time. His shoulders were low, his face grim, and his eyebrows were slashed down, hooding his worried eyes. My bright, humorous man wasn't taking this any better than I was, for all that he'd just given me a tiny ray of hope. I touched my water meter, processing his sudden change of mood.

"Why do you look so freaked out?"

"Besides the fact that we just saw how they were treating the "laboring class" and what they did to your brother?" he asked.

I nodded, focusing on his body language.

"Nyx, I've said it before, but did you ever consider that maybe Chace left you behind on purpose?"

I sucked in a startled breath, and now I was angry for another reason. "River, we've been over this, there is *no way*—"

He held up a hand and interrupted. "To protect you. Not because he wanted to go. But because he didn't want them to know you existed. There are hardly any records of births or deaths anymore. They had no way of knowing he had a sister—not until we got here—if he didn't tell them. You two had different dads, right?"

I nodded, mind whirring at the possibility.

"He probably knew what was going to happen. You saw those people, Nyx. They were beat up, not one of them looked to be in good health, and they were doing hard physical labor under guard. Bastion City has working *jets*, so I don't buy that they don't have machinery to move those rocks. They're trying to break them." His tone was dark, and my mood matched.

What he said made sense, and I'd been too heartbroken to think it through. That could get me killed. I knew my way around a desert, an abandoned building, and low-level gang bangers. These people were every bit as relentless and abusive of their power as King and the Sidewinders, but they hid it behind a veneer of civilization and scientific wonder.

I ground my back teeth and clasped my fingers together behind my back so tightly that my bones hurt.

I had to push my emotions out of the way, and analyze this with a clear head, or I'd have no chance to get us *or* Chace out of here. But there had to be a way. There was no chance in the god-forsaken Wastes that I would leave this place without Chace. They'd have to kill me first. And if River was right, if Chace had disappeared in the dead of night to protect me, only to have me wander into this beautiful prison of my own free will, well . . . that wouldn't do.

Two timid raps on the door froze me in my tracks and pulled River to his feet. We stood shoulder to shoulder and faced the door, waiting for Morgan's friendly face.

But it wasn't Morgan. A thin man in his early twenties stepped in, the usual tray on his narrow shoulders, head ducked so as not to make eye contact.

"Good morning, I have your breakfast rations here. The leadership panel is still deliberating, and unfortunately you won't be allowed to leave again until they've reached—"

I strode forward and snatched the tray out of his hands. His head flew up, terrified eyes meeting mine.

"Where's Morgan?"

"Who?" he asked but wouldn't meet my eyes. *Yeah right, buddy. You know who.*

"Don't play games with me. You'll lose. You tell the leadership panel that this ends today. They let us out of here, or we starve. This is their notice. Now, if you'd be so kind, step aside for a second when you open the door to leave."

"You won't be able to escape, even if I step to the side. And I'm afraid the leadership panel doesn't negotiate, so you will need to keep your strength up until they've decided what to do with you."

"Just humor me."

He backed slowly away, glancing between me and River, silent and steady as a rock at my side. When his hand was on the doorknob, I called a reminder.

"Don't forget to step to the side and tell them we don't want anyone back besides Morgan."

He ducked his head and pulled the door open. For a moment, I thought he would ignore my request, but when he stepped out of the door, he left it open, and turned and walked out of the way. Before one of the guards could lean in and close it, I reared back with the covered tray, and threw it with all my power straight out the door. The lid flew off in the middle of the hallway, and green plant matter and delicately trimmed fruits flew and spattered across the far wall. The tray itself bounced off with a satisfying crack, and a guard leapt to shut the door.

I raised my voice and called again. "This ends today!"

I stalked back into the room to pace some more, and River crossed his arms and sighed. "Did you have to throw out the food? I'm starving. Besides, how are we going to stage an escape on empty stomachs?"

"They want us. For free labor and for their reproductive program. If we starve to death, they can't have us. They'll fold, and then it'll be time to deal."

"Deal?"

"Everybody wants something, River. It's time we practice the art of the win-win."

His eyebrows climbed up skeptically, but he didn't push me further.

A full day passed and they sent a new person in to deliver the tray each time. And each time, we refused to speak with them, and I chucked the tray out behind them, untouched.

That spot in the hallways was scrubbed shiny, a hint of gray concrete peeking through the paint where it had been scrubbed too hard. There was still a green smear on it, and I found that more satisfying than I should've.

Was it logical? No.

Was it all I had? Yes.

The next morning, a swift double-tap on the door came, and I slid carefully down from my top bunk to see who it was this time.

To my pleasant surprise, it was Morgan. And then I watched her walk in, and all pleasantries went away. She wore a white tank top, and a ring of bruises in the shape of fingerprints marred her upper arm. She was also limping and moving much more slowly than usual—she was clearly in pain, though no other injuries were visible.

"What happened to you, Morgan? Are you okay?"

She laughed and dropped the tray on the desk. "You should see the other guy." She winked, but the wince that replaced it when she leaned her hip against the side of the desk told me all I needed to know.

"Those mother—"

River cut me off. "Nyx, let's let her talk."

"Yes, please, tell us what's happening," I ground out, and then clenched my teeth shut. *Calm, collected, trader mask.* Maybe if I repeated it to myself enough times, that sense of calm would come back to me.

"I was punished for taking you off the approved track, but my uncle made sure it was kept light. They're all ticked off that you know your brother's here, and that they had to subdue him. His cohort of transplants has been rioting almost nonstop since they hit him with the neural agent, and four more of them have had to be given the same treatment to get them to stop. They're also pissed that you're not eating, and don't like feeling like you're forcing their hands. Personally, I say keep it up." There was a hard glint in her eye, and I knew she was a kindred spirit.

I crossed the few feet between us and gingerly hugged her. She froze a minute and then wrapped her arms around my middle and returned the embrace. She felt so small in my arms, so fragile. And they'd hurt her. When I stepped back, it was with determination.

"Thank you for risking yourself to help me find my brother. I owe you a debt, and I won't forget it," I promised. "If we're able to get out of here, I'll take you with us, and teach you how to survive in the desert. If you want to go, of course. There's nothing else like this place on the outside, and it is a hard life."

"Better a hard life on your own terms than to have no choices."

"Amen," River agreed.

"So, are they going to bring us back in?" I asked, getting back to the matter at hand.

She shrugged. "I don't know. How determined are you to stick to this no eating plan?"

"Highly."

"Well, get busy chucking this out the door, and we'll see what happens." She shrugged. "I was told to convince you to eat, but instead I'll remind you that they can monitor your water intake from the faucet, and that humans can live a very long time with no food." She nodded once, and then half-strolled, half-limped to the doorway.

"River?"

"My pleasure." He hefted the tray and Morgan gave us a mocking salute before flinging the door wide and getting out of the way.

River sent it flying with even more force than I had, the metal dome clanging into the wall with the discordant notes of a broken bell as the greens-laden breakfast flew through the air like limp shrapnel.

"That was every bit as fun as it looked." River smirked as an irritated guard pulled the door shut, and once again, we waited, hunger our constant companion.

Twenty-One

The Dotted Line

After eight hours of no water—and my hydration meter reading below eighty percent for the first time in a *long* while—Morgan once again appeared at our door. She was moving slightly better this time, and I hoped that meant she'd been given some medical aid for her injuries. She didn't come in far this time, though.

"I have to ask you to come with me," she said, face grim.

"What's wrong?"

She sent a pointed glance at the familiar faces of Excursion Team One hovering over her shoulder and didn't answer.

River and I walked out behind her side by side, and they swallowed the three of us into the middle of the group. My stomach growled loudly, breaking the staunch silence, and River smirked over at me. I resisted the urge to do something *really* mature, like stick my tongue out at him.

We were led directly to the same room where we'd originally met the leadership panel, and they'd all taken their same spots. Apparently, order and routine were big with this group. So was child abuse, slave labor, and blowing up other cities just trying to scrape by, so, really . . . they were swell.

I stood tall and said a silent prayer that my stomach wouldn't make any more noise in the middle of this meeting. I had a lot of ground to cover, and I needed every scrap of my professionalism to get through it.

Commandant Kieran sat at the far end of the room, that ankle crossed over his knee so flippantly. He hadn't spoken a word—his fingers lazily rested against his mouth and covered his expression—and already I wanted to stomp over and shove that ankle off his knee and tell him to sit up straight and *take us seriously*.

The door clicked shut behind us, with only Gabriel and Nanette standing inside shoulder to shoulder to keep an eye on us.

To my surprise, the man we suspected to be Morgan's uncle Vander was the first one to speak. He had a broad grin on his face, and he nodded to his niece. She wiggled her fingers at him but didn't interrupt his opening foray.

"Well, it's lovely to see you two again. I hear you've gone on a bit of an *unsanctioned* field trip?" He glanced between River and me, and River bobbled his head side to side, neither confirming nor denying the statement.

"Right, well, we're all hopeful"—he used his hands to gesture in big circular motions around the room—"that after getting to see a bit more of Bastion City, you're willing to accept this generous offer, which we have worked over diligently for the last few days." He smiled warmly, and I almost, *almost* believed it.

"Now, typically there is no contact between new members of our reproductive and laborer classes, however, since you two have come in together, we are willing to make a very generous exception in your case. The two of you will be assigned one of our couple's apartments, overlooking the park—a highly desirable location, which has a several-year waiting list typically—and at the end of each day's contributions to our small eco-society, you will be able to retire to your mutual quarters. This is, of course, assuming you don't have testing or other assignments as part of your reproductive responsibilities." He leaned forward, a glimmer of excitement in his eyes as we quietly let him finish. "The only thing standing between you two and a beautiful life that people out in the Wastes would never dream of is our DNA testing—it sounds scary, but it's just a few blood draws—mandatory birth control implants for you, River, and eventually you as well, Nyx, if you choose to leave the reproductive class when your time is up. Do you two have any questions?" He brushed it all aside so quickly, it caught my attention. He was hiding something important, but what?

I looked over at River and gave him a little nod, so he swayed on the balls of his feet and began peppering the man with questions while I wracked my brain over what it was the man wanted to brush under the rug.

"What's the currency here, if everyone receives the same amount of water?" River asks, curiosity in his tone.

"There isn't a formal currency per se, as we all work together for the common good. However, our working class citizens, if found to go above and beyond, are rewarded with extra water quotas, and occasional other perks—like access to a luxury shower, up to twice per month, or increased access to other, nicer goods."

I wonder how often the leadership panel gets to make use of these luxury showers? I brushed the bitter thought aside and continued thinking it over. Mandatory birth control was a big one. Freedoms being chipped away, bit by bit, seemed to be the MO here. But was that such a big deal, in a world where so many children died? I wasn't guaranteed to get to have kids, even if I wasn't inside these walls. It rankled, but ultimately the most important thing was to get Chace out of here, whatever the cost. Surely it wouldn't be permanent, right? I tossed that possibility aside.

River continued to distract them with questions so I could think. "I see. And how long would I be a member of the laborer class, before I could move on to a higher-level job, such as, say, security?" He cast a pointed glance over his shoulder at Gabriel and Nanette, who stood stony-faced and silent, as usual.

"Clever man. Laborer class requirements can be anywhere from four to ten years, depending on your work ethic and performance."

I was missing *something*. But what? I resisted the urge to drum my fingertips against my thigh.

River cut his eyes over at me, then asked, "Is it the same for a woman on the reproductive team? Also, what would, say, punishments be if my performance were *lackluster*?"

Vander's eyes narrowed, and he cast a quick glance over at the commandant before answering. "Yes, women on the reproductive team can serve anywhere from four to ten years. They most frequently transition to lifeside duties when they complete their service. That involves food production, animal husbandry, and numerous other tasks taking place in the life-side structure. And as far as punishments, I don't think that's a concern in your case; you're such an affable fellow."

"And less affable fellows? What about them?" I cut in, the edge on my voice sharp enough to cut him out of his well-tailored white suit.

The look he gave me was patronizing, and I realized it was best not to waste any more time. I was hungry, angry, and ready to get to the brass tacks. "Or we could go with a better option. You take us on as something more *useful* than a rock mover and an embryo donor. We work as emissaries and bring trade into the city. Give you people a little more *color*." I ran an intentionally scathing look down their bland clothing. "I'm sure that in a city this size, you burn through resources rapidly, for all you've got a lot. Whatever you need, I can get it. I'm somewhat of a . . . procurement specialist. I've been training River for several months, and he is more than qualified to work alongside me."

"And what might you want in exchange for the use of these talents? We've already offered you the best accommodations available, and I have to admit—it would be highly unorthodox. Every new member of Bastion City must pay their dues, and we don't much engage with the outside populace—"

"Dues? Is that what you're calling slavery and abuse? Because, really, I think you need an updated dictionary. The conditions we saw were nothing short of *barbaric* and I'm not dumb enough to believe that you want us here so desperately to move rocks." I spat the words with more venom than I intended, and clamped my lips shut as I struggled to regain my impassivity.

Wait. Suddenly, all the pieces coalesced in my brain, and I shot a look at River.

"But you don't actually want us here to give you babies and free labor. You want us to think so, but that's not what you want at all, is it?"

Vander straightened in his seat, and the sound of panel members shifting in their seats echoed in the suddenly still room.

"Besides, you have a carefully controlled population size, and you *kidnap* the people you need to fill in the ranks. If you needed two more people, you'd have taken them a few months ago, right along with my brother. But you *didn't*." I narrowed my eyes at Vander, who'd gone pale, and turned toward the commandant. He still held his casual pose, but his back had stiffened, and it no longer looked natural.

"Why don't you tell us what you really want, Commandant?" I demanded.

River shifted slightly, putting his shoulder between me and the commandant, as if that would save me from danger. I knew it was pointless, but I loved him for it anyways.

The commandant dropped his hand gracelessly to the arm of his plush white chair and leveled an icy gaze on me. Everyone else was so silent, you could have heard the quiet hiss of a water orb sealing a mile away.

"You're right, we don't need more muscle, or another person for our reproductive team. We're not sure we need you at all, but according to our laws, we have to offer you citizenship to find out." He spat the words like they tasted foul.

"What is that supposed to mean?"

"You came here claiming Kokinos; kinship with Chrysanthe, one of the great founders of this place. We need to verify this claim through DNA, but we cannot without your consent. I was willing to brush it aside as coincidence, some writing you'd found or swindled from a ne'er-do-well in the Wastes, except you've got that locket."

That was a hair too close to the truth for comfort. I resisted the urge to shift on my feet.

He pointed at my neck, where the silver chain disappeared beneath my tunic.

"Excursion Team One's scans found a match for it, from the private collection of Chrysanthe herself. She has no living relatives inside these walls, but we have a sample of her DNA on file, as we do for all citizens, so we can verify your claim."

"And why does it matter? If I'm not really a relative, the password doesn't work?"

"It does not."

"If you're kidnapping people anyway, why does it matter if we have a password? So what if we're her long lost relatives?"

"Your brother Chace *isn't*. But it has been pointed out by my astute leadership panel that you two have highly different features, and likely didn't share both parents. The chances are infinitesimal, but we must investigate the veracity of this claim."

"You're just going to skip over the *why* part of the question?" I snarked, even though I shouldn't have. Something about his *pretend* gentility pissed me off. *Evil marshmallow overlord.*

"As I stated before, it's written into our bylaws that relatives of all founding families must be granted an offer of citizenship. You will receive all of the benefits of living in this oasis of civility. We're offering you much in exchange for very little: your agreement to abide by the same rules of every citizen here. No more, no less."

"No deal." I said the words calmly, and maintained eye contact. His eyes narrowed, but he didn't look away or blink. "If being related to Chrysanthe is so important, I should get something important in return for following your *stipulations*. I'm not joining your baby-making club, and my brother's not part of your laborer class anymore, and we get regular visits. We'll do honest work for you—source something you need, set up trade avenues, even, with some of the other desert dwellers. But when your first round of trade goods arrives, you let all three of us leave, *unharmed*."

Vander cut in, incredulity ringing in his tone, "Why on earth would you want to *leave*, Nyx? There's nothing out there; you of all people should know! This is the most bio-diverse, thriving place left on the planet. There is nothing out there except strife, death, and *sand*. This is an opportunity that anyone else in your shoes would kill for!"

"Not everyone. And I'm serious. We don't want to stay. You agree to our terms, you promise to let us leave, or you don't get our DNA, we don't follow your citizenship rules, and we continue our strike. I don't know how long it'll take for thirst to kill us, but we're what—nine, ten hours in now? Don't take too long to decide. I don't have any kids, so there's nobody else for you to chase down for this DNA."

I spun on my heel and gestured for Nanette to open the door. She didn't, of course, until she looked over and received a nod of approval from the commandant.

Morgan joined us outside the door and Excursion Team One escorted the three of us back to the C Barracks and sealed us inside once more.

Morgan rounded on us, excitement in her tone. "You really don't want to stay? There's something out there worth going to?"

"No, I really don't want to stay." A horrifying thought struck me, and I grabbed River's hand. "Do you, River? I should have asked before I told them I was taking you with me."

He gave me a reassuring, lop-sided smile, flashing that dimple in his right cheek. "Where you go, I go. That hasn't changed."

"Can you tell me about the outside? Like, how do you find water? What do you eat? Are there other people out there? Well, you came from somewhere, so there have to be people. Do they all live in a city like this one? Where is the city, and has anyone from the Bastion ever made it there?"

"Whoa, whoa, whoa," River teased. "One question at a time so we can get through them all." He settled down on the edge of the bed and leaned forward to rest his elbows on his knees. Morgan sank into the desk chair, and I leaned against the back wall, where I had a line of sight on the door. "Now, what do you want to know first?" he asked, and we started again.

It only took an hour of answering Morgan's endless stream of questions before a tablet containing *terms of acceptance* was brought to our door. Morgan was ushered out before they'd allow us to see it, and that concerned me. What was in here that they didn't want us to discuss with her? River and I sat cross-legged on the floor, our backs against the bed frame as I held the tablet between us, and we carefully scrolled through.

It seemed pretty straightforward, and mostly matched what we'd demanded in the room, although they'd rejected removing Chace from the laborer class, or allowing continued visits—there was a note about unwillingness to cause strife amongst the remaining laborers. It made a wary tingle zing up my spine that they'd just accepted all of our other terms. They *really* wanted to DNA test us. Well, me. River was along for this unfortunate ride by default.

Once we reached the end of the terms, we sat and stared at each other, indecision hanging thickly in the air.

"There's got to be a catch. We don't know enough to know what it is," I grumbled, once again swiping back up to the top of the page, ready to read it through for a third time. River reached out and captured my hand, pulling my finger away from the screen.

"Nyx, if they want your DNA so bad, what's to stop them from taking it if we turn down this deal? They're big on looking civil, but we already know that they're not. This might be the best offer we get, even if we *are* missing something. If it says in there that all three of us get to leave after we deliver on trade goods, Chace won't be getting beaten anymore, and all we have to do is let them take a blood sample and set up trade, well, I think we need to take this deal."

I pursed my lips, digesting his words. He wasn't wrong, even if my inner trader could smell something off. I just didn't know *what*, and what you don't know very much *will* kill you in the desert. I worried the same applied to technologically advanced, militant government compounds, as well.

But did I really have a choice? I could accept these seemingly advantageous terms, or I could get nothing, and they'd take what they wanted by force.

Or blow me up, like they originally threatened.

With a sigh, I pulled my hand out of River's, scrolled down to the bottom, and signed the terms with my finger. River did the same, and a big green checkmark appeared on the screen, before it went dark.

River grinned and hopped to his feet. "Well, now that that's settled . . . let's get something to drink. I'm parched."

Twenty-Two

ADRIFT IN A SAND SEA

The next morning, Morgan arrived early with our breakfast tray, and two white satchels. "You two are moving out of the Barracks today, so eat up and let's get this show on the road."

"Where are we going?" I asked while shoveling the formerly-gross-but-now-tasty greens into my mouth. They were weirdly addictive after you got used to them.

"Ahh, well . . . remember that fancy apartment overlooking the park they mentioned?"

"Yes . . .?"

"It's not there. Apparently your renegotiation meant they got to renege on that. But, you are still together, at least, and they're not sending

261

you to the laborer quarters or the reproduction hospital wing."

"Well, that's still a step up from the initial proposal," I grumbled, finishing my meal with a little less vigor.

She laughed. "The initial proposal is usually, 'Come with us quietly if you don't want to die,' so I think you're right. We have to make a couple of stops along the way. These are for your stuff." She tossed each of us one of the white bags, but we didn't have much to put in them. River finished his food first, so he walked into the bathroom and came out with our new tooth-brushes, and the gooey tub of toothpaste. The sight reminded me of something I'd forgotten to negotiate for.

"Hey, what are the chances we'll be allowed to retrieve more belongings from our Bronco, now that we're going to be official citizens?"

She frowned. "Uh, good question. Usually no one goes outside the wall at all. What's so important?"

"Well, all of our stuff is out there. But I'd love to stop using the weird tooth goo. My tablets from home are a lot nicer."

"You don't have toothpaste?"

"No, and that stuff's gritty . . . and slimy."

She made a confused expression. "Are you wetting the toothbrush, and then rinsing your mouths after?"

River and I just stared, first at her, then each other. When River shook his head no, she rolled her eyes. "That's how you're supposed to use it. It doesn't stay on your teeth. You rinse it out and spit it down the basin."

"You spit out perfectly good water?" I asked incredulously.

River put a hand on my arm to stop my squawking about their wastefulness. "It's still weird, but we'll try it. Can you ask about us getting let out sometime soon, at least?"

"Sure. They're going to say no, though. And if they say yes, everything you bring *in* will have to be decontaminated."

I grimaced, remembering the horrible, body-wracking reaction I'd had to the decon room. "We'll make do for now."

Our apartment sucked. The little holey tent the red riders had given us was more spacious, and at least came with cutlery and a breeze. This place was a glorified closet, with no windows and a set of metal bunk beds barely wider than I was. River's shoulder hung off the side if he lay flat, even when his other touched the wall.

We did have a private bathroom, but it had a toilet, a pedestal sink with a small square mirror above it, and a single bulb for illumination. There wasn't a spare foot of space in it, either.

Somehow, we'd gotten our semi-freedom, and gotten put into a worse housing situation than the barracks jail. At least it was a different set of walls to look at, and we weren't locked in. I hoped. After we dropped our near-empty satchels off in our rooms, we stepped back outside where Morgan and our two silent escorts still waited.

"What do you think of the new digs?" she asked, as she led the way towards the medical center.

"They're smaller than my Bronco."

"Really?"

"No, but it's close. And the Bronco has windows."

"Windows are nice," River agreed, scanning our surroundings closely as we walked. We were on the opposite side of the compound from the C Barracks, just inside the city walls. There were only two turns between our room and the courtyard, so hopefully we'd be able to find our way back after our tour was over. A muted bell tone echoed through the cavernous space, and Morgan froze mid-stride.

Morgan snorted. "Well, regardless, you should be happy. That part of the city is old, and there are at least no cameras or monitoring equipment, like in the barracks holding rooms. You finally have some real privacy."

I knew they'd been monitoring us before.

An AI voice spoke in the same register as the tone. "All citizens, please report to the gate. All citizens, please report to the gate."

"Oh crap," Morgan breathed, and made an abrupt turn.

"What's wrong? Why are we all going to the gate?" River asked as we turned to follow her now-hurried footsteps.

"There's only one reason we go to the gate," she said, keeping her voice low as people poured out of the doorways and the park area on both sides of us.

"Which is . . . ?" I prompted.

"Someone's getting exiled into the Wastes," she said grimly.

As more and more people clogged the walkways, we slowed to a snail's pace. Eventually, the throng ended up at the interior of the gate—an exact replica of the exterior; its high, swooping arch gave me flashbacks of being dragged through it and thrown into the decontamination room. I shifted on my feet, and River looked my way. I forced a smile for his sake and pointedly looked back to the front, where everyone was anxiously staring at the gate.

Within minutes, all of the available space behind us had filled with hundreds more people, and a murmur of unease ran through the crowd. I periodically scanned for Chace, or any other familiar faces, but I didn't see any. We were so crammed in, my own father could have been in here and I'd never have known.

Suddenly, the crowd fell still, and the sound of footsteps drew my attention back to the gate. There on top of a platform was Commandant Kieran, and a man I didn't recognize in the marshmallow soldier uniform.

The commandant slowly rolled his gaze over the crowd, a somber expression on his face. "Citizens of Bastion City, it is with grave sadness that I stand before you on this day. Amongst your fellow residents, there has been a grievous error, which we cannot allow to go unpunished. Officer Kutsuki, please explain the crimes for which these residents must be punished."

Morgan gasped and sank a handful of nails into my forearm as he gave a grave nod, and the soldier stepped forward, stiff as a board and at attention.

"What is it?" I whispered to Morgan.

"These residents. Plural. They're exiling more than one citizen. That's never happened before in my entire life." Her sorrowful whisper tugged at me, but there was nothing I could do. I had no way to get out. Yet.

Unlike Commandant Kieran, Officer Kutsuki made no attempts to address or interact with

266

the crowd. He barked out the accusations one by one, keeping his eyes above the crowd and his spine stiff. "These residents have misused resources, as outlined under penal code 87b-k, contributed to the degradation of the life supporting ecosystem under their care, as referenced in penal code 221g, and lastly, they have failed to correct these actions through mandated reparations to their fellow citizens, sir!"

The commandant nodded, and Officer Kutsuki stepped back to his place at the back of the platform, still gazing out over our heads. "Thank you, officer, for your service and dedication to the well-being of all. It is time to bring forth the criminals."

We all watched in dread-laced silence as an elderly man and woman were ushered onto the stage. They clung to each other, the woman struggling to hold the man upright as they were dogged up the stairs by a passel of guards.

A ripple of unease went through the crowd, but the commandant raised one hand, and silence fell once more. It was quiet enough, in fact, that we could hear the small sobs and struggling breaths of the woman.

My throat tightened, and when I took my next breath it felt like I was trying to suck air into my nose through a straw.

"Please, Commandant! We've done nothing wrong, there must be a mistake! Frank and I have served for decades, and we've never been anything but faithful!" The woman reached out a hand for the commandant, but Officer Kutsuki stepped between them, and gave her a cold look. Her frail hand dropped away, back to grasp the man's white sleeve and give it a shake. He didn't seem to notice her clinging, and when he stared out at the crowd, his eyes were vacant, confused.

"Lira and Frank Grenkel, you have been found guilty of crimes against the people of Bastion City."

"No! Please!" she cried out again, but the commandant continued his deadly proclamation.

"As a result of these crimes, you will be released into the Wastes, to live and die by your own hands. From this day forward, you are no longer entitled to the rights of citizenship, or the protection granted by these walls. Excursion Team Three—" He gestured them forward, and the platform was suddenly full of the guards who'd pursued the elderly couple up the stairs. Two of them patted them down, while the others pushed open the massive gate, revealing the empty white hallway behind.

Items were dumped from their pockets onto the stage, and I watched in sickened silence as a water orb bounced down and rolled off the edge of the stage.

"They're taking everything? They won't have any water?" River asked, having seen the same thing I did.

"No, they get nothing. Before they step outside, they'll even take the jumpsuits." Her voice cracked as she whispered.

My stomach was a mess of knots as the guards took the two elders by the upper arms and hauled them down a set of stairs behind the platform, into the hallway, and shut the interior gate. Only the commandant remained, and he clasped his hands behind his back, not a crack in his solemn mask. I wanted to shove through the crowd and smack the righteous look off of his face. These were people! People he was throwing away, with no remorse and no care whatsoever. I shifted forward on the balls of my feet, but before I could do anything, River's fingertips came to rest gently on my bicep.

I looked up and met his troubled gaze, remembering why I couldn't throw myself up there. Demand something different. Donkey kick the commandant off the stage with my door-kicking boots and make the people see that they should rise up against the atrocity happening in front of us. It hurt me to my soul, but I stayed still and quiet.

"It is never easy to see our own fall, but these laws are necessary for our very survival. We must ruthlessly uphold them. We are the Bastion, last hope for humanity." I felt sick, the horror and disgust churning like bile in my stomach at his callous words.

Around us, the crowd spoke as one; "We are the Bastion, last hope for humanity."

The robotic words gnawed at my soul, and I knew I'd be hearing them in my nightmares, underpinned by poor Lira Grenkel's hoarse cries as she was hauled from the stage to be sent to her death. In that moment I knew, humans might live here, but their humanity was long gone.

Twenty-Three

MEDICAL
MALFUNCTIONS

T he next day dawned with me once again sleepless, but this time with less room to pace. Due to our status as *new citizens*, we were not allowed to leave our shoebox without an escort, or between the hours of nine p.m. and seven a.m. At least now that we knew the room wasn't bugged, River had felt comfortable planting a good-morning kiss on my lips in between rounds of pacing.

At seven on the dot, Morgan waited outside to take us to do the mandatory DNA testing, as everything had closed yesterday after the exiling. Apparently, the entire city shuttered after an exile as the only memorial allowed for the "criminals."

Frankly, no crime those two could have committed would convince me they deserved to be turned out to die, alone and thirsting in the desert. I wasn't convinced there was any crime, beyond being old and less useful than they supposed their newest unwilling recruits would be. What a repayment for a lifetime of hard work *that* was. Frankly, if the walls hadn't already felt like they were closing in on me, yesterday's exile would have sealed my decision to get my brother and get us the frack out of here as quickly as possible. Anybody that turned on their own was no better than the gangs that ran the outside.

"So, how was your first night as citizens of Bastion City?" Morgan asked as we slowly trailed her towards the medical center.

"Those mattresses leave something to be desired," River grumbled. It was uncharacteristic of him to complain ever, and I turned and took him in. His hair was mussed, his eyes tired, and his shirt rumpled; he had the looks of a man who hadn't slept well. I reached over and slipped my arm around his waist and gave him a small squeeze.

"Want to try switching bunks tonight? Mine wasn't so bad."

He sighed. "Maybe. It might have been not as bad because you're lighter than me. I sink right through, and I can't lay flat without my arm dangling over the edge. It's making my fingers fall asleep." He flopped his hand around dramatically.

"We'll think of something," I promised.

"Mattress upgrades only happen on a set schedule, unless you choose that as a bi-annual service reward. Although, most people don't choose to replace what they already have, they choose to get something new they don't have."

"Service reward?" I asked with a squint as we left the stark tunnels, my eyes struggling to adjust to the bright natural light.

"Yeah, if you have no infractions for six months and you meet all of your work deliverables satisfactorily you are eligible for a service reward. I wouldn't expect to get one your first time because there are a lot of rules that are easy to mess up." She frowned, and I realized that us convincing her to take us on a side-trip to find Chace had likely cost her a reward this time.

"What's next on your list?" I asked, feeling uncharacteristically guilty.

She looked over her shoulder to see how far back our guard was before answering in a low voice, "I'm saving up my credits to delay entering the reproductive program. Eventually I want to upgrade to a higher-level room with a view of something, but for now I want to change career tracks."

"That's cool. What do you want to do?"

"Well, there's only so many entry-level options, but I was hoping to join the excursion teams. It's not allowed until you've got five years of service under your belt, so I've got a while to go"—she dropped her voice to a whisper—"if I'm still here by then."

A frisson of unease flowed under my skin at her words. She meant that she was going to leave with us, right? And if she didn't, what was I going to do about it?

She raised her voice back to normal levels, and pointed to the side, where a window was cut into the side of the wall, and a queue of people wound between small tables. "By the way, that's the closest place to get your meals, now that I'm no longer your personal waitress."

She didn't say anything further about the escape, instead continuing on down the sidewalk past the eatery, and gesturing to a fogged-glass door. Surprisingly, it had a large red plus symbol on it, the only thing I'd seen with color that didn't grow out of the soil.

"This is the medical center. Another career option besides the reproduction program, and also where some women go when they're done with the reproductive team," she said louder than usual, as if for the benefit of our trailing guards.

A strong, sharp smell washed over me as she pulled open the door and held out a hand indicating we should go in. River led the way, and I followed reluctantly. Morgan didn't follow, however.

"I'll be right outside when you're done." The smile she gave was little more than a grimace, and the door swung shut between us with a decisive *thunk*. I turned around to take in the waiting room, clean and polished, every surface from floor to the line of identical chairs against the wall to the reception desk were white and slightly shiny, the concentrated smell of—what *was* that, alcohol?—giving me an instant migraine. Or perhaps that was anxiety, but who was counting.

A woman with midnight skin and tight, straight braids stood from behind the desk and offered us a kind smile. She exuded warmth in an otherwise cold place, and I had to resist the ridiculous urge to step closer. I hadn't felt like a child even when I *was* a child, and here I was wanting to cling to this stranger's skirts.

"Nyx and River, I presume?" she asked, a beautiful, lilting quality to her voice. She had that soothing aura thing down *pat*.

"That's us," River said with a smile. Apparently the overly-sterile enclosed space didn't give him the heebie-jeebies like it did me.

"Excellent, you're right on time. Please follow me, and we'll get you on your way quickly." She gestured to a doorway off to the side and met us there. Like an utter chicken, I made River go first. He shook his head at me, but led the way, gripping my fingers tightly in his. Whether in comfort or to keep me from hightailing it, I didn't ask.

The walk was short, and the room she led us to was even more claustrophobic than the waiting room. It held four strange-looking beds; a wall with a bank of monitors and equipment I had never seen before—and had absolutely no clue what it did; and a sheet of blue-backed gauze laid out on a short countertop. The gleaming metal instruments lying on it made my heart skip a beat, and *not* in the way that River did.

I quickly looked away, scanning the blank walls as if they were fascinating.

"If you'll each take a seat on a table, we'll get started." Her soothing voice helped, but didn't stop the erratic racing of my pulse.

River hopped right up onto the closest bed-table and offered her a genuine smile. "I'm sorry, I didn't catch your name . . . ?"

"Miriam, thank you for asking," she said with a polite nod.

"It's lovely to meet you, Miriam. What exactly will we be doing today? We weren't given a lot of information."

"Ahh, yes. Well, we'll start with a simple blood draw. This allows us to test your DNA for anything too concerning, and also see what place you both might have in our reproductive programs. We also have birth control implants, and depending on your initial titer results, you could have quite a few vaccinations due. Beyond that, we take it on a case by case basis." Her smile was warm, and I let it lull me into pretending I knew what anything meant beyond *blood draw*. The only times blood had been drawn in my life had hurt like the devil, and had usually been due to blunt injuries from scavenging . . . and on one or two occasions, from fights on the streets. I assumed her method would be more civilized, at least. Hopefully *also* less painful.

"Would you like to go first, River? You seem calmer than your lovely lady."

"Sure, I'll be the pincushion."

She wrinkled her nose at his statement but didn't comment as she pulled over the tray of shiny tools. "This will only pinch for a second, so please hold still. It hurts worse if you move." She wrapped a solid white cuff around his tanned bicep and pressed a button on her tablet. The cuff started to hum and inflate as she reached over to the tray and picked up a handheld scanner. She ran it briefly over his forehead, down the side of his neck, and then pressed the device to the crook of his arm. He flinched a second later, and a tube I hadn't noticed on the underside of the scanner quickly filled with red. I looked up at the ceiling, feeling queasy at the sight of River's blood.

A few short moments later, the machine emitted a cheerful series of beeps, and she untwisted the tube from the bottom, and stuck a white patch over the small wound on his arm.

"Excellent, River. The machine will analyze your titers right away, and the rest of the vial will go into the bigger system for full processing."

She tucked his vial of blood into a glass-doored cabinet full of indents the perfect size to hold it, and as soon as she closed the door, it rotated deeper into the machine and disappeared from sight. Crossing back to River's side, she looked him over.

"Feeling alright? Some people get woozy at the sight of blood, especially if it's their first medical check."

"Nah, I'm good." He gave her his patented one-dimple grin, then looked over at me. I was still queasily examining the ceiling, and it wasn't even my blood.

"Wonderful. Nyx, if you'll please come to the table, we'll do your scan next, so the titers can run while I do your physicals."

"Okay," I agreed, trying to keep the anxiety out of my voice. River reached over and squeezed my hand supportively as the nurse twisted a new tube onto the machine and punched in a series of digits. The scanner let out an angry chirp, and she furrowed her brow at it before unscrewing the tube again.

"Excuse me for a moment." She gave me a smile that didn't reach her eyes and walked out of the room.

"What was that about?" I asked nervously.

"I don't know, maybe it needs to be charged or something."

I shifted on the table, unease like lead in my gut despite Miriam's calm and polite manner.

She was back quickly, a small clear pouch in her hands, attached to a tube with a circular head on the end. She screwed the head into the machine in lieu of the tube, then began the same process she'd performed on River. First the big white inflatable cuff, which was uncomfortable but not painful, then scans of my forehead and neck. When she got to my arm with the scanner, I stiffened.

"Don't tense, dear, it really does make it worse." She patted me gently on the shoulder, and I let out a shaky breath as I willed my muscles to relax. With no further warning, I felt a sharp jab, and hissed out the last of my breath as I heard the trickle of my own blood into the tube. I looked back to the ceiling, counting my inventory in my head—anything to distract myself from that slow, awful trickle and the weird suction feeling at my vein.

"Nyx? Nyx, look at me, I need you to take some deep breaths, now."

"What?" The word came out sounding distant, and I furrowed my brow and looked down from the ceiling in confusion. The woman swung through my vision sickeningly, and I scrunched my eyes closed at the nauseating sight.

"She's really pale. Is she supposed to be that pale?" I heard the twin thuds of River's boots hitting the floor, but I didn't dare risk opening my eyes.

"Let's see if removing the cuff helps; we still have a ways to go," she murmured to him, and then all the tension on the white cuff vanished.

I felt a second of relief, and then in the next breath, everything went black.

"Nyx, Nyx! Come on, Nyx!"

"Stop, don't shake her! It's not helping!"

"*You* said the pill thing would work! She's still out, we have to try something!" River's sharp bark of anger shocked me into opening my eyes, but the bright overhead lighting made me squinch them immediately shut.

"Smelling salts *do* work, just give her a moment! She had a minor reaction to the blood draw. It happens every now and then." Miriam's stern tone didn't deter River. He leaned in close, and I felt the warmth of his breath on my cheek, as his big palm came to rest on my forehead.

"Nyx, baby, please open your eyes. Nyx! You're scaring me here, don't check out on me yet. Think of how pissed off Chace would be. We have too much to do still, and I can't take care of your brother or anyone else without you. Nyx, Nyx, Nyx . . . Come on, come on." He breathed my name out like a prayer, and I carefully peeled my eyelids open one more time, careful to go slow.

"There you are," Miriam said with a smile. "You had us worried for a moment."

"Thank God." River searched my face with laser-level intensity, as the sensation of his fingers clasped around mine anchored me back to the present. "Don't ever do that to me again."

"I'm not sure what—" I cleared my throat, my voice still sounding a bit far off and weird. "I'm not sure what happened. Sorry. My head is still muzzy." I gestured vaguely towards my hair, and River honed in on Miriam.

"How do we fix it?"

"I don't know because you made me remove the scanner—" River shot her a sharp look, and she quickly backpedaled, and began shifting my position on the table so my head was further down, and my feet were raised up higher. "She just needs time. Although there is one more thing that may speed up the process."

"Do it."

Miriam shook her head as she crossed to the small countertop, and I closed my eyes again against the overwhelming lights. River clutched my hand tightly and ran his fingertips through my hair as I heard the sounds of cabinets opening and closing, followed by a short burst of running tap water.

"Lift her arm over her head," Miriam ordered, and River used our entwined fingers to comply.

A second later, something cold in my armpit shocked the bejeezus out of me, and my eyes flew wide open.

"Camels on crack, what in the desert dump—"

"She's back!" River smiled down at me happily, completely ignoring my anger at the polar assault. "Can you sit up?"

"Take it slow! We don't want to go backwards," Miriam chided.

"You heard her. Slowly, and hold my arm." He offered up his other hand and forearm, and I wrapped my fingertips around his warmth and clung, while he pulled me upward at a snail's pace.

"Now that you're feeling better, we'll need to finish—"

"Absolutely not," River cut her off, his tone deadly serious.

"River, I understand your concern, but fainting at the sight of blood isn't all that uncommon. Now, the commandant—"

River took an agitated step towards her, and she froze mid-sentence. "Do you think we didn't notice the little switcheroo, there, with the vial and the whole bag? We might not know what he's planning to do with her blood, but I think he's got plenty for whatever *test* he needs on her DNA. Now, you'll excuse us, because I'm taking Nyx back to our room."

"Fine! I can explain about the blood, but you *can't* leave without your birth control implants. Really, it's just a quick injection, and no one is allowed in the city who isn't on birth control except the reproductive team." She raised her hands in a pleading manner.

River cast a quick glance over at me. I wanted out of here more than anything, but if we didn't do this now, we'd have to come back. I found I wanted that even less. I hesitantly nodded, and he stepped to the side, allowing Miriam access to both of us with the smaller device she picked up.

"River, yours will go into the top of your thigh, so I'll need you to lower your waistband a few inches. Nyx, yours goes into your inner arm. Whichever side you'd prefer, both of you."

I offered her my left, since I'm a rightie. Miriam didn't wait for River to protest that I still needed to rest, swooping straight over and pressing the device to my arm. It was more than a pinch, but it was over much faster than the blood draw. My head spun again at the intense pain in a tender area, but I was pulled out of it by River's yelp.

"Holy mother of camels, you didn't say you were going to shoot it into the top of my *groin*," he wheezed pitifully.

"Sorry, that's the only place it's effective for men."

She didn't look *even a little bit* sorry.

"Are we free to leave now?" he gritted out through clenched teeth.

"Yes, though your titers just came through, and it looks like *neither* of you have had any of your basic vaccinations." She made a displeased tutting sound under her breath. "You'll need to come back within three days and get started on the first course. There are at least fifteen here that every other citizen has had, and you'll be limited on your movements until you're fully cleared—"

Not liking where that line of conversation was going, I slid to my feet, ignoring the woozy feeling sloshing in my stomach, and gripped the back of River's arm. "We'll deal with that in three days, thanks, Miriam." I force a half-hearted smile, and River and I beat a hasty retreat.

With any luck, I'd never come back inside this room, vaccinations or no frickity-fracking vaccinations.

Twenty-Four

Trade Negotiations

T he next day found us recuperated from our ordeal in the med center, and Morgan once again waiting for us outside the door promptly at seven a.m. I had a massive bruise on the inside of my arm from the implant, and I could only imagine the state of River's groin. He hadn't shown me, but he had a slight limp, and I could connect the dots.

"Morning, love birds." She waggled her eyebrows, and I snorted in response. "You two ready for the *grand tour*?" She began walking backwards as we talked.

"Does it involve a visit with Chace?"

Her weary sigh answered that. "Not yet. Uncle Vander says there's been push back on you hav-

ing any interactions with someone in the laborer class—besides moi, of course—until you've
proven that you're an ally to the city."

"So, they don't trust us," River summarized.

"Well . . . there's already unrest amongst new
laborers. They don't want to worsen that by
giving Chace what would be perceived as unfair
treatment. Frankly, if anybody asked me, I'd say
that's why we even *have* a laborer class—sweat
the resistance right out of 'em. That's beside
the point. What it boils down to is, nobody else
in his class is allowed to fraternize with people
outside the laborers and the overseers. You're
going to have to pull off a pretty big win to
secure those visits." She pressed her lips into a
grim line and turned around to lead the way.

What constituted a big win to these people?
They'd accepted my offer to be a trader, and
diplomat—however ridiculous the idea of *diplo-
macy* felt with the people that had wiped my
hometown permanently off the map—but what
could I trade that would get me another face to
face with Chace, and then get us out of here?

Morgan was still chattering, and I forced myself to focus as she led us on a winding path
through the greenspace. Letting a finger trail
over a tree's bark, I did my best to pay attention.
She was our best hope of understanding the
people of Bastion City.

". . . there aren't many jobs on parkside outside the wall—only a few people are allowed to work to maintain the park and harvest the produce. There's a strict schedule and a really long course of scientific training to even test to take over one of those positions. Frankly, you'd be better off looking for *anything* else. Biodiversity is prized here, and while over thirty percent of our working-age population has taken the training courses and added themselves to the wait list, only five percent of our people are qualified to work in the park. The vast majority of our people are employed in service positions inside the wall like me, lifeside, or in security."

"And you want to go into an excursion team, right?" River asked politely.

"Yes. There aren't very many women—three, currently—and one is about to age out of service. Nanette. She was the first woman to make an excursion team in my lifetime, so she's kind of my idol. Err, don't tell her that, okay? Awkward."

"Our lips are sealed," he promised.

"Good. Okay, so, you've seen the park. You've seen enough of the wall, I assume?"

"More than enough," I agreed with a shudder.

She chuckled. "Thought so. Okay, then, let's go see the parkside. It's a completely different world over there, and you're going to love it. I'm not sure exactly what you'll be able to do as far as trade, though. Isn't it pretty barren out in the Wastes? I mean, when we get exiled, we die. So . . ." She trailed off and waited expectantly.

I pondered a moment, grappling with the best way to explain the Wastes to someone who'd never experienced them. "It's barren, yes, but there's a lot that humanity left behind." I shrugged. "Just because they abandoned it, doesn't mean it's not useful. There's a big difference between old and useless."

She pondered that as we exited the park area, and came to a large, towering back wall. A gate about half the size of the front gate—but every bit as impressive—was carved into it. She placed her palm over a scanner off to the left, and it swung towards us slowly. The motion was smooth, and silent. We stepped into one of the ubiquitous white halls that made up the inside of the walls, but within three minutes we were at a much smaller door and she was palming us through.

"Things are a lot different on the lifeside, but the rules not to touch still apply. You two are on thin ice here—even a small mistake could be bad." She gave us the highly unnecessary reminder and pulled the door open.

We stepped through into another world, and my breath caught. Where behind us was a sprawling indoor forest with green spaces for humans, this side of the Bastion felt like walking into a pastoral scene from a book ages past. The rolling, green space was dotted with all sorts of wild grasses, flowers, buzzing insects, and most impactfully—animals. A flock of sheep grazed just a few feet from where we entered, and most didn't even look up at our sudden appearance. A black-faced lamb bleated at us and hid behind its mother, who barely flicked an ear.

"Well, those are adorable," River mused as we followed behind Morgan dutifully away from the sheep. An alarmed squawk caught our attention next, as a large chicken with a bright red comb chased a smaller one, who was bobbing and weaving through tufts of tall grass. The larger one caught it and seemed to tackle it to the grass.

"Uh, should we help that chicken?" I asked, pointing to where they'd disappeared in the knee-high grass, only the top of the red comb visible.

She sniggered and turned an incredulous eye on me. "Really? Not too familiar with the birds and the bees?"

It took a moment for what she was implying to click, and then my face colored in mortification. "Uh, I didn't realize—I've never seen chickens before. Or bees," I finished lamely.

Morgan held her ribs she laughed so hard, but she didn't stop walking. "The head farmer is going to get a kick out of you."

"Happy to oblige," I said drily, casting an embarrassed look at River. He had a broad grin, but beyond a friendly elbow bump, he didn't mock my ignorance. We walked a few more minutes, passing a surprisingly huge variety of life for such a seemingly flat and simple landscape. We saw two different varieties of animals with horns, one huge and red-brown with spots which lumbered slowly past, and another which leapt out of a cluster of tall grass and scared us half to death. Even Morgan jumped when it bolted by, the impressive cluster of horns on its head enough to make us scramble backwards.

Eventually, we came upon a small brown structure, the roof made of ancient tin and well-weathered from endless years of sun. It was small and homey, and the polar opposite of anything on the parkside of the city. I instantly loved it.

A balding late-middle-aged man ambled out wearing rubber boots and coveralls over an amply stained white linen shirt. He scratched the side of his arm idly while he took us in, our clothing identifying us as outsiders before we'd said a word.

"These the new people? The traders?" He addressed Morgan.

"Yes, they are. This is River, and Nyx. Guys, this is Griffin. He's the head of the field operations on the lifeside. They're here for a tour, and to see if there are any needs they can fill by trading with people *from the outside*. She's the real deal." Her tone was one of barely concealed excitement, and I had to resist the urge to shuffle my feet at the attention.

He patted her gently on the shoulder with a smile, and then his gaze slowly drifted back to us. "Well, come on, then. Lot to see before chores."

Griffin led us around the great indoor plain and pointed out various species of plants and animals. What to me was just a wonderful kaleidoscope of grass, to him was called fescue, Bahia, Johnson, Kentucky blue, and an endless stream of other names I'd never recall.

Though the man seemed simple at first glance, he rattled off the scientific names of many of the insects as we walked, and knew the precise species of every animal under his care. Once we reached the far side of the pasture, he palmed us into a large greenhouse structure, where rows and rows of white tubing lined every single surface, with seedlings and plants of various sizes and colors sprouting out of them. A woman in a white coat worked with a tablet at the end of the first aisle, and she looked up at our unannounced entry.

"Griffin! Good, I need you to look at these peppers. Our nightshades are not performing at the levels we need, and frankly, I'm concerned.

We've adjusted the nutrient ratio as far as we can without throwing off the rest of the system, and yet they're still weak and we're seeing the early rot before they've ripened. Thirty percent of the crop hasn't made it to seed, and it's still early." She proceeded to rattle off a string of numerical and chemical values which meant nothing to me, but Griffin rocked back on his heels with his hands in his pockets.

After a long minute of us standing around in silence, he shook his head slowly. "That ain't good. Our last batch of seed stock hasn't taken to the conditions. They need more water, and more space. They weren't made to grow in test tubes, Darinna. Plus, the pollinators don't like it in here."

She let out a dispirited sigh. "I know that, and you know that, but there's nowhere else to put them."

"All we can do is try."

"Yes, but if these fail, we'll lose the species. This is the last crop of nightshades we have, Griffin. We're going to be taking a long walk into a hot dune if we lose the *last* nightshade!"

He flattened his lips and shook his head again. "There's nothing for it. Scrape any seeds you can from the top part of the peppers that haven't rotted."

"They're immature, and we both know it."

"You got another suggestion?"

"No."

"All right then. I'm going to show our guests around." She blinked rapidly, as if finally noticing the three of us—the guards opted to wait outside the door due to the narrow aisles—and gave us a curt nod. Spinning on her heel, she stalked back down to the end of the aisle, presumably to continue poking the ailing peppers.

"Sorry 'bout that. Darinna's a high-strung filly."

"It sounds like you've got some troubles with your seed stock, if you don't mind my saying so," I interjected, ignoring the dismissive comment about his female co-worker. It wasn't the first or the worst I'd heard said about women, and it wouldn't be the last.

"No sense mindin' the truth. We've got trouble. All the science in the world, but sometimes a crop just fails. Unfortunately, over the last ten years our nightshades and some of the other species have started to lose vigor."

"You don't have backup seed stock?"

"Sure, we do. But the stuff that grew under twelve hours of sun and a steady dose of rainfall from the seed bank have a hard time surviving, even with our hydroponic setup." He stopped in front of a large circular tank, all white except a glass viewing panel. Behind it, a schooling mass of silvery bodies swam and gulped under the water.

"Are those fish?" River asked excitedly, dropping into a crouch to get a better view of the tank.

"Carp. They help balance the water and live symbiotically with the plants."

"Wow," he breathed out reverently. "Can you believe it, Nyx? Real fish. I never thought I'd see anything that *swam*."

It was cool, if a little sad. Those might be the only living fish left on the planet, and they lived stuck inside a high-tech barrel, no freer than anybody else inside these walls as they lived and died swimming in an endless circle. The watery reminder of my current captive status made the skin between my shoulder blades itch.

At least the sheep seemed happy out there, eyeball deep in the grass. They might have been the only ones besides the leadership panel who had any kind of good life here.

The wheels turned in my brain as I watched River ooh and ahh over the fish.

"Griffin, what's your number one challenge here as you provide the food for the entire city?"

He rolled his lips in and out, thinking it over in his usual unhurried manner. "Lack of genetic diversity. We've got the animals we got, and no more. We've got a cryogenic bank we pull from, but even that's only so deep of a bench. Same with the plants. If these next few crops don't produce, we could lose a plant species altogether. Once it's gone, there's no comin' back." He shook his head gravely.

Simple words, but with a deep meaning. The fewer plant options they could grow, the less variety of food they could produce, and in another ten, fifty, hundred years, when a different plant started to fail, it would grow even more limited. Until what? There were no varieties left, and even people inside the city were forced to go out and scavenge like the rest of us? Assuming they left any of the rest of us alive; there was only so much food left to find in the world. Though, the Red Riders had managed to grow that spongy green goo, despite being constantly harangued. It wasn't the most exciting, but it was hardy, and nutritious.

It was a sobering thought. All the technology left to humanity, and even inside these walls, they weren't untouchable. Nature had a will of its own, and we couldn't create life from nothing.

I tapped my fingers on my thigh, thinking it over. I had seeds. But more than that, I knew the location of Armand's greenhouse, where lush greenery covered the whole tower, with very little water in the system, and no human intervention for seemingly hundreds of years.

I also had his notebook, detailing the varieties and methods he used when he cultivated those plants. It would be a hefty trade, yes, but could I afford to part with that knowledge?

That resource was supposed to set us up in the north. Although—I cast my gaze around at the high-tech setup—there was no way we had the knowledge or materials to create something of this level. If they couldn't keep plants growing reliably with hundreds of years of scientific development and research, what hope did three untrained people have in the wilds of the north? I'd assumed we would eventually find a temperate region where the seeds could go into the ground.

Maybe it was *exactly* the chip I needed to play to see Chace and start formulating a plan out of this place.

Time to shoot for the moon. "What if I told you that I had access not only to seed stock, but also a current, live greenhouse with several hundred thriving plants in it?"

Griffin froze, his eyes going narrow. "I'd say you're full of hot air. This is the only live greenhouse left on the planet."

River stood from the fish tank and retook his place at my side.

"I'm not full of it, and there is a greenhouse. I'll have to talk to your leadership panel—or whoever is going to be my trade liaison—but it's a long, long drive. There's a closer location with some grain seed, but it's from a different source."

"What kind of grains?"

I tossed a gaze over to River, trying to remember exactly what we'd left behind in that hidden solar-powered safe room.

He must have been thinking the same thing, because he helpfully jumped in. "Barley, wheat, peas, millet, oat, and . . . the last one had a funny name. What was it?"

"It started with an S."

"Sorghum by chance? You really know where those seeds are?" Griffin cut in.

"Sorghum sounds right. And yes, really. Those bags are closer. The rest is deep south, probably two months' drive from here."

"Bags? What size? All my training says old earth seeds came in little paper packets."

I shrugged before holding up my hands about two feet apart. "They were big sacks. We didn't have room for all of them in the truck."

"Sweet water fairy in the desert. Darinna! Get over here. I need you to go talk some sense into the leadership panel."

"Coming," she groused, but walked with purpose. "What is it?"

He gave her a brief rundown of what we'd shared, and her eyes grew wider as he spoke.

"Can you help them establish the value of that quantity of seed stock for our seed bank? The leadership panel doesn't put a lot of stock in what I think," Griffin said with a smirk.

"Or mine. They don't think anything outside is worth having, but I tried to tell them," I added.

"Absolutely." Darinna set her jaw. "We'll tell them in no uncertain terms that we need these seeds, and *make* them listen."

Our trade liaison was a chubby man with over-long hair and round glasses, and he was un-moved by the initial explanation of what we wanted to do; the details had settled in my mind on the walk back across the length of the city to meet him. Setting up a trade envoy with the Sidewinders and providing them with the co-ordinates of the bags of seed grains we'd found between here and there made the most sense. Once they'd arrived and we were clear of the gates, I'd provide them with the journal as well as the coordinates to Chrysanthe's southern home and Armand's greenhouse.

King wanted an in with the city? Check.

The city needed outside goods? Check.

I'd make the connection, supply the valuable information, and get all of us safely out of this place as soon as they arrived with the seeds? Check.

It was the best plan all around. Now I just had to convince Horace.

"I don't see why we would risk sharing our location with outsiders in order to obtain a few ancient bags of seeds, when we have a cryogenic seed bank inside the walls." He sneered down his nose at us, and Darinna rose slowly from her chair.

"Did I not show you the projections? We do have a seed bank, but we haven't had new stock to bring in for nearly *three hundred* years. Do you think we should wait another three hundred in the hopes of another opportunity? No more seed stock is being grown, and we desperately need to gather any that's still out there."

He leaned back in his chair and rested his hands on his protruding stomach with a sigh. "Yes, yes, if you insist. But why must we involve the riffraff?"

I glared at the insinuation, though in regard to the Sidewinders, they *were* a rough lot. I wasn't going to tell him that, though.

"You involve the people of Coyote Springs to foster goodwill, and also to have a permanent connection to the outside. We aren't staying. It's symbiotic to have people on the outside willing to bring you things that they find in exchange for trade goods you can easily produce inside. Some of the technology you have inside these walls—the higher grade of replicators, for starters—don't exist anymore outside. That has value to people who might like to manufacture new parts for their vehicles, or better housing for their people."

He blew air between his lips as if my speech bored him, but Darinna wasn't put off.

"Sit up straight and take this seriously, Horace, or I will tell your mother about that *thing* in tenth grade."

River's eyebrows shot up, and mine must have been just as high.

Horace stammered as Darinna stared him down. "You wouldn't dare. That's ancient history!"

"I absolutely would dare if it got me these seeds. You should *want* to get them for the city because this is an unprecedented opportunity."

"This is *highly* unprofessional, Darinna. I take offense."

"Take all the offense you want—right out the door and down the hall to get the approval for this deal. We get seeds, a new desert liaison, and they get to walk. Stamp it, seal it, get me what I want." She pointed to the door, an unflinching look on her face.

He blustered and protested for several more minutes, but when it came down to it, Darinna was a fearsome ally for us in working with our Bastion City trade liaison. Up from his seat and down the hall he went, and I exchanged a smile with River, before turning to Darinna.

"Thank you, Darinna. There's *one* more thing we could use your help with to seal this deal."

Twenty-Five

Reunion

I paced the small room—apparently the only thing I did inside these suffocating walls. It held me, a small square table, and two chairs. Nothing more, nothing less. When the door cracked and swung open I froze, holding my breath until I saw his face.

"Chace, thank God." I bolted across the room and nearly tackled him, flinging my arms around his neck.

He stumbled back a step, but caught me, squeezing me so tight around the ribs, I thought they'd crack under the welcome assault. We shuffled a few steps further into the room, and the unfamiliar guard outside growled at us, saying, "You've got half an hour," as he left.

The door clicked softly shut, and we were alone; face to face for the first time in months.

"Are you okay? You're bruised up, but you're still standing, so—" I turned, pulling out a chair for him as I talked.

"What were you thinking?" His cold tone shocked me, and I turned back around to face him.

"What do you mean?"

"I left to save you! I tucked you in at Marl's and went out *alone* when I heard they were doing a roundup. They knew about us, *knew* exactly how many people in our age bracket lived in Coyote Springs. I lied. Told them you were frail, and barely hanging onto life. Nyx! You were never supposed to end up here! This place is prison! It's *death*, and you just waltzed in—"

"For you! I came for *you*. Don't lecture me, when you made a stupid decision to leave me without a word in the middle of the night. I thought the 'Winders took you, killed you, were lying—something! They took advantage, and I pushed until I found the truth." I jabbed the table with my fingertip and realized absently that my hands were shaking with fury. How dare he chastise me, after all I'd been through to find him?

My mind was spinning in overdrive at his words. How did they know so much about us? Did they have someone inside the town? Did they *capture* someone from outside the town and pump them for information?

"I did it to protect you!" His angry outburst knocked something loose in my chest, and I realized that he wasn't truly angry. He was sad, and frustrated, and he'd gone thinking he would never see me again.

"Well, I came to protect *you*, Chace! This is a two-way street, you moron! You think I care any less about you than you do about me? You're my brother. My everything. *Of course, I came for you.*"

"I should have expected it, honestly. You've always been the stubborn one. But Nyx, I'm the big brother. It's my job to protect you. The only way I could do it was to leave. Get ahead of them. Tell them what they needed to hear. I thought . . . I thought they'd let me go back and pack, tell you goodbye. Explain why I had to leave." His anger seemed to dissolve, his shoulders slumping at the memory of that night. "They didn't, Nyx. As soon as I walked up, I was interviewed for no more than three minutes, and somebody grabbed me from behind and jabbed a needle in my neck. I woke up here, in a weird blinking room, buck naked with a dozen other people and with nothing but a white freaking slave jumpsuit and a headache." He angrily slapped the loose fabric on the side of his jumpsuit and dropped like a stone into the low-backed chair.

"It was all for nothing, because you still ended up here." When he looked up and met my eyes, sorrow was the overwhelming emotion in them.

I sank into a crouch next to the chair and flung my arms around him. He laid his head on top of mine, and we were silent for a few breaths, clinging to each other, when I broke the silence.

"It wasn't for nothing, Chace. We know so much more, and I've got a plan to get us out of here. The Bronco's right outside, loaded down with food and a decent amount of water. And I've got credits now. A *lot* of credits."

He lifted his head and gave me a quizzical expression. "How'd that happen?"

I grinned. "Turns out, I'm really freaking good at my job. But we'll have time to catch up when we're on the road. Give me the scoop about this place—what's it been like?"

"Geez, loaded question. I don't even know where to start."

I pulled the second chair around the table, so we were sitting knee to knee. "Start at the beginning."

"Well, I told you about the drugging and then waking up in the weird glowing room."

"Yeah, I got to experience the joys of decontamination, too. They wouldn't let us in without stripping down and being put through the cleaner." I huffed at the unpleasant memory.

"Us? Who's with you?" His eyes narrowed. "It's not Hoss, is it? If he moved in on my sister as soon as I left—"

I rolled my eyes. "Seriously? I'm grown. Get over yourself. And no, it's not Hoss. His name's River. It's part of a long story, but I picked him up in the desert, and he helped me find you."

"I see."

"You don't, but you will. He's great. Anyways, you were telling me a story, and we only have so much time."

"Fine, fine. So, we woke up in the decontamination room. There were a handful of us from Coyote Springs, but also people from two other cities I'd never heard of. We put on the clothes and were herded out and through the hallways back to a couple bunk rooms. We're six to a room, men and women separate."

"Jamie from back home—was she in the group that got taken?"

He nodded. "Yeah, she went to the reproductive team. Not surprising; she was in good health."

"Were all the women sent to the reproductive team? They tried to convince me to do that, too. So far, though, they've accepted a bag of blood and the promise of trade goods."

"No, not all of them. I think you saw two that stayed with us as laborers? It's the most asinine thing you've ever seen, the jobs they have us do. Move rocks. Break down scrap with sledgehammers. Physically exhausting, and little to no value. But what do you mean, a bag of blood?" He leaned forward in his chair, concern chiseling his forehead into sharp frown lines.

"They made us do the regular intake testing, and only took a tube from River." I held up my fingers a few inches apart for reference. "Then she left and got a bag for me. I . . . had to do some arm twisting to get us in the door. They're verifying my story." I shrugged, completely leaving out the part where I fainted like a sissy.

"They blood tested all of us, too. Freaking unpleasant." He rubbed the crook of his arm for a second before dropping his hand back to the arm of the chair and tapping his fingers on it. "Nyx, what did you say to get in? There was an anomaly in one of the guy's blood results, and they took him out of our group for further testing, said he wouldn't be back for a few days. We were all jealous, because by that point three of us had already fallen out from exhaustion and dehydration." He scrubbed the side of his head absently with his palm. "We have half the numbers we had when we got here, between disappearances, overwork, and the *punishments* they like to dole out. Hopefully the women have fared better."

That fact sent me reeling back in my chair. Half. *Half* the men they'd abducted were already dead. Anger roiled in my belly at the reminder of the thinly veiled cruelty of this place.

"Well, you keep your head down, and we're getting out of here. I've already got the city to agree to a trade. All I have to do is get in touch with the 'Winders and get them to make a delivery. They were hoping for this outcome, so it should be a pretty easy conversation. It'll take them a few weeks, but once they get here, we're home free."

He clenched his jaw and stared me down. "You really think they're going to hold up their end of the bargain? What happens if they don't actually let us out?"

That possibility made cold fear run down my spine, but I wasn't going to tell him that. He had enough to deal with. "One thing at a time, Chace—we have options. It'll work out."

"Here's hoping it goes that easily, but you still didn't tell me what you said to get in the door."

"It's a gate, actually."

"Nyx," he growled my name like a cuss word.

"Ugh! Fine! I told them I was a descendant of one of the founders. Her name was Chrysanthe. She lived hundreds of years ago and left a locket with a map for her family."

He groaned and dropped his head in his hands. "Why would you say something like that? You don't think they can check? They have more technology here than we've ever seen."

I shrugged one shoulder, brushing off the concern. "If I couldn't get in, I couldn't get you out. End of story. I would have told them I was descended from the moon's president if it got us in the door. Don't worry about it, okay? I'm holding up my end of the bargain. Even if their test comes back that I'm not a descendant, I'm still giving them what they want."

"You think they're going to tell you what they want? And it clearly does matter to them, if they took extra blood. Nyx, the guy who had the blood anomaly? He never came back. We asked, but the bastards they assigned to guard us don't give us any information. I don't know why they blood test everybody, but it feels like they're looking for something. Maybe it *is* significant being that lady's relative."

I snorted. "She died hundreds of years ago! Can they really tell this far down the line? Besides, I might *be* her relative, anything is possible. In fact . . . well, let's just say that stranger things have happened in the last few months."

He narrowed his eyes and leaned forward, his voice a hushed whisper. "Why, Nyx? What aren't you telling me?"

I leaned forward as well, slipping my finger under the chain and fishing the locket from the neck of my shirt. "This was hers. I found it in her house down south—almost died getting there, and the three men King sent before me *did* die on the way."

Chace swore under his breath.

"No sense swearing about it now. I lived." *Barely.* "The point is, I made it, and I found this locket. I picked it up and it spit some green powder that knocked me on my butt. Out cold, don't know how long. It's . . . affected me, ever since. Subtle things, but over time I can tell it did something to me."

"Nyx, I don't like the sound of that."

"Yeah, well, there's more." I bit my lip and let the rest of it flow out. The people it killed. The fact that it was impenetrable until I'd bled on it. The short version of the message inside. When I finished, Chace was grim.

"Nyx, this is not good. You might have stumbled on something, but you also might be her *real* relative; have you considered that? Maybe whatever is in that locket is meant to kill anyone who's outside her family?"

"Chace, *seriously*? What are the odds of that? Whatever powder it spewed probably did something to me which let me open it."

"What are the odds that that locket sat there for hundreds of years, and no one stole it be-

311

fore you? You need to find out what the significance was of this woman, and why they want someone related to her so badly. Nothing good comes from being on their radar—you may have stepped into something bigger than you planned."

"I don't freaking know. It is what it is, now. I said what I said, and I'm here to get you. I have a plan, Chace! You're supposed to be happy to see me," I snapped, irritated by his questioning.

His facial expression softened, and he let out a sigh. "I am happy to see you, and I'm not. I was trying to keep you out of this. But . . . of course I'm glad to see you. You're my baby sister, and there's nobody I love more on this planet. Only family I've got worth having." He chucked me under the chin lightly.

A rock formed in my stomach, as I realized there was more I needed to tell him. "Chace, there's something else."

The door cracked open behind him, and a guard stepped in. "Time's up. Let's go, Brandt."

He rose slowly to his feet. "What is it, Nyx? Tell me quick."

"It's Jaen. I'm sorry. She's dead—Nagesh killed her." I bit my bottom lip as the shock and anger crossed his face, the guards each took one of his arms and pulled him from the room.

"I'm sorry, and I love you! See you soon!" I called as they took him out of sight.

It was time to call 'Conda and get this ball rolling.

Twenty-Six

BACK DOOR POLICY

T he Sidewinders were happier to get my second call than the first. I had to promise them just shy of El Dorado-level scavenging to get them to agree to accept the rest of the room's contents as payment, but in the end, 'Conda's greed won out. They took down the coordinates and instructions on getting in and promised to deliver the requested bags of seed—and their choice of "diplomat"—to Bastion City.

I figured it would take them less than a month, and then we'd be out of here. Unfortunately, the leadership panel had made it very clear that I wouldn't be allowed to see Chace again until the goods had been delivered.

That night, when the guards walked me back to our room to be locked in for the evening, I had a smile on my face for the first time in a long time. River had already cleaned up for the evening by the time I made it back from my reunion with Chace, and he was sitting on the edge of the lower bunk waiting for me.

When the door clicked shut and the lock turned behind me, he stood and crossed the room to stand in front of me. "How'd it go?"

"Better than I hoped. We've got a trade agreement underway, and Chace is still alive. He doesn't look any worse for wear after the taser net, and he doesn't have any new bruises. They haven't been continuing to punish him for our run-in, at least." I shrugged one shoulder, trying to filter through the jumble of feelings in my chest. Relief. Anxiety. Determination. Hatred. Attraction. It was a mixed bag.

"That's huge, Nyx. You've pulled off the impossible. How do you feel, after seeing him?" The question was reserved, but I could see the concern underneath his calm exterior. He'd agreed that I should go alone so I could have a private moment to see my brother without the "who's that guy?" distrust. But I know it had to have been hard on him to sit here and wait.

"I'm . . . apprehensive. I haven't pulled this off yet—there's still plenty that could go wrong. But, I'm hopeful. Ironically, more hopeful than Chace, and he's the one we showed up for." I shook my head at his insistence that I'd stepped into something.

"What? What did he have to say?"

I sighed and crossed to drop to the edge of the mattress. He joined me and slid an arm around my shoulders.

"He had a lot to say. They're not treated well, which we knew, but they're also dying and disappearing. He's concerned they won't stick to their end of the bargain."

"Yeah, I am too—but we can't do anything about that. Not without access to our *back door*."

"Good point." A little C-4 would go a long way to reassuring me we'd get out, that was true.

"I've actually been thinking about that, while you were gone. I have an idea, but you're not going to like it."

"What's that?"

"What if we could get them to lend us some marshmallow suits, so we could retrieve some of our stuff from the truck?"

"I mean, we could ask. I'd kill to have my own tooth tablets, and something with pockets." I looked over with a scowl at the pile of boxy, shapeless white sweats and t-shirts they'd provided us with. "But why would they?"

"That's the part you won't like. You bargained for the seed stock from that room specifically to involve the Sidewinders, which is smart. But we both know there's more."

"Yeah, but they don't. And it would be best for us to keep it that way if at all possible. Assuming we make it out of here and can head north, how are we going to feed ourselves? We don't have replicators, and we have no way of knowing how many people are north. We could ask the people here—they probably know, since they have access to jets and are monitoring the desert people—but I don't trust them to tell us the truth. Even if they did, I'd rather they assume we're going to head back east. Frankly, the quicker we're off their radar, the better."

"I get it, I really do. But we're scrappy, Nyx. You have practically superhero-level powers of turning nothing into gold. Literally, in some cases. Giving up those seeds might be the only thing which gets us access to the truck."

"Okay, let's say we *do* convince them. They're going to make us put everything through decontamination. How are you going to get anything useful in? I'm not giving up our private seedbank for tooth tablets. We'll survive without them for a month."

"They can't put seeds through decontamination. Think about it. Whatever they sprayed on you couldn't be good for the seeds. They'd have to let *something* through. We could find a way to capitalize on that."

"Yeah, they're gonna notice C-4."

He sighed and dropped his ear to the top of my head. "I want to try. Do you trust me?"

My knee jerk reaction was to brush off the question, but instead I stopped and really thought it over. Did I trust him? We'd been through a lot; some good, some bad. He'd left. He'd come back. He'd protected me, he'd abandoned me. He'd kept secrets, but then he'd opened up.

And somehow, we were here at the end of the journey.

He'd followed me to the ends of the earth.

But did I *trust* him?

I'd learned long ago to never trust anyone but Chace. Other people wanted to use me, own me, hurt me. So, I'd built a wall of skepticism, and an impenetrable trader's mask behind which I hid all my emotion, all my desire for human connection.

I'd let River closer than anyone else in my entire life. But was that trust?

I trusted him to drive the Bronco, and not to run off in the middle of the night with my gear. I trusted him not to use his superior strength to put me out in the middle of the desert, which was about as important as it got in the Wastes.

But was that it? Or was there more?

I didn't know, and he still needed an answer.

"Yes, I think so."

He gave me a small squeeze in response.

"I'm going to get cleaned up for bed. Since I'm letting you go out on a limb, I want you to try something with me," I said.

"Uhm, okay. What's that?"

The curiosity in his voice made me bite back a chuckle.

"Pull the mattresses off the frame and put them on the floor. I'll be back in a minute." I quickly shut the bathroom door and blew through my nightly clean up. We had a small daily allotment of water for personal grooming, and regular laundry service. It was one of the few benefits of being inside the city walls. Though a month from now, I knew I'd be happy to give it up to get our freedom back.

Feeling fresher and in my ugly, standard-issue pajama tee, I opened the bathroom door to find a confused River staring at our mattresses squished into the little floor space we had. The bathroom door *barely* opened, and I had to turn sideways and shuffle to squeeze through the narrow gap.

"I'm not sure what you had in mind, exactly . . ." He hesitated, opting to gesture to the tight quarters, rather than keep talking.

"Uhm, sleeping? Hop in." I stepped on the closest mattress and sank all the way down to lie on my side. Propped on my elbow, I patted the space next to me.

He slowly followed me down, balancing on his own elbow in the mirror position to mine.

"How do you like to sleep? On your back, right?" I asked.

"Yeah, back. Flat is always preferable, which has been a challenge here."

"Exactly. Lie down and get where your arm's not hanging off the edge. We can share."

"Nyx, I feel like you're trying to get me into bed," he joked.

"Oh, shut up and lie down. You're exhausted. We're grown adults, and neither of us has cooties." I rolled my eyes as he winked and settled onto his back. His right shoulder was fully eight inches over the middle seam, so it was no wonder he'd been getting crappy sleep.

"All jokes aside, I'm taking up too much of your space. I don't want you to be uncomfortable either." He propped his arm under his head, opening up the middle space again.

"Shush," I scolded, and settled onto my pillow at his side. Not touching, but close enough to feel the warmth radiating from his side. His very *muscled* side. "I'm a side sleeper. This is plenty of room."

We lay in comfortable silence for a while, and then River surprised me by speaking up.

"Earlier you said Chace was primarily worried about us getting to leave. Was there something else?"

I sighed, not wanting to rehash it. So, I gave him the short version. "He's worried they're going to be mad I'm not related to Chrysanthe, or worse, that I *will* be her great-great-great-granddaughter, and that will be a bad thing. That they'll want to use me."

He stroked his beard for a second and looked over at me, a worried look on his handsome face. "I hadn't thought about the fact that you could actually be related. I wonder if that's why they want your blood? It opened the locket—maybe they need it for something else she left behind."

Putting it that way gave me pause, but what was done was done. A niggling voice in the back of my brain reminded me that Commandant Kieran had refused to say *why* it mattered if I was her relative. "Who knows. There's no point worrying about it when we don't even know if it's true. Maybe it's designed to only open for a woman; everyone else who tried to touch it was a man. We really can't know, unless we're willing for some other people to die."

"True, and we don't need to risk that. We'll stay on our toes. At least if they need you, they'll keep you alive."

"They don't need me; he's just being paranoid. Everything's going to work out," I insisted, in equal parts for myself and him.

The lights flickered off at the scheduled time, and in minutes, River's breathing evened out in the soft rhythm of sleep.

◈

When I woke the next morning, River was already out of bed, dressed and doing push-ups on the lower bunk frame.

"Morning." He grinned over at me, but he never stopped moving. Sweat beaded on his forehead as he pumped himself up and down without pausing.

"How are you so awake? Geez, it's still early." I scrubbed at my eyes with the heel of my hand and checked the time. Six thirty. Oof.

"I know, it's great. I actually slept last night, thanks to you." He shifted positions, putting one hand on the small of his back, and continuing the pushups with one arm. Psycho.

I scuttled out of the bed like a half-asleep crab, then shut myself into the bathroom. When I came out a while later, he'd finished his pushups and was toweling sweat off his neck with a grin the size of Texas. The mattresses were also stacked neatly on the bottom bunk and out of our walk space. There was nothing left to do except go sell Horace on River's plan, whatever that was. Easy-peasy.

"Absolutely *not*." Horace slammed his fist on the table, a bit of spittle flying off his bottom lip along with the outburst. "What kind of idiot do you take me for? We know you've got weapons in that vehicle, and you want us to give you the chance to smuggle one in? No! Darinna, even you can't seriously think this is a good idea." He turned an incredulous gaze on her.

"Horace, no one's suggesting we *arm* them. All they're requesting is a suit, and the ability to provide us with seeds. From what they've said, there is seed stock in there from varieties we're actively struggling to maintain. This is a win we need, at a time when the whole community needs a morale boost. You *know* how it gets when there's an exile. And Lira and Frank were *beloved*. Putting them out into the sands . . . that was a serious blow. We need a win, not just for our biodiversity sustainability—though we desperately need that—but for the *people*. These two are offering us both. We'd be stupid not to take it."

Time to drive in the final nail. "I *also* have a garden journal. I would like to retain a copy when we leave, of course, but I'm happy to have it brought in for your people to scan and analyze. It belonged to Armand, Chrysanthe's husband, who cultivated all of the seeds in our possession. From what I've read and experienced, he was a master gardener. He could have notes in there that will mean more to your people than they did to me." I shrugged, feigning ignorance. I'd asked Morgan on our walk this morning if she had any idea what a nightshade was—that Darinna had said was doing so poorly—and she had explained it was a genus of plants including tomatoes, peppers, and a whole host of staple food crops. I'd seen both tomato and pepper seeds in the book, as well as detailed instructions from Armand. They *needed* what we had.

"So what, to hell with our decontamination protocols? Seeds won't survive the solution. It's specifically designed to kill any pests and invasive species that might be hitchhiking along with someone."

"Surely there's a scanner in the decon room which can scan their seed box without applying the solution? Let's consult a tech. That way, we'll still know if they try to bring anything else in. We can verify, and still get what we need unharmed. All I'm asking is that you work with us. Griffin and I are more than capable of setting up a temporary quarantine greenhouse where we can start grow-outs on the seeds separately from our existing stock. In fact, I'd insist."

Horace sighed, seeing she wasn't going to drop it and had a rebuttal for each of his protests. "I want it on the record that I say this is a *terrible* idea. And there's no way they're going to let her out of the walls. She's a flight risk."

"I'll be the one to go," River jumped to reassure him. "I know that Nyx is the valuable one—she's the descendant. I'm happy to suit up and get what's needed from the Bronco." He gave Horace his most unthreatening, puppy-dog smile, dimple on full display and head cocked to the side. He could really ham it up when he chose to.

Horace scowled at each of us in turn, then shoved his chair back from his desk, the scraping sound grating across my nerves like sand rash.

He stomped out of the room and down the hallway, and we waited.

Three hours later, River was suited and I was in a small control room in a line of rolling chairs with three members of Excursion Team One, watching him on a monitoring wall. It ran floor to ceiling, dotted with camera views of the entire exterior of the city. There were gaps that usually held interior views, but they'd flipped a switch to hide those when I was escorted in.

They weren't taking any chances in giving me too much information. Though, even seeing how much visibility they had to the entire perimeter was huge. We'd have to get over two rows of dunes minimum to be out of their sight, assuming they didn't follow with any of the drones. I couldn't watch the views from those, though, because they made my stomach twist painfully.

For now, my gaze was riveted on River. He stood with Gabriel just inside the front gate of the city wall. The Bronco keys were clutched in his gloved hand, and Gabriel was pulling the helmet portion of the suit up and over his face, covering the familiar dishwater blond hair. Once it was in place, from the camera angle behind him, he could have been any other marshmallow soldier in this place, and the feeling was unsettling.

Almost as bad as when he'd shown me his Sidewinder tattoo.

With his helmet fastened, we heard a comm crackle through the room. "Give me a thumbs up if you can hear this." Gabriel's no-nonsense tone was loud and clear.

River gave him a thumbs up.

"All right, now say something so we know we can hear you."

"Uh, hmm. I'll be right back, Nyx."

"Loud and clear. Straight to the vehicle, retrieve *only* the seeds and the journal, and no more than two personal items. Stop outside the glass dome for a preliminary scan. Once cleared, approach the gate and wait for the secondary scan, and then the gate will open fully. We are monitoring you at all times; we *will* see if you try to smuggle in a weapon, and you will be placed into the laborer pool for punishment if you do. We clear?"

"Loud and," River responded, his tone dry and sarcastic.

My fingers gripped the arm of my swivel chair so hard, I felt a thread pop under my fingernail. I forced myself to relax, look at ease as River walked with painstaking slowness through the now-open gate, and out into the intermediate zone. While no one in the room appeared to be paying me any attention, I should have had no reason to be nervous, and I didn't want to raise red flags or make them suspicious. Frankly, I didn't know what River had in mind to try. He'd insisted on keeping it to himself, just in case.

As far as everyone was concerned, this was an easy walk to the truck and back; something River and I had done every day together for months. Just throwing in a freaking space suit, airlocks, and multi-million water credits worth of security and surveillance. No biggie.

He took the first steps out into the intermediate zone toward the dome wall with painstaking slowness, and I leaned forward to get a closer look at the screens. Was he struggling with the suit? He continued plodding along, at a third of his usual speed, and I realized he must have been. River was so athletic, it had never occurred to me that he might not take to the suit like a fish to water.

The excursion team mumbled some complaints as we watched his snail-like progress—he tripped and fell over twice as he hit the deeper sand closer to the perimeter—but finally he made it to the dome.

Since it took so long for him to walk, by the time he made it out of the bubble and halfway to the Bronco, my nerves had settled. But as he neared the Bronco, they began to ramp back up. Nobody had mentioned their plan to send him into the laborer's class as punishment if he tried to sneak something in. Was he going to risk that? What *was* he going to do, dang it?

I hated being in the dark.

It required a lot of trust; and while I trusted River not to hurt me, I didn't trust he wouldn't hurt himself *for* me. It seemed like exactly the kind of stupidly heroic thing he'd do—sacrificing his own time in the trenches with the laborers to give me a way to escape. But I wouldn't escape without him any more than I would without Chace, and him being locked up would make things harder. Plus, if they caught a weapon, they'd take it, and it would be for nothing.

I hated this plan. I should have tried to talk him out of it.

He fumbled the keys and struggled with the button to get the door open. The excursion officer closest to me groaned and rolled his eyes.

"They should have sent one of us, and we'd be back in the Barracks already."

"Can't; it's their property. We can't just go search it—they wouldn't consent," a second officer said with a pointed glance at me.

"I know, I was just saying," he said sullenly, and took a chug of coffee from an off-white mug.

They fell silent as River's torso and arms disappeared into the back of the truck.

I kept the frown off my face as I watched. The seeds and journal were right behind the front seats. Why did he go around the back? Did he not remember, or was this his play for a weapon?

Keeping utterly still, I let my eyes flicker to the other camera angles, checking to see if the interior of the truck was visible from any other view.

No, no, no, ahh—black fabric. He was going for the C-4. I kept my breaths steady, but they wanted to shallow out.

This was worse than anything dangerous I'd ever done myself. Being in the action, I could slip into it and let the possible consequences fade out of my mind. Watching? All I could do was sit on my hands and try not to clue the guards into his plan.

To his credit, as slow as River had been getting to the Bronco, he wasn't inside long. When he leaned out of the back, he had my leather satchel slung over one shoulder, the seed box clutched under one armpit, and the journal in his opposite hand. He shuffled them oh-so-carefully into the same hand, then closed the back hatch and re-locked the truck.

Then began the slow trudge back. To my surprise, though, he came back a bit faster than he'd gone. Maybe he was getting used to it, finally.

The occasional mutters continued in the control room as he made his way back and into the bubble, but when he approached the inside gate, River's exuberant face was clear as day inside his helmet. He was proud of himself.

When he was only a few feet from the giant gate, he looked straight up at the camera above him, and held the seeds and journal up proudly over his head, like a triumphant hero returning home. To my surprise, there was a smattering of applause from the guys in the room at his accomplishment. And then, so close to the goal, he tripped over a rock in the path, and fell head first between the wall and a giant organ pipe cactus.

"Ooh," everybody in the room groaned sympathetically as one.

"That's gotta hurt!"

"What a doofus. He almost made it," another mocked.

I watched with my hand over my mouth as River struggled to rise and extricate himself from the prickly situation, helpless to get to him and give him a hand.

It took several minutes, but he managed to get upright again and gather the few errant seed packets back into the box—all without ripping a hole into the suit, which would have meant he had to be decontaminated again.

Once he was upright, he sheepishly took the last few steps to the gate, and watched as it swung open, letting him back into the cold, heartless fold.

I leapt to my feet and darted into the hall but didn't get far before one of the guards caught me by the arm. "Hold up—he's got to take that stuff into the decon room to get scanned before he can come out of the suit. You can't touch him or it."

With a sigh, I stopped and waited just outside the door. River passed us, ten feet away, and

I gave him a supportive wave as he lumbered past.

Half an hour later, he was back in his normal clothes, walking briskly but still looking sheepish with my satchel over his shoulder. "So, that was harder than I expected," he admitted as he ran a hand through his hair.

"You did fine. We good to go back to our room?" I asked the guard over my shoulder.

"Yeah, you're cleared. Go." Gabriel, suddenly next to me, gestured with his chin to where Morgan waited down the hall as he walked up beside us.

I jumped, having not seen him coming, so focused had I been on River. "Thanks. Come on, pokey Joe."

"Aww, not you, too! That suit's heavy. It was hard to walk in. They've all practiced, and they make it look easy!"

Sniggers from the guards echoed behind us as I looped my arm through his and we exited the bleached-white hallways, to walk through the park back to our room with Morgan.

As soon as we were in the open air—well, *more* open air—Morgan was the first to speak.

"Did it go okay?"

He nodded. "It was harder navigating in the suit than it looked, but I got it done. Pretty sure everyone was laughing at me when I fell into the cactus, right by the front camera." He sighed, looking at his boots.

A giggle escaped her before she schooled her expression. "I'm sorry. But I'm sure everyone has a hard time their first go around."

"Yeah, maybe," he hedged. I gave his arm a supportive squeeze, but didn't chime in. It didn't seem to be helping, anyways.

"Hey, I wanted to ask you two something. Would you be amenable to joining me and some of the other citizens for a . . . dinner?"

Her hesitation piqued my interest. "Dinner? Like, a friendly dinner, or . . .?" I squinted at her, trying to pick up on any small signal that might give me a hint of what she was inviting us to.

"Very friendly. You might even say, we're like a family." She gave me a knowing look, and a miniscule nod that I should say yes.

"I don't see why not. When is it?"

"Next week. I'll pick you up just after curfew."

River was the one to question that little tid-bit. "*After* curfew? Won't the door guards have something to say about that?"

"Well, let's just say that your guards that night will be part of the family." She gave us a wink as we arrived at our door. "See you soon." With one last finger wiggle, she turned and disappeared back into the twisting, turning hallways.

When the door shut behind us, I locked it and pressed my back against the frame, making pointed eye contact with River.

"Well?"

He grinned, ear to ear. "We have a back door."

"*How*? I watched you every step of the way. The only time you weren't in direct line of a camera's view was when you were inside the back of the Bronco. And even then, I did see you pull up the . . ." I thought about it, deciding not to lay it all out there, in case someone was listening in. "*Black bag*," I hissed.

He did a victory lap around the itty-bitty room, fists pumping in the air with exuberance. "That means you didn't suspect me!"

"Suspect what? I knew what you were trying to do."

"You didn't suspect I was clumsy on purpose." He stopped and stared at me, waiting for me to put two and two together.

"Do you mean to tell me, you weren't struggling in the marshmallow suit?"

"I was *not* struggling in the marshmallow suit."

My jaw dropped. "You little faker! So, the big stumble at the end . . . ?"

He bobbled his hand back and forth indecisively. "It's more of a front door than a back door, but, we've at least got a helluva distraction."

"I could kiss you—that's utterly genius!"

"Well, come on . . . I won't ever complain about a kiss." He held up his hands and gave me the universal sign for *come on over*.

So, I did.

Twenty-Seven

ENVOY

The next week passed in a sluggish crawl, each day feeling like pointless torture—besides the fun bit where we ducked the daily summons to come back for vaccinations. *Not happening, lady.* Morgan had to go back to her regular duties, and any time we left our room our guard detail followed hot on our heels. Kind of took the fun out of tramping through the meadow and petting the sheep. The worst part? We had two to three more weeks to go before the Sidewinders showed up with the trade goods, and we had a chance to get out of here. Assuming the leadership panel stuck to their end of the bargain. Assuming there were no issues with the trade. Assuming . . . well, it was a lot of assuming. Other than the secret dinner tonight with Morgan, though, we had nothing to do but sit around and wait.

River also exercised a lot, but he was weird like that. I was used to it.

When the mid-day pounding at our door came, I was lying on my back on the double-stacked bed reading a borrowed novel, and River was doing sit-ups in the middle of the floor. We both sat bolt upright and exchanged a worried glance.

He popped up and beat me to the door, but I was hot on his heels. River swung the door open, and I peered past his arm to see two of our guards standing stiffly. They worked in a rotation, but today it was Germaine, an abrasive man with an off-color sense of humor, and Lou.

Lou, usually our most reticent guard, was the first one to speak. "Your presence has been requested by the leadership panel."

"O-kay. Is there a reason? They just missed us, or . . . ?" River said jokingly.

Lou scowled, and pressed his fingertips to his ear, listening to someone over his earpiece. I spotted a small, black swirling tattoo there which I hadn't noticed before.

"I've been informed that an envoy has arrived, and you're needed in your official emissary capacity." His eyes lowered from River's to mine, and he cocked one eyebrow in question.

"Oh. Well, okay then. Give us just a minute to grab our stuff."

He nodded, and River pushed the door to so we could have a moment of privacy.

"Didn't you say it would be three to four weeks for the Sidewinders?"

"I did. It can't be them, unless they've got something a whole lot faster than ancient muscle cars we didn't know about."

"Is that a possibility?" he asked as I shoved my feet into my boots and stuffed a water orb in my pocket.

I couldn't help a snort at that. "No. It's not the Sidewinders."

"Who do you think it is?"

"I honestly don't know." I cast around the room for anything else I needed, but we had very little here that wasn't provided for us. "Let's go find out."

We followed the guards in silence, and they didn't provide any more information about who the mysterious envoy was. They led us to the familiar leadership panel meeting room, but the chairs had been completely rearranged. There were four chairs on each end of the room, with a few placed surrounding a short table turned parallel to the room's length. Apparently, they intended to watch as River and I spoke with whoever had arrived.

Although . . . how long ago had they arrived? They'd have been put through decontamination like we had, right?

"You can wait here. The rest of the group should be arriving shortly," Lou gestured to the table—a.k.a. hot seat—in the middle of the room, and then stepped out and shut the door.

Thankfully, we didn't have to wait more than ten minutes before the door opened again, and four members of the leadership panel walked in. Morgan's Uncle Vander, another man, and two women. One had been angry—Celeste? Was that her name?—while the other two had sat quietly and observed during our previous interactions with the leadership panel, so I didn't know their names, or what they thought of us. There was no sign of the commandant, but that was good. I didn't need him breathing down my neck while I tried to negotiate with whoever this was. The four of them settled behind us in the row of chairs against the wall, but other than brief pleasantries we waited in silence.

Two minutes later, the door opened again, this time admitting six men dressed head to toe in black, their faces covered. I felt River freeze at my side, and horrified worry washed over me. They paused briefly, in which time my blood pressure ratcheted through the roof, and I checked my water meter out of life-long nervous habit—green, ninety-two percent—two of them approached the table while the other four took the seats against the far wall, much like the Bastion City representatives.

When my eyes met Hema's, it felt like an electric jolt through my body. This was the man—the complete stranger—who'd saved me from the brink of death by dehydration in the desert. And now, fate had brought us here, back together in the last place I'd ever expected to see the reserved nomad. It was a long, long way from where I'd seen him last, and by the look in his eyes, he had experienced much in the time since—just like we had. He flicked a disinterested glance over at River, before settling back into the silent connection with me.

River squeezed my knee lightly under the table, and the simple contact snapped me back to the present. This wasn't all those weeks ago on death's door. This was the here and now, and Hema was—I now knew—a Nightblood. His presence could mean death for River, and that was the *right now* problem.

My, how things had changed.

I slowly rose to my feet, inclining my head respectfully towards him, and then his companion. Thankfully, I didn't recognize the other man as any of the men who'd roughed us up on the way here. That would have been awkward.

"Hema, my friend, I have no words to describe exactly how shocked I am to see you. We were expecting a trade envoy soon, but I admit, we did not expect you. And your . . . Nightbloods?" I couldn't help but glance across his gathered men as I threw out the question. I hadn't known *then* what I knew now. My hazy, grateful memories of Hema the nomad were clashing horribly with what I knew of the Nightbloods, ruthless killers and terrorists of other desert dwellers. How could he be both?

"Nyx, I am likewise pleased, and surprised. Καλημέρα στην άμμο, η επί χρόνια φίλη μου." He gave me a grave nod. "When I learned of your passing through our territory, I was intrigued, and decided to follow."

That was unexpected. It also made me question his real intent. I was marked to be released in their system, but River . . . River had technology that they wanted, sitting outside unprotected in the Bronco. The very thought made my shoulder blades itch and my palms sweat. How high was Hema in the Nightblood hierarchy? River hadn't mentioned him—or anyone—by name, and it was too late to ask if he knew him. The team who'd seen us hadn't seen his alert, but if Hema and his companion were sitting at this table, they had to have some power—and knowledge.

Did any of them know River on sight, and of what he'd run with? Could I find out without blowing his identity if they didn't?

"I'm honored that you found me intriguing. Now that you've found me, what is it you hope to accomplish? Are you interested in trade with the city?"

The man to his right shifted in his seat. Not a lot. I caught it in my peripheral vision—the small stiffening of his spine, the twitch of the muscle above his left eyebrow.

Not trade, then.

Hema held up his hands. "We came for curiosity, but we'll never turn down a mutually beneficial arrangement."

My mind was spinning, trying to figure out if that was a veiled threat to River, to me, or the city. When had my life gotten so complicated? Trading coffee beans for water credits to stay alive was one thing. Trading convoluted pleasantries with a veiled man for unknown stakes was enough to drive a girl insane. *Keep it cool, Nyx. You made it this far, and he's saved your life before. He isn't an enemy, at least.*

"You and me both. Was there anything in particular you'd like to see from the city, something your people need? Are they *your* people, by the way? I'm a bit blurry on how the Nightbloods operate." I gave him a lopsided smile and wobbled my hand back to illustrate my uncertainty.

His eyes crinkled briefly at the corners, and I imagined the outline of a smile under the black fabric swathing his face. "We are a private people. For now, that is enough to know. Our people lack for nothing but information. We have heard rumblings that there is a highly important project here that could benefit all mankind. If there is to be progress with this project, we would like to be a part of that."

Okay, *what*?

"Hema, I must admit— we haven't been here long, and we're not confidantes of the city. Merely temporary allies, as a means to an end. If there's something specific, I'm afraid you'll have to speak plainly, or I won't be able to help." It felt odd laying it all out there, but I was curious, now. I thought the city *was* the project.

One of the women behind us stood abruptly, waving a hand. "Bastion City will neither confirm nor deny any of our technological projects, and we are not interested in trading our intellectual property—"

Hema's eyes grew cold and hard as steel as he cut his gaze to her. He shook his head, tutting lightly. "You have technology that could change the course of history for *all men*, and you wish to play coy? It is unwise to assume that you are safe inside your dome. It may be impressively tall, but even mere men can reach its foundations."

Okay, that was *definitely* a threat. I shot a quick glance at River, hoping my worry at the turn this was taking wasn't too obvious. But my curiosity was winning. If there was some top-secret, earth-shattering science project here, I wanted to know about it before we left.

"It is *unwise* to threaten the people who have the power to wipe you off the map," the woman said with a pointed snap of her fingers.

Hema didn't flinch, and he didn't seem impressed. "You threaten us at mere mention of the water generator. Perhaps this technology is not as advanced as I was led to believe. Surely the sharing of the device with all across the lands who have the means to deploy it would be beneficial, no?"

"This meeting is over." Vander stood, causing a ripple effect as the two remaining members of the leadership panel rose, uncertainty painted across their faces. "We'll take your request under advisement, and let you know within seventy-eight hours."

Three days. Apparently they liked to piss off the most notorious bullies in the whole flippin' desert—while we were trapped inside their walls. Joy.

"Hema, I'll see what I can do to find out more about this water generator. I hope we will have another chance to speak before we part ways." I gave him a nod, which he returned slowly, deliberately. When he rose and left the room with his people trailing him, it was like all the air left with them. The guards shut the door behind them, and a small object went flying across the room and crashed into the glass wall separating us from the park. The pen bounced away to land harmlessly on the white floors, but I stood regardless. If people were throwing things, it was best to be on your feet.

"Consequences! What did I say but that there would be *consequences*? We should have sent these two away the first day! He threatened our bio-dome!"

"Enough, Celeste! Remember the decorum due your position!" The petite, fine-boned woman at her side spoke, sharp disapproval coating her words like acid.

"Yes, Sakura, where *has* her decorum gone?" Vander was visibly angry, clenching and un-clenching his fist at his side before turning towards River and me. "You two—dismissed. Back to your rooms."

"Shouldn't we help negotiate—" River started but was quickly shut down.

"Absolutely not. You don't have clearance for what they're asking, and it's a nonstarter. We'll notify you when you're needed again." With that, he turned his back, and started dressing down Celeste in a low tone.

I reached for River's hand, and together we headed out of the tense meeting room.

Twenty-Eight

A Different Kind of Negotiation

River and I had barely shut the apartment door between ourselves and our guards long enough to gape in silent shock at everything that had transpired before a hurried knock rang out.

He took the two steps back to the door and pulled it open to reveal Morgan, earlier than expected and with her hair flying wildly about.

"Change of plans. You guys free now?" She shook her head. "Who am I talking to? You don't have anything to do, you lucky ducks. Come on."

Without waiting for a response, she turned on her heel and speed-walked away. We hurried to follow; despite her shorter legs, she was freaking fast. If we didn't keep up, she would disappear around a corner without us.

True to her word, the guards didn't follow us for the first time since we'd been inside the city. They resumed their posts, backs to the door and bored expressions painted on as if we were still inside. What would they do if the leadership panel came looking for us again?

Hopefully we didn't have to find out; Hema's request should keep them busy for a while.

Morgan led us through a veritable maze of hallways, for longer than she ever had before. After a time, the pristine white gave way to a kind of dinginess we hadn't seen before. From the front gate to the sheep's pasture, everything in this place seemed obsessively clean and well kept. But here, the halls began to feel more like tunnels. We approached a door, the same dingy-white color as the rest of the walls, with a keypad dangling from a nest of wires, lazily blinking yellow in the harsh lighting. She didn't try to palm-scan in, instead knocking three times in a rapid staccato, then pulling open the door. There was a man and a woman in lifeside jumpsuits inside, instead of guard uniforms. They gave us curious looks, but nodded for us to continue down the smaller, shorter halls.

River reached up and trailed his fingertips briefly over the low ceiling. We walked another ten minutes before reaching a sharp right corner. With one last turn, we reached a door. It was nondescript with no windows or any markers besides another sad, blinking palm scanner, but Morgan repeated the knock. This time, she waited for the door to crack and a woman's head to peek out and nod us in.

I hadn't been sure what to expect from this family dinner, but a long room stuffed to the gills with angry people wasn't it. Heat from so many bodies packed in close enveloped us as we squeezed into the back of the room and stood elbow to elbow with the woman on door duty. She gave us a welcoming nod, but otherwise seemed disinterested in anything except the front of the room; a small space was cleared except for an overturned ancient wooden apple box.

A middle-aged man with a bald cul-de-sac cut from his russet hair stepped forward and easily up onto the box, giving him two feet of height over the crowd and making him visible to all.

"Welcome, family." Two small words sent a hush over the buzzing crowd, and he gave us all a warm smile.

"We've gathered this evening to discuss the sudden changes happening in our city. Many of us have been concerned—disturbed—by the leadership decisions in recent years, but in the past months these bad decisions have compounded to a new level. We have long toiled in silence, accepting our roles as the labor that keeps this great city flourishing. But one among us wishes to speak, and I know his family wishes to hear. Frankie, please." He motioned a younger man forward, and stepped down from the apple box.

Morgan leaned in closer to River and me and whispered, "That's Frankie Grenkel. His parents were the ones who . . . well, you remember."

He was tall and lean, with deep chestnut hair cropped short. His eyes burned with anger as he gazed out over us all, and I could see the man his father must have been, before old age clouded his memory. "Family, a great wrong has been committed by those in power, and we cannot let it stand."

A murmur of agreement rippled through the crowd, and I could feel the tension hanging thick in the air.

"My parents, who've served the Bastion throughout their long lives, were cast out for crimes they did not commit. Is it a crime to be aged? Is it a crime to move slower as a life of hard work stiffens the joints? Is it a crime to use your knowledge to help instead of your back? No, it is not! My parents committed no crime, except to have reached the natural waning of physical strength." He paused and ran his gaze over the people, seeming to see into our souls.

"I ask you, family, if any of us will do any less? Will we sweat, and toil, and strain under the weight of hard labor the whole of our lives faithfully, only to be cast out by the ones we feed and clothe?"

"We will not!" a woman in the middle of the crowd shouted, raising an angry fist in the air.

The crowd roiled, and more shouts rang out. The heat of danger rolled over my skin. This was a mob in the making, and we were strangers. The ones who'd probably been the catalyst of the exile. I mentally cursed the leaders of this city for not letting me keep so much as a pocketknife.

"It is time for change!" Frankie exhorted, his voice raised and echoing around the upper reaches of the chamber, until the raucous cheers of the angry throng drowned him out. With a satisfied nod and a near-religious fervor in his eyes, he stepped back down and melted into the crowd. The first man stepped back up and raised both hands, but it took several minutes for the fevered cheers to die down.

"Family, we all agree that this grave injustice cannot be allowed to stand. If they have no love for the greatest and most honored among us, how can we give that same honor to them?"

"We don't, Yu-riel!"

"We can't!"

"I say it's time to fight!"

Shouts rang out around the room, and Yu-riel once again patted the air, attempting to quiet the crowd. "The interests of the people have long been denied. The time has come for change; the only question is, what should that change be?" He held up a pre-emptive hand as he continued to speak, gazing around the room until his eyes fixed on River and me, standing tensely in the back of the crowd.

"We have among us newcomers, rare people who not only survived on the outside, but journeyed across the Wastes to make it safely to our hallowed walls. They have befriended one of our own—Morgan—and supplied seeds to bolster our desperately waning stores. While their appearance may have been the cause of Lira and Frank's unjust exile, we cannot place the blame on them. From what I hear, they have made this long, treacherous journey to right a wrong that was perpetrated on them by our leadership, as well."

This time the noise from the crowd was troubled, and my sense of imminent danger spiked, leaving me hearing the blood pounding in my ears, and mentally disabling the woman watching the door so that River and I could bolt down the long halls if this turned south.

"I would like to ask these newcomers to come forward and speak to us about what they've experienced. While it would be easy for us to blame them or cast them aside, perhaps a better solution can be found that rights the wrong for us all, if we work together. Nyx and River, please come forward."

Morgan tapped the shoulders of the few closest people, and they shuffled to the sides to make a path for us towards the front of the room.

The room with no doors, windows, or exits, and several hundred furious people ready to throw down.

I took a deep breath and lifted my chin, trader face intact as I stepped forward, the crowd continuing to part like sand under the Bronco's tires as we walked to the front of the would-be mob.

I looked up at Yu-riel, and he looked us up and down in our drab and ill-fitting Bastion City sweats. "Whose brother was taken as a transplant?" He asked the question quietly, and I answered.

"Mine."

He nodded. "Please step up, and speak honestly," is all he said before stepping down the far side of the box.

I glanced at River, and he gave me an encouraging nod before I stepped up on the wooden box. I braced myself for it to rock under my feet, but it was steady and grounded, much like these people surrounding us. Looking out over a packed room of people was a new and unsettling experience, but I forced down my uncertainty as I raised my voice.

"My name is Nyx Brandt, and I've driven weeks across the Wastes and nearly died more than once in an effort to find my brother, Chace."

The people closest to us shifted uneasily on their feet, and I could tell they didn't want to see us as human, as victims. I was nobody's victim, but I was not the enemy, either.

"A few months ago, the brother who raised me disappeared from our tent city in the middle of the night. He's been my caretaker since my mother cast me out at the age of seven, when he was only ten. It was because of him I survived the cruel realities of life in the Wastes, and I knew there was nothing short of death that would keep him from me. So, I made it my mission to find him, find out what happened to him."

Silence was the only answer, so I continued.

"I suspected the gang leaders of our city; many people had been killed and tossed to the dunes over the years, but we were always careful to steer clear of them. As the days passed, I learned of other young, fit people from our city who'd also vanished. Not many, but enough to know it wasn't just my brother. A beautiful young woman, another man in good physical health and a year younger. Vanished. I searched the dunes for their bodies, but found none. I spoke to every person in every tent who was over the age of five and finally, approached the gang."

I cleared my throat, unused to speaking for so long at a time.

"What I found—after much pain and punishment—was that they didn't have my brother, but knew where he was. Weeks of travel led me to a map, left by one of your founders."

Soft gasps and whispers of unease wound around me as I finished the story. "River and I used that map, crossed the Nightbloods' territory, and came here, where we found my brother, and at least a dozen others who'd all been taken from cities like mine, struggling to survive in the Wastes. We've come to deal with the Bastion and get my brother back." With a quick look down to River, I looked back out at the people. "It was never our intention to cause the people here any trouble, and we are deeply sorry that your elders were thrown out in our stead. We've made it abundantly clear to your leadership that we want Chace returned, and we'll leave in peace. We've agreed to trade outside goods for his freedom, and have acted in good faith, supplying the seeds. Still, they haven't released him or us, and they attacked him when we found him and tried to get to him."

A sudden lump rose in my throat, and my attempts to swallow it down failed. An unfamiliar hand on my wrist caused me to look down, and Yu-riel gave me a grave nod before gesturing that I'd said enough.

As soon as I stepped down, he stepped back up and addressed the people. "Our leaders have committed crimes against us, and they have committed crimes against these people as well. I propose that we band together, and work with them in friendship as should have been done by our leaders. They have great knowledge of survival on the outside, and an exile to these two would be no death sentence. Family, it is time we take our power back."

The resulting cheer was so loud, my eardrums hurt, and it felt like the floor vibrated under my feet. After that, we were escorted from the room. As we wound back through the crowd, it was to slaps on the shoulders, and repeated welcomes from the people we brushed past.

Morgan waited just outside the door, and Yu-riel and a handful of others exited with us, and headed further down the dingy hallways to a much smaller room. The furniture was ancient and made of wood, a scratched and dented long rectangular dining table surrounded by mismatched chairs—a few with missing spindles—on three sides, and a flat bench on the other side.

The door clicked closed softly on the sounds of the meeting hall emptying, voices echoing and clashing as the people dispersed, and I breathed a small sigh of relief. River and I took the seats closest to the door, and my hand sought his under the table like my lungs sought their next breath. Our fingers lacing together grounded me, and I forced myself to assess the few leaders who'd moved to this room with us.

Yu-riel was clearly their leader, but the other five people were a mystery to me. They were a mix of ages and colorings, men and women. None seemed overtly angry or dismissive, which was a good sign.

To my surprise, Yu-riel wasn't the first to speak. A petite woman with smooth and tawny skin and deep black hair, she spoke softly but with conviction. "We of the Bastion are sincerely sorry for the wrongs done to your family, and hope that from this ugliness, something beneficial for all can be born. Are you willing to negotiate with the people, as we've been told you have negotiated with our leaders?"

I studied her, deciding how to proceed. "Thank you, and of course we're open to working with you. I admit that I'm not sure what I *have* that would be of value to so many, besides the seeds which I've already traded to the leadership panel. What is it your people need from us?"

She steepled her fingers lightly and looked at Yu-riel and the others.

"You want to leave with your brother, and you know how to survive. Could you help us to do the same?"

"All of you?" I asked, unable to keep the surprise from my voice. Smuggling Morgan out and bringing her along with us was one thing, but when Yu-riel nodded that they *all* wanted to leave, I leaned back in my seat as the enormity of that rocked me.

"I'll be frank with you—while I have the knowledge needed for desert survival, logistically your request is . . ." I pressed my lips together and carefully considered my next words. "I only have one vehicle, and enough water for a few people. To take everyone away from here, we'd need enough vehicles and supplies for everyone. Tools, clothes . . . tents would be nice, but I suppose optional if the vehicles are big enough. I . . . I don't have that kind of resources as a single person. I'm happy to advise, and I do have a location where a new city is being built around a water source. But, as we could both tell you, life in the desert is not perfect. We live with much less than you are accustomed to here."

"And with more danger," River added, leaning forward on his forearms. "Are you aware that your city's excursion teams regularly bomb and attack the people trying to live too close? We met a group—the Collective, they call them-selves—a few hours south of here who are walk-ing wounded, even some of the children cov-ered in burn scars because the Bastion doesn't want people living close to the walls."

Around the room, lips pressed into lines of distress, but a black man on the end shook his head slowly. "Exile is no threat if another civilization waits on the doorstep. They've en-forced this no-man's land for many, many years. It is unfortunate, but it is one of their methods of keeping the so-called peace."

A pit formed in my stomach at his words, but I could see the logic in them as River continued. "We've given the Collective the coordinates of the new city, Wolf Well, but we don't know if they've decided to leave the area. We haven't been in contact since we've been inside these walls. I'm sure Nyx would agree that we could share this information with you as well."

"Of course, but you should know that you'd be trading a corrupt and controlling leader-ship panel for a gang run by a madman; the Sidewinders have claimed control of the new city. And you'll be free, but you'll have to watch your backs. It's . . . a complicated life."

They sat in silence, thinking on what I'd shared.

"If you are willing to teach us, we are willing to take the risk." Yu-riel finally spoke again. "We are used to hard work—at least there we would know that the work is for our own people, and not the luxuries of the leaders so willing to discard us as useless. Eventually, I am sure we could find a way to self-govern. We'd like to discuss what you'd like in exchange, though. What is your plan for freeing your brother from the laborer class?"

"As you seem to know, we've struck a deal to set up trade and supply seed stock in exchange for his freedom. It will be a few more weeks, but they've promised to release all three of us when the seeds arrive. Though, we've had doubts about whether they will keep their word."

The dark-haired woman's pained expression told me all I needed to know. The council had no intention of letting any of us go, as we'd feared. The weight of River's gaze on my cheek added to the heaviness already on my shoulders.

"None have permanently left these walls, outside of exile, in living memory." It was the black man who confirmed it.

I nodded in appreciation for the honesty. If we couldn't trust that they'd keep their word, there was no point in waiting weeks for the Sidewinders to show up. There was *certainly* no point in attempting to trade goods to a city who didn't intend to hold up their end of the bargain.

I drummed my free fingers against my thigh, thinking. I squeezed Rivers fingers for a second, then let go and placed both of my palms flat on the table, a sudden calm settling into my bones after so long of being on edge. "I guess we're just going to have to work out a plan to get ourselves exiled, then."

Twenty-Nine

PASSING NOTES

The next three days passed in a rush of constant meetings with the lifeside leaders and various experts among their people from the lower echelon of the city. Because they were the ones who produced all of the food, they had people with access to the high-powered replicator machines who could create a large stash of meal bars; and water was simply a matter of them stockpiling direct from the source, which they assured me they could handle. Ground vehicles were the biggest limitation we faced, and it would take time to fix that shortage.

We also hashed out some ideas for high-value trade goods they could make quickly that would convert to water credits outside the walls. It was a new concept for most of them—the fact that labor alone wouldn't sustain them, and they'd need currency. River was great at helping me explain, and far more patient than I had any hope of ever being. The two of us fell into our floor-mattress together each night with bone-deep exhaustion and slept like the dead. I was pretty sure by that point that talking to people was much harder than scaling old building walls and prying valuables out of the desert's grip.

We'd already given them the coordinates to Wolf Well and begun mapping out the multiple routes they would need to take, in case the military of the city tried to force them all back. Contingencies upon contingencies were discussed until we were blue in the face, but slowly, painfully, the plan came together.

Finally, it was time for us to execute the first part—getting the three of us Waste-landers exiled from the city. According to Yu-riel, it would be surprisingly easier than expected. There were certain things that were verboten, even the youngest child among them knowing not to cross that line.

All River and I had to do was pick a piece of fruit off the giant fig tree inside the park, and it would equal immediate expulsion from the city, in nothing but our underclothes, and River would activate the radio to help the Red Riders as we were stripped and dragged out. At that point, there would be no further harm that could come to any of us if they detected the signal, so it would be the perfect opportunity.

I lamented the loss of the clothing we'd worn in—spare clothes didn't grow on trees, after all—but having to buy scavenge or new clothes at the nearest populous city was a small price to pay for getting the heck out of this biologically advanced hellhole.

The resulting hubbub should keep the leaders busy for a while, taking the scrutiny elsewhere and letting the uprising finish their preparations. The three of us would high-tail it north-east, overshooting the top of Wolf Well by a wide enough margin that we wouldn't lead any Bastion tails there, but close enough that we could swoop in and help make introductions and ease their transition when they arrived.

They gave us a pencil-lead sized comm device, much like the one I had from the Sidewinders, so that we could stay in touch as they made their escape, and River installed it into his water meter so we wouldn't lose it in the stripping portion of our plan.

Getting Chace out, however, proved more problematic. He didn't have access to the park at all, let alone the giant fig tree that was our escape route, and any attempts to get there would see him trapped in another taser net and drugged, unable to reach us. They offered to let

River and me leave, and bring Chace as part of their mass exodus, but I hotly refused.

There were *no* circumstances in which I left this pile of rocks without my brother. I did, however, have to trust them to help us in order for this plan to work. We still needed to clue Chace into the plan so he would cooperate, though, and that was nearly as difficult as getting him out.

The day before our planned exile, Morgan snuck to our room after curfew with a pair of guard uniforms. We pulled them on in silence and followed her out of the main corridor and into a small service hallway, which ran between the living and working quarters and the exterior stone walls. As we followed Morgan, I found it strangely soothing to run my fingertips over the cool, gritty surface of the city wall.. It was a long walk to the far side of the city, but eventually we made it to a smaller, darker version of the C Barracks we'd been kept in.

Everything was still white, but the spacious halls and generous lighting were gone, replaced with narrow walkways and flickering, wan light coming from ancient lights lining the ceiling.

We stopped at a corner, and she peeked around it, gesturing for us to wait. I heard the sounds of shuffling feet and a few grunts as if someone was being punched, and then a door shutting.

She pulled her head back around, and spoke in a barely audible whisper. "Okay, the laborers were all just locked in for the night. Guard change is in fifteen minutes, and they'll leave the door unattended for ten minutes while they debrief the new round of guards. You have the uniforms, but the best thing is for no one to see you, so you need to be out in nine minutes or less. This city isn't so big that they wouldn't recognize everyone except new recruits, so don't get caught up talking to your brother and expect the uniform to help you out for long. I have this to get you in past the scanner."

She held up a small, beige piece of leather with two finger holes and a thumb hole. "Slip this on your palm carefully." She passed it to River. "It's got a copied print from the commandant's favorite boot-licker, Kutsuki."

The officer who'd exiled the Grenkels. If anything went south, he would be implicated, and that ire would be directed squarely at us. Even in helping us, this was highly personal for them, and I wouldn't forget that. Forgetting someone's motives—whether ally or enemy—could be a deadly mistake.

River slid the piece on to cover his own palm print, and the next fifteen minutes were the longest of my life as we waited in silence. Finally, we heard the sound of boots thumping away down the hall, and when they faded around a corner, we moved.

Morgan whisper-yelled, "Remember, nine minutes!"

We bolted down the hall as quietly as we could, the little squeaks and thumps on the smooth flooring under our boots sounding like bullets ricocheting through the soundless space. River palmed the scanner, and I held my breath until the scanner blinked green, the lock clicking open.

He turned the handle and slipped inside first, with me hot on his heels. When the door shut behind us we froze, blinking as our eyes tried to adjust to the sudden lack of light. There was a very faint glow from the end of the long, narrow bunk room that was likely the bathroom, but nothing else. Narrow bunks like ours lined each wall, head to foot with no spaces in between, and nothing else in the room. Most of the beds appeared to be occupied, the male laborers on their sides facing towards the wall with their backs to us.

I scanned the bunks for my brother as fast as possible, and we made it to the middle of the room before I spotted him and his dishwater-blond hair. I hesitated, unsure how to get him to the bathroom without arousing suspicion from any of the other laborers.

River didn't hesitate, though, and barked out. "Brandt! On your feet, now!"

Chace's shoulder blades drew together, anger and tension radiating off of him as he rolled over and got to his feet. Defiance was quickly replaced with confusion as he recognized me and looked quickly between me and River in our uniforms.

I placed a finger over my lips, as River barked out again, "Report to the facilities for questioning, Brandt! We know that sister of yours has been up to trouble, and now you're going to pay the price!"

Not a bed sheet ruffled, as the beaten-down laborers huddled in their beds, unwilling to draw attention to themselves, no matter what was happening to their fellow laborer. It was no better than prison, and it hurt me somewhere deep down to know I was leaving all of these people to their fates.

Chace stomped to the spartan bathroom in silence, and once we were all inside, River shut the door, and gestured to the far end, as far from the door as we could get. There was nothing in here but a row of toilets along one wall, and a row of sinks on the other. Chace stood with his back to the wall between a toilet and a pedestal sink, arms crossed across his chest, and a glare in place.

"What the frack is going on, Nyx? Are you with a *guard*? These guys are scum!"

"No, he's not a guard, Chace, and we don't have much time." I glanced at my water meter, seeing we'd used a third of our time to find him and get him in here. "I only have six minutes. We're getting out of here tomorrow. River and I have been working with some dissatisfied people, and we've got a plan. The two of us are going to get publicly exiled, and while that's going down, one of them is going to come back here and sneak you out. We're going to set it up as if you attacked a guard when you heard about the exile, and he killed you. I know it's not perfect, but it's the best we've got to get ourselves out of this place."

"It's a good plan, Nyx," River said soothingly and reached up to squeeze my shoulder.

"Are you kidding me? Keep your hands off my sister! We are prisoners here, and you two are making moon-eyes at each other like teenagers! God, Nyx, where are your priorities? How do you know you can even trust this guy?" The acerbic jab from Chace took me completely by surprise, and I stiffened under River's gentle touch before turning back to him.

"Seriously, Chace? I've crossed the whole fracking desert to get you, and you're going to complain about my choice of partner? Now is *not* the time. Tomorrow is the day we get out of here. When they come for you, go with them. I've got the Bronco outside, and our supplies should be waiting for us."

"Fine, but you better promise me your head's on straight. The sister I remember wouldn't let anything cloud her judgment."

It stung—no, it *cut* deep that he didn't trust me to keep his best interest at heart, and I found in that moment I couldn't argue with him. I didn't have time to explain it all, and what would cloud my judgment was breaking down into an emotional standoff with my brother.

I narrowed my eyes, but kept my mouth shut over the angry words that wanted to fly free as we walked out the bathroom door. We left Chace to find his own way back to his bunk as we slipped out of the prison-like bunk room, the door automatically locking as we bolted back down the hallway to where Morgan waited.

Now Chace just had to cooperate, and we had to go fig-picking. Easy-peasy.

Thirty

TRUSTING

O nce we were back in our room and the guard's uniforms had been returned to Morgan to dispose of, we did our usual clean-up for the night, using up all of our water quota for a good hair-washing, since we wouldn't be able to again for a while. I went first, and then waited, lying on my back and staring up at the ceiling as River cleaned up. The contentious scene with Chace played on repeat in my head as I lay there, unable to close my eyes or drift off, despite how tired I'd been for the last few days. Talking to River would help.

River emerged from the bathroom, his eyes meeting mine across the room and holding them. In that moment, he focused every last ounce of that raw, boundless energy in my direction, and it felt like electricity in the air. His hair was still damp, and I couldn't place the look on his face. He was intent, sure—he was the most intense man I'd ever met, and that was saying something. A flush rose up my neck, and I had to resist the urge to touch it, cool it somehow. He was standing still, as if torn between leaving, and staying—even though we had nowhere else to go in this tiny shoebox apartment except to sleep. The nighttime routine was done, but he was still half-turned towards me, as if he couldn't decide if he should walk towards me or back through the bathroom door. Tomorrow, we'd leave this place and never walk through that door again.

He swallowed, and the motion pulled my gaze downward. I watched the rise and fall of his throat, as my eyes slowly traveled down the broad expanse of his chest, his own white tank top clung to his enticing pectoral muscles and brought out his deep tan. I was overcome with the desire to touch him there, feel him warm and vibrant under my hands. And yet, I couldn't move. I was a snake under the lull of a charmer, unable to do anything but what he asked. The tense power of his thighs broke my wandering gaze, and I snapped my eyes back to his face. There was tension there now, too and I knew that he'd caught me so openly perusing him, like he was mine to ogle.

He wasn't, though. Yes, there was an attraction, but we were friends, comrades—co-workers, perhaps. But more? No, we hadn't agreed to more. A few kisses didn't entitle me to assume we were anything serious romantically, even if it felt like we'd been toeing an invisible line for weeks, now. We hadn't *spoken* anything. Changed anything.

Did you have to agree to be more, or was this how it happened? One tense moment, and someone made a move? I didn't know, I'd never done this before. Never wanted to, frankly, because it meant giving up my control, and a level of trust I would never consider with *anyone*. But River . . . it was my turn to swallow.

He reached up and used this thumb to rub the small, silver scar that marred his left bicep, a nervous habit of his I'd noticed early on. Am I making him nervous? Why isn't he saying anything; coming to lie on the bed like we did every night? I chewed my lip and fought the urge to glance down at my water meter, my own nervous tell. Just as worry began to take over, he spoke with a slow, cautious tone.

"Chace told me to stay away from you. I really should move my mattress back up into my bunk." His eyes hardened, angry at the order.

I was surprised, but Chace wasn't in charge of either of us. We were adults. "Luckily, Chace isn't here. Or in charge of who I spend my time with. Besides, you need your rest before tomorrow. It's going to be a long day." I held his gaze, steadily showing him that I wasn't worried. I'd do what I wanted, and as soon as we were out of here, I'd tell Chace as much. *What did I want, though?*

As he raked a hand through his hair, that golden skin of his calling to me like sirens called to the sailors in the old tales, I knew. If I didn't go to him, I was going to burn up. If I did, I might crash and burn anyway. He was worth it, though. I knew it in my bones. The fever he stirred inside me lived there, begging for him. Demanding him.

He took a step forward, then another. My eyes were riveted to his every move as he sank to his knees on the mattress, the small room disappearing between us. I pushed myself upright, matching his pose on my knees. When only a few inches remained between us, we both stopped again. We were closer, but not close enough yet. He searched my face, looking for something. I stared back, curious and wondering—begging for something I couldn't explain, couldn't name.

He lifted one hand, and brushed his thumb across my eyebrow, tracing it as lightly as a feather. My eyes fluttered closed for a moment, but I forced them back open. Whatever it turned into, I wasn't going to miss a second of it. He traced an invisible path down the side of my face, across my jawline and to the corner of my mouth. He paused and ran back the other way along my jaw down to the base of my throat, where my pulse leapt under his fingertips. I was sure he could feel it pounding wildly, giving away my inner turmoil. He rested his hand there, tracing my collarbone with the lightest of touches, but nothing more. It felt like a challenge. Would I rise to meet him, or turn away? I'd never been one to run, and I wouldn't now.

I reached up and traced my own path from the corner of his mouth to his ear, down the strong column of his throat and back again. I didn't stop at the corner, though. I brushed my fingertip across his full lower lip and paused in the middle. It was softer than I remembered. The heat in his eyes seared straight to my soul, and when he nipped my finger between his teeth I almost levitated out of my skin. Then he kissed it softly, and I pulled it away to rest on his shoulder. His muscles bunched under my hand, ready to spring.

He leaned forward and pressed a kiss to my collar bone, right above his fingertips. Then he left a blazing hot trail across my skin as he planted kisses one after the other up my neck, and jaw, until he was hovering there, short inches away from my lips. "Nyx . . ." My name was a sigh on his tongue, and the sound sent a shiver through my frame. He steadied me with his other hand on my waist, and pulled me closer to him, bringing my body flush to his. "Shh," he soothed, and my eyes fluttered closed again.

This time, I let them stay closed for a moment to center myself. When his lips touched mine, the sensation was better than anything I'd ever dreamed. Soft and warm and sensual. I leaned into him, wanting more. The hand on my shoulder ran down my arm to hold me firmly in place at my waist, locking me in place now with both hands. I was his captive, and I loved every second of it. He deepened the kiss, slanting his mouth to the side over mine. I mirrored the position and sucked lightly on his bottom lip.

With a groan, he pulled back so there was a little more distance between us. Indecision warred on his features, and I could feel his shoulders tense under my hands. I gave him a small squeeze of reassurance.

"Tell me to stop, Nyx." His voice was a low rumble, and I hated every word.

"Don't stop," I blurted before I could second-guess myself over what this meant. "Stay with me."

His eyebrows shot up for a split second, and then he dove back toward me with renewed urgency. His lips claimed mine with unrestrained fire, and I felt it brand every piece of me. I matched him kiss for kiss, and I knew to the depth of my soul that I was his. But for the first time in the whole of my life, he was mine, too. And somehow, I knew deep down, that was exactly how we were meant to be.

Thirty-One

LOCKDOWN

T he next morning, I woke later than usual, and was surprised to find the ever-energetic River passed out, an arm thrown over his eyes. A blush crept over my cheeks at the realization that we were still wrapped together, and I was clinging to his side like blooms on a cactus, with his other arm wrapped around me. I quickly extricated myself and made my way to the bathroom, where I donned my personal clothes underneath the big, baggy white clothes the Bastion had issued us. I wasn't sure if they would strip off my outer layer and allow me to keep my personal clothes, but it was worth a shot. As I pulled the boxy tee over my head, I realized that this was it. My big chance to get Chace out of here; get back to living on our own terms.

Though now we had commitments to the life-side leaders and their people, the Red Riders, and even the Sidewinders, so it wasn't like we were scot-free the second we cleared the bubble.

Still, it was a step in the right direction.

I searched my face in the mirror as I braided my hair back away from my face. For all that last night with River felt like a huge leap, and a momentous change, I looked exactly the same. I hadn't changed one bit, for all that I'd changed so much inside. I was surprised to see that my hands shook as I tied off the end of the braid, and I quickly clenched them into fists and leaned against the counter for a second. A few deep breaths to calm my nerves, and I'd be ready to go out and face the day. And River. Who I'd spent the night with.

I brought one of my hands up to my lips and closed my eyes, letting the full range of emotions wash through me in this quiet moment. I hadn't realized how afraid I was that things might change between us until right now, this very instant.

Even with everything, we hadn't exchanged any promises, or any words of love. But I . . . I had feelings for him. Strong feelings, perhaps even bordering on love. I'd never loved anyone besides Chace, and he was my brother—it was entirely new and different, and I didn't know how to process it. So, I stood, and I breathed, and I schooled my features back to normal. I could play it cool, be normal. I had a trader face that never let me down; I'd pretend this was a trade. Focus on the day's plans, not the night's decisions.

With my back straight and my chin high, I exited the bathroom, to find River up and leaning against the corner post of the bunk bed. When he saw me, his face broke into a slow grin, and it sent warm shivers down my spine.

He crossed the room, confidence oozing with every step, and folded me into his arms. His head tilted over to rest on top of mine, and I breathed in the rich masculine scent that was so uniquely him, and closed my eyes.

"You're not running scared on me, are you?" The question was quiet, and while I sensed a hint of River's usual good humor, there was a surprising thread of fear underneath.

Was he unsure of himself, too?

I pulled back a few inches and studied his face more carefully. His relaxed grin was there, and of course his handsome features and beautiful golden tan hadn't changed overnight any more than I had. But there—something about the tightness at the corner of his eyes. Concern. For me? That we had changed?

I lifted up on my tip-toes and pressed a soft kiss to his waiting lips. "You don't scare me, and I'm not running anywhere. Are you?" I challenged.

"Never, Nyx. I told you, I'm in. For good."

"Well, okay then."

"Okay, then."

We exchanged smiles and another slow, sweet kiss before he went to get ready for the day as well. We'd planned it so that we'd pick the fruit at noon on the dot, so there would be time for all of the exile proceedings to happen, and then give us only a few hours before nightfall hid our direction from any watching eyes.

So, we had time for one last late breakfast. River and I left the room hand in hand, our guards trailing along a few feet behind us, thoroughly bored with the job. We'd proven to be a low-maintenance assignment, and often one of our guards would disappear entirely before wandering back with a snack for the two of them.

We picked up a breakfast tray from the closest eatery, and sat at the table closest to the grass, where we could smell the trees, and hear the occasional chirps from birds in the canopy. It was sad, really, that we'd never see this again. Even if there was a green space up north like we hoped, I doubted it would have this much carefully curated variety.

So, we took our time and ate slowly, languorously sipping our water orbs, and chatting about nothing. I checked my water meter, and saw we had an hour left before go time.

"We should probably go and check in with Morgan," River suggested.

"Okay. Let me finish this orb, and then we'll go." I quickly tipped the small, squishy container up, and nearly dropped it when an alarm started blaring from every corner of the city. River and I were both on our feet in seconds, the water orb abandoned on the table, forgotten.

A baby somewhere was crying, and people were scrambling towards the front of the city, leaving trash and knocked-over chairs in their wake as they fled the eatery. We weren't frozen long before our guards rushed us.

"To the front, go! This is the emergency announcement alarm," one of them hollered over the din. We joined into the flood of anxious humanity, and once again wound up towards the back of the crowd, without the comforting familiarity of Morgan at our sides. My mind spun as we watched the commandant, the entire Leadership Panel, and two excursion teams' worth of soldiers take the big stage at the front. As soon as everyone was assembled, the alarm cut off.

The silence in its wake was deafening.

The commandant paced across the stage, looking agitated, and the little hairs on the back of my neck stood up. Something was *very* wrong. We had forty minutes until we were supposed to pick the figs that got us booted permanently from the city, but even if we did that right now, no one would be there to see and report us. The question was, had the people who were set to smuggle Chace out realized that? Would we just . . . try again tomorrow?

A chilling thought struck me. Had our plan been leaked? Was that what this was about?

I scanned the crowd for Morgan, but there was no sign of her in the sea of white-clad humanity.

The commandant finally spoke, but he didn't stop pacing. "My people, there have been some unsettling recent developments, which is what brings us together today. As a result of these developments, we are enacting martial law to ensure the continued safety and well-being of all citizens." He paused, allowing for the panicked murmur that rippled through the crowd.

"As a result, there will be no excursions out of the city, and no new entrants accepted into the city, effective immediately. Martial law will remain in place as long as necessary for these new situations to be dealt with. Officer Kutsuki, if you would join me."

The officer stepped forward, his marshmallow uniform blindingly white under the midday sun while he stood at parade rest.

"In these trying times, Officer Kutsuki will be placed in charge of law enforcement. Exile-punishable crimes—"

"He doesn't deserve the uniform! Down with Kutsuki! Down with Kieran!" somebody hollered from the crowd. Everyone's attention fixed on the location the voice had come from, and I watched in mute surprise as a full water orb flew through the air towards the stage. The orb's top spiraled around and around until it splattered against the commandant's side, exploding and sending water everywhere.

"For the Grenkels!" someone shouted, and then suddenly, people all around were rushing the stage. The cry of, "For the Grenkels!" echoed off the dome's metal rafters as more and more people surged forward.

The guards on the ground in front of the stage tried to fight them back, but they were soon overwhelmed with the sheer mass of humanity pressing in from every side, and their helmets disappeared under the crush. A single man made it onto the stage, climbing up with help from his peers, running full-tilt as if he was going to tackle one of them off the stage and into the roiling crowd below. Chaos; it was utter chaos. I gripped River's forearm so hard, I might have left fingerprints.

The man was four feet away from the commandant when the shot fired.

More than one woman screamed as Kutsuki bellowed, "Cease and desist!" He gave a hand signal, and the two excursion teams on stage swarmed forward to form a wall of bodies between the people and the commandant. "The next person to unlawfully threaten Commandant Kieran will meet the same fate!"

As one, a horrified hush fell over the space. Nausea nearly choked me as we watched the man's lifeblood run to the edge of the stage and begin dripping down the side in a scarlet stream, tarnishing the ubiquitous white planks.

Seeing the moment of calm, the commandant stepped out from behind Officer Kutsuki, adjusting his jacket's sleeve with practiced ease before looking up to address his people once more.

"As I was trying to inform you all before this ugliness ensued, due to the lockdown, exile will not be possible. All exile-punishable crimes will be met with capital punishment."

I blinked once, then twice as his words sank in. They were going to start killing people in the streets, like the poor man lying dead on the stage?

We had to get out of here.

People began backing away from the stage, and in all the ruckus I didn't notice the vibrations at first. It was a steady hum, building slowly to a monstrous crescendo. It wasn't until the dome overhead began to rattle with the force of it that I looked up.

What I saw made my heart skip in my chest.

"River . . ." My voice quaked as I shook his arm, drawing his attention upward. The city itself seemed like it was threatening to fall down around our ears, and we watched in terrified shock as sand flew up into an opaque wall all around the city—it blasted against the side of the dome, causing us to lose sight of anything outside the walls, and an eerie loss of light inside.

People screamed all around us and ran in every direction, some slamming into each other and falling in the process. Another series of shots rang out, but we didn't move, didn't breathe, didn't do anything but watch and cling to each other . . . as suddenly, the rattling stopped. It felt like I was watching from somewhere outside my body as the dust began to settle outside, revealing the truth.

A massive, silver spaceship was sitting on our doorstep.

Thank you for reading Finding the Bastion! I know, I know—another cliffhanger. Don't throw your book! What can I say—I really enjoy writing them. They keep me coming back for more of the story, and I hope they do you, as well.

If you want to be notified as soon as book three is ready, you can **pre-order it here.**

In the meantime, you might enjoy hanging out with me in my new reader's group, **which you can find here.** Hope to see you there, and keep turning the pages for some fun tidbits/behind the scenes notes about the story.

Thirty-Two

NOTES FOR THE CURIOUS

Purple water basis (the fun starts about one minute in!): https://www.youtube.com/watch?v=jI__JY7pqOM

Did you catch Nyx's Collective call sign? https://en.wikipedia.org/wiki/Nyx

Hey, uhm, what about those coordinates for Wolf Well? It's the location of the springs with the largest amount of measured output in Utah: https://www.allbryce.com/nature/mammoth_springs.php#

I thought it was a cool idea to choose an actual water feature, and roughly in the right area of the country. It's possible that the people of the future would have chosen the place as a monument to the beauty and wonder of water, so it seemed fitting.

Pssst, hey! Over here! Would you like a bonus deleted scene? You can join my newsletter, and **get a free deleted scene here!**

Before You Go . .
.

Thank you so much for reading Finding the Bastion! This book . . . this book was hard for me to write. I don't know why; I suppose art is that way sometimes. But the immense joy I feel at completing it and sharing it with you . . . it was worth the effort.

If you enjoyed this book, I would so appreciate you taking the time to **leave it a kind review, or some stars.** Reviews and Ratings help Indie authors like me get found by more readers, and help the stories you love reach more people. So, thank you in advance! I read and cherish every kind word you share with me.

If you'd like to sign up for my mailing list so you never miss a new release, and get fun freebies from time to time like recipes, short stories, and more, you can do so **here,** and receive a free deleted scene from this book! This is a really fun deleted scene where Nyx and River try those MREs they found—I'm always sharing things like these with my newsletter first, so you don't want to miss out!

I've also recently started a **Facebook group for readers, who enjoy YA Dystopian books** (with romance, like mine!). If that sounds like your cup of tea, please **come and join us.**

I am available by email at kagandyauthor@gmail.com as well, if you'd ever like to drop me a line directly!

More by K. A. Gandy

Post-Apoc

In The Dust

Finding the Bastion

Descendants of Rust – Pre-order Now!

Dystopian

Dwindle (Populations Crumble, Book 1)
Torn from her home and family. Forced to marry a genetically matched stranger. Will she find love, or destruction?

Rise (Populations Crumble, Book 2)

The man she thought she knew truly is a stranger. Swept away on their honeymoon, the stakes have never been higher. Will his identity be their undoing, or will they rise together?

Reign (Populations Crumble, Book 3)
Kidnapped from their honeymoon resort, nothing is as it seems. Betrayal, intrigue, and secrets abound as Sadie works to free the captive women. But will she end up the savior, or the next captive?

Marked(Populations Crumble: Resurgence, Book 1)
She doesn't want to get married, but with her would-be captors on her heels, she's got no choice but to hope the NLC's strict security protocols will be a safe haven. Marriage is a small price to pay for her life, after all.

Fantasy

Aerthen Sight (An'Loran Chronicles, FREE Prequel Short)

The Lost Talisman(An'Loran Chronicles, Book 1)

The Hatchling – Pre-order now!(An'Loran Chronicles, Book 2)

Clean & Small-Town Romance (as Kristen Dixon)

Bea Mine (Sweet Nothings Bake Shop, Book 1)

Will Travel for Love (Sweet Nothings Bake Shop, Book 2)

Waiting on Forever (Sweet Nothings Bake Shop, Book 3)

The Bachelor Bargain (Sweet Nothings Bake Shop, Book 4)

Sweet Romance Anthology (Paperback Only)

About the Author

K. A. Gandy was born and raised in Jacksonville, Florida, and is married with two kids. She has worked as a restaurant hostess, library book shelver, ranch hand, tour guide, Realtor, tech whiz, landlord, and small business consultant, all in addition to pursuing her passion of writing. As a person of many interests, her life has never been boring. She likes to write late in the evenings and thinks drinking hot tea and baking great cookies fuels hopes and dreams. If you would like to find more of her works, you can sign up for her newsletter at https://www.subscribepage.com/e0v1b5. You can also get updates on Facebook at https://www.facebook.com/KAGandyAuthor.

www.ingramcontent.com/pod-product-compliance
Lightning Source LLC
Chambersburg PA
CBHW030352030726
47497CB00002B/308